INSIDE ALIEN RUINS

Slowly, her eyes adjusted to the light. The outline of buildings began to appear in the dimness. Here and there, shafts of light stabbed through the tangled growth overhead and illuminated subtle colors, something that moved and shifted, something that seemed to cover every inch of surface. Someone who had never seen anything like them might have thought they were insects. But An had seen them before, on other ruins.

They were Glyphs.

She *saw* them, but was unable to let them slide by without *reading* them. They were like a silent crowd among which she had not yet spotted a particular face. They all seemed to flow into arrows, which pointed to a small archway to the right. An moved towards it with a feeling of joyous and terrified anticipation. She stepped through and let her eyes rest on the wall immediately opposite her.

Her mind went blank.

EggHeads

Emily Devenport

A ROC BOOK

ROC
Published by the Penguin Group
Penguin Books USA Inc., 375 Hudson Street,
New York, New York 10014, U.S.A.
Penguin Books Ltd, 27 Wrights Lane,
London W8 5TZ, England
Penguin Books Australia Ltd, Ringwood,
Victoria, Australia
Penguin Books Canada Ltd, 10 Alcorn Avenue,
Toronto, Ontario, Canada M4V 3B2
Penguin Books (N.Z.) Ltd, 182–190 Wairau Road,
Auckland 10, New Zealand

Penguin Books Ltd, Registered Offices:
Harmondsworth, Middlesex, England

First published by Roc, an imprint of Dutton Signet,
a division of Penguin Books USA Inc.

First Printing, April, 1996
10 9 8 7 6 5 4 3 2 1

For Pat Luna and her family:
Albert, Rochelle, Albert Jr., and Damien.

And for Mike Burman and Jennie Akin,
who understand why.

ACKNOWLEDGMENTS

I would like to thank Rick Cook, Gia DeSimone, and Ernest Hogan for brainstorming sessions at the Denny's Restaurant at 35th Ave. and Bethany Home Road, during which we discussed different sorts of suns, the sorts of planets one might expect to orbit them, and the odd sorts of plants (not to mention people) that might grow on them.

I borrowed the concept of the RNA drip from John M. Ford and his book *The Final Reflection;* and the Johnny Mercer song about the Egghead is from the musical *Daddy Long Legs,* starring Fred Astaire and Leslie Caron. I never could remember all of the words to that song, and as soon as I made up the title, *EggHeads,* it started to plague me. So I figured I might as well make the best of it.

PRONUNCIATION GUIDE

An	ahn
Jo	joh
Ra	rah
Te	tay
Ro	roh
Le	lay
Jokateanke-Re	joh-kah-tay-ahn-kuh-RAY
Javici	JAH-vee-chee
Geo	GEE-oh
Teo	TAY-oh
Qiop	KEE-ahp
Rego	RAY-goh
Egan	AY-guhn
Kokoboro	koh-koh-BOHR-oh
Mohamonero	moh-hah-moh-NAIR-oh
X'GBri	ex-GIB-ree
TTra	TAH-truh
GNno	GUHN-no
CVvu	COO-voo
MJki	MAHJ-kee

Vorn (if you want to pronounce it like the natives):
vvvvvvvvvvVVVVVVVVVVVVVVOOOOOOOOO-
OOOOOOOORRRRRRRRRNNNNNNNNnnnn

BETRAYAL

An was just coming out of a deepsleep cycle when her Egg popped open and tried to spit her into the void.

"Jo!" she cried, as if her lover could help her when she was a billion miles out in the nothingness. But her hands were smarter than her heart; one grabbed at the torn hose of her breathing mask and the other grabbed the handle at the lip of her Egg hatch, clutching it desperately while the escaping atmosphere tried to tear her loose. She felt instantly frozen despite the insulation of her safety suit, and only the fear of certain death kept her fingers tight around the handle.

Then the air was gone, along with every item that hadn't been bolted down or stored away; and An was floating, hauling herself back into her tiny habitat. The meager air left in her mask was already used up.

You're dead, she told herself, but she sealed the Egg back up, anyway.

An began to black out as she pried open the compartment with the emergency air masks in it, two of them that she had checked before takeoff. They should have read two hours each, and she fully expected that they still did. But she checked them again, and saw two glaring red lights. *Danger. Zero. Empty.*

You're dead, she told herself again as she flipped on the repressurization controls. It would take several minutes for the Egg to fill with breathable atmosphere, and An could barely see now. She could taste her own blood as the starving arteries pounded in her head.

Her hand fumbled another compartment open. Emergency stims were inside. *What the hell do you think you're going to do with these?* she asked herself as her hand pressed the stim to her neck, against the artery that led to her brain. Then the darkness began to recede, and An remembered that stims had oxygen.

But she still had to breathe. Her lungs needed something in them. Soon she couldn't resist the urge to inhale. As she started to black out again, she pressed another stim to her neck. *This is impossible,* she warned herself. *This won't work.* But she kept pressing the stims to her neck anyway.

An put her face near one of the vents and tried to breathe with short pants what was coming out of it. But it wasn't long before blood was bubbling out of her nose and floating around in little purple balls. *Supposed to be red,* her starved brain told her, and she pressed the stim against her neck again. She tried to look at the chronometer to see how much time had passed, but her vision was too blurry. She decided she didn't want to know anyway, and went back to her strategy of the short breaths and the stims.

Five minutes later she was alert and breathing normally.

"I don't believe it," she croaked, then tried to laugh; but that sounded even worse. This was going to be a story to tell in the bars, to other EggHeads who would nod sagely and tell her they'd already gone through the same thing. This was one to tell Jo. *Do you know what almost happened to me?*

An just floated there for several minutes, congratulating herself for being alive. Her brain was undamaged by the experience; it was already trying to figure out what had gone wrong. She looked around—where was her gun? It must have gotten sucked out with everything else that hadn't been in compartments. She should have strapped it to her body, like Jo always did.

Blood was floating around, clinging to everything, little globules colliding, bouncing, and sticking. It was the proper red color, at least. She took a vacuum tube and started sucking up as much of it as she could. And in the meantime, she typed a query into her main computer system. First thing was:

LOCATION?

A map appeared on her screen. An's vacuum sucked the globules off it and she read the bright print at the bottom. CABAR SYSTEM. It had a type-G sun and five planets, with half a dozen little planetoids in the outer orbits. Her jump drive had dropped her well outside the orbit of the fourth planet, and now she was at full stop, drifting there.

She was reminded of the first time she had been there, the time when she hadn't even been sure she would find it. An had taken a big chance, jumping there that first time; the biggest chance an EggHead could take, since there might have been nothing there at all. She would have had to jump right back to known space with nothing to show for her trouble, to a credit balance that was so far into the red, she doubted she would have even had enough to get a new supply of jump juice.

Lots of EggHeads got stranded that way. But when An had seen "Cabar System" on an outdated map, a map so old that she had had to compute a new position for the star, a feeling had tickled the back of her neck.

"Thank goodness that went right, anyway," she said, and coughed as she accidently swallowed one of the blood drops. The taste had already been in her mouth anyway, so she didn't waste time feeling disgusted about it.

SYSTEMS OK? she asked the computer, then looked at the readouts. Everything checked out. But that might not mean anything. She checked the supply roster, especially the part about her emergency air masks.

The log stated that all supplies were properly stocked and both air masks were at full capacity, two hours each.

An looked at the air masks again, just to be sure that they really read empty. They did. She clearly remembered having them filled, so obviously they had malfunctioned and leaked out their air supplies.

But both at once? She had bought them at different times, from different companies. Two malfunctions might be possible, but the Egg had popped open, and that was a third malfunction. That was too many to believe.

She looked at her main screen again, and at her peripheral screens. All of them were giving her readouts that said NORMAL, NORMAL, NORMAL.

An kept looking at them, anyway. They could say whatever they wanted, it was what they *did* that counted. You couldn't prospect unknown space in an Egg for as many years as she had without learning that at least.

You're still alive, she told her dazed brain (or maybe *it* told *her*). *Now fix the problem.*

An typed VOICE CONTROL into her keyboard.

"Ready," said the mechanical voice.

"Replay all voice-activated codes," An said, rather lazily. She didn't think this would tell her anything, but it was a nice way to put off the inevitable. If the manual codes were okay, she always listened to the voice codes. After that, there was nothing left to do but run a diagnostic, which was a slow process, and one An wasn't looking forward to.

She sighed and kept vacuuming the blood droplets as she listened to her own voice giving all the voice commands she remembered perfectly well having given. Several droplets were sticking to her honey-colored skin, which was a little disgusting to look at, like some dreadful plague. Another corner of her mind was mentally reviewing her contract with Iknaton Inc., which had financed this expedition for Early ruins. She wondered if their insurance would cover any repairs her Egg needed, or if she would have to pay it out of her own pocket.

The drops that clung to her long, black braid looked like rubies. If she found Early ruins on Cabar 4, she could buy as many jewels as she wanted, real or synthetic. Just one Early glyph contained enough information about Early technology to pay An's bills, and the ruins would be covered in them. They always were.

"Even the most primitive Early technology makes ours look Stone Age," the agent from Iknaton Inc. had told An. "If you translate new glyphs for us—our galaxy, as we know it, could be transformed into something you and I might hardly recognize."

Our galaxy? An had thought to herself. *Your part of the galaxy maybe. The Inner Worlds will be transformed. But you'll make sure us peasants from the Outer Worlds stay in the backwater.*

Not that An intended to stay a peasant. Even if there were no ruins, Cabar's type-G sun and its lovely, human-habitable fourth satellite would fetch her a good prospector's fee. Home Corp always preferred planets that were as much like Earth as possible: planets with nice, yolk-yellow suns in their skies. An didn't have a contract with Home Corp at the moment, but one would be hastily arranged for a prize like Cabar 4.

Don't be so pessimistic, she chided herself. *Earlies loved those yellow suns, too. You're going to find ruins here!* Any EggHead who was sitting where she was right now would be thinking the same thing. Jo would.

An smiled at her good fortune—and her good judgment, for taking a chance on a star that had been nothing more than a speck on an outdated map when she had first seen it.

Then a man's voice filled the egg.

"Jo!" An said, and stopped to listen.

Jo had an extremely masculine voice. He was also a man of few words.

"Sleepcycle 0001," said Jo's voice. "Sleepcycle 0999. Jump 0001. Jump 1000. Abort planetfall. Abort planetfall. Sleepcycle 1000. Planetfall 0999. Abort aircheck. Emergency open 0999. Emergency open 1000."

That was all nonsense. That was a bunch of command codes all jumbled up. He had told the computer to start the sleepcycle, start the jump cycle, end the jump cycle, end the . . .

Emergency open 1000.

But it made no sense. An had done two other jumps before Cabar: One to Omsk to get the RNA drip—memories implanted from a glyph expert that would allow her to read the Early glyphs—then one to Mythos for supplies and a rejuve treatment. Why hadn't the Egg popped open on one of those?

She listened to the voice codes over again, this time paying attention to each one. She knew the answer before she was even halfway through them. Jo had placed his jumbled command in the middle of her Cabar program. He must have known what she would be looking for there. And that was her answer, why her lover had tried to kill her.

Money.

Soon, tears joined the drops of blood that were still floating around An's tiny habitat. She dutifully vacuumed them up, too.

Jo only remembered meeting An fifteen years before, when she was twenty-five; but An believed she may have met Jo on Storm when she was fifteen. Fifteen was when she had left home, with a caravan.

Her mom hadn't even wanted to say good-bye to her. Sometimes Mom didn't talk to An for days on end. She was prone to depression; every year she seemed to sink a little deeper into it. But An knew she should try to say good-bye. Otherwise she would be *running* away, not leaving out of her own choice.

"It'll be easier for you without me," she said to her mother's back. "Your energy bills will be lower."

Mom didn't turn around. Her shoulders were squared in that same relentless, exhausted position they had maintained for all of An's life. Gray had long since crept into the thick, black braid that hung down her back. The braid was just about the only physical trait An shared with Mom, who was square and sturdy. An must have gotten her slender looks from her legendary, rarely spoken-of Dad. He had been an offworlder.

"My bills won't be that much lower," said Mom, with no emotion. "I needed the rent you were paying."

"You can take in boarders now."

"From the losers around here? They're all parasites."

An was sorry that things were hard for Mom. She had worked at the same poultry processing plant for twenty years. She worked ten-hour shifts, five days a week. Her hands were getting gnarled; they were covered in scars. Mom would never do anything else in her life, except die.

But *An* was going to do something else.

"Good-bye, Mom," she said, and would have hugged her. But Mom walked away, so An left her alone. She walked out into the harsh early morning light, into the streets of TradeTown, her only home since birth.

I'll come back and visit her when I'm a pilot, she told herself. *I'll fly out here and surprise her.*

But An never saw her mother or TradeTown again.

Her best friend was the one who saw her off. Le had had three babies by then; her oldest was four, conceived when Le was eleven.

Le, An, and the three babies were swaddled from head to foot in protective clothing, against the damaging UV of Storm's type-F star, the hot, bright monster who burned in their sky. They wore protective goggles, too, though you weren't supposed to need them under the covered streets of TradeTown. There were so many holes in those covers, at least on An's side of town, you didn't dare go without them.

Le's eldest boy tugged at Le's skirt and kept hiding his face whenever An smiled at him. It was as if he knew that she didn't want one like him, didn't want any at all. Maybe he thought she was the Anti-Mom.

"I wish I had your looks," Le sighed. "Maybe I could have made something of myself, too." She pulled a long strand of brown hair away from her goggles and blinked at An with eyes that, even through the UV-screened plastic, were the same gold color as her skin.

Looks had been Le's problem all right, but not the lack of them.

"Never too late to get your equivalencies," said An.

"Yeah." Le shifted her youngest to another arm. She was crying a little, and trying to look cheerful. She had a black eye from an argument with her boyfriend, who hadn't wanted her to see An off.

"Remember how we used to play war out here?" Le asked.

They were passing through one of the ruined places. Drugged people squatted in what was left of the buildings. Children couldn't play here anymore. But there had been a time when this had seemed the perfect playground. You could play some pretty serious hide-and-seek back then, in the half of the town that had been decimated in the last Vorn war.

Practically all An could remember of those early days was the playing. The boys liked to be marines, and they told the girls they should be nurses. But An had wanted a more active role than that—she had wanted to *be* one of the heroes, not to doctor them. Besides, they were never properly grateful for the doctoring.

The boys would play really hard; they couldn't be bothered to worry about weaker people. An got hurt plenty of times. So she thought up another angle.

"I'm the space pilot who flies you in every day," she said. "So you can fight. Besides, the Vorn warriors are female, and you need someone on your side who can understand them."

An had always had a gift for persuasion. Eventually, everyone came to accept her in the role of space pilot; no one more than she herself.

How they had loved those early games in the rubble of TradeTown. You could look out one of those ruined windows and see nothing but destruction for blocks around you. The tinted adobe was fading, day by day. The shade from the covered streets became dubious. Not all of the holes in those buildings had been blasted by the Vorns; but An hadn't known that, back then. She and the other kids had loved their protective clothing—it made them feel like real marines.

After a Superstorm, sand would pile up over Trade-Town in huge drifts: red sand if the storm was from the west, yellow-white sand if it was from the east; and a sort of tan-colored sand where the two types had mixed from the north and south. It would look like the whole town was being wiped from the face of the planet. An would imagine herself flying everyone out of there, back to the wonderful ship where everything was clean and modern, and everything still worked; where they would all live one day, after they won the war.

Maybe it would even be like it was in the Inner Worlds. Once the war was over, the Outer Worlds would be welcomed back like long-lost brothers. They would be treated to all of the wonderful technology, all of the comforts they were denied now because Central Command on Earth didn't want the Vorns getting their claws on Human secrets. Maybe Storm could join the marvelous Net instead of using those clumsy message drones that took months and months. Maybe An and her friends, and even Mom, would be like the people they saw in the entertainment vids, the heroes and the beautiful people. Once the war was over.

After all, the war was the reason everything was so bad.

For eleven years, she had indulged herself in that fantasy.

"And then the game was over," An said, half to herself.

"You're amazing, An," Le said. "Where do you find the courage? You've always been a step above everyone else."

An was embarrassed, so she couldn't think of what to reply.

Le didn't mind. She almost seemed to be thinking aloud. "I don't know what I'll do without you to look up to. But on the other hand, if you had stayed, I think I would be disappointed in you."

"I couldn't stay," An agreed.

"I almost hope I never find out what happened to you. I can imagine wonderful things about what you're doing. Promise me you'll do wonderful things, An?"

"I promise."

"You always keep your promises. That's why we've been friends so long."

So long. Fifteen years. It had seemed very long, back then.

Stay off the drugs, An wanted to say. *Don't have any more babies. Get your precollege equivalencies.*

But she had said all of those things to Le before. Either she had listened, or she hadn't, and that was that.

"I'll miss you," An said. "Thank you for coming to see me off."

"I wouldn't miss it for anything. I have to see it with my own eyes. I want to tell my kids about it, when they get to be old enough to make their own way."

Le said this with such determination and seriousness, An's heart expanded with pride, and for a moment she felt very brave and important.

They walked into the caravan district, the one place in TradeTown that could still honestly claim to do any trade. Big outdoor markets sprawled across the roadways, places that almost never saw automated vehicles anymore.

Storm has a Star Port, An thought to herself, not for the first time, *but you sure wouldn't know it by looking at this place.*

Still, her heart lifted at the sight of all that hustling and bustling, all that activity. *I'm going!* she told herself. *I'm really going!* She felt like pinching herself.

What makes you think they'd want to hire you on a caravan? her mother's voice said at the back of her mind. She had said that four years ago, when An had first concocted her scheme. *They've got strong men to do that job,*

Mom had said. *They can pick and choose. And if you think the men in this town are going to let the women escape from this life, you've got another think coming. They get us pregnant, they leave us here, and they go on to better things with no one to point a finger at them and say, "Hey, how about your other family? What are you going to do for them?"*

An glanced sideways at Le's bruised eye.

Le looked so different from that eleven-year-old An had known, the one who had jumped and scrambled through the ruins, who had lain in hiding with An, panting, scared and excited, while a troop of "Vorns" had slithered by. Now she looked like a grown woman, ten years older than she really was.

Maybe it was because Le had started her period so early. She had barely been eleven. But An had started a month later, and she didn't look like Le. An could still remember the look on her mother's face when she had told her she was menstruating.

"What's wrong, Mom?" she had dared to ask.

"I can't afford a grandchild," her mother had answered. An had been completely baffled by the remark.

And then Le got pregnant.

An hadn't realized you could do that at eleven. She had thought you needed to be a grown-up.

But then, An hadn't taken drugs, either. Her friends had learned to pass them around her.

"Why don't you just try it?" Le had asked her.

"I did try it, once," An had said. "I got a bad cold, and I felt stupid. You can't be stupid and be a space pilot."

Le had been taking the drugs when she got pregnant. An had thought it was a pretty clear lesson.

She still thought so. She, Le, and the children had to keep to the center of the street to avoid the drug addicts who were sprawled on the sidewalk. No one tried to shoo them away from there anymore, except on the rich side of town.

Collectors shared the sidewalks with the addicts. They wore crisp, cream-colored uniforms. They moved here and there, using their vacuums to suck up likely piles of sand. An couldn't help watching them; she had been fascinated by them ever since she was a child.

On the rich side of town, they took the sand that blew in from the storms, separated it into its various colors, and made beautiful Zen gardens out of it. An had always been amazed by the variety of colors they could find. She had thought Storm was red, yellow, white, and brown. But the sand collectors found turquoise sand in the mix; they found pink, cobalt, green, black, cream, taupe, orange, and sometimes even gold. When the storms messed up the gardens of the rich, they sent their collectors out again, and started all over.

What an odd existence it must be, An thought. *To have the time and the money to become so absorbed in the colors of the sand.*

As if to punctuate the thought, a flyer buzzed over their heads, out and away over the desert. It was yellow and red, the colors of TradeTown's only university. An had thought it was a personal flyer; but then, it was almost certainly being flown by a rich person, anyway. Only the rich could afford to go to the university. The flyer would compete in a matter of hours the journey it was going to take An three weeks to make.

The sound of its engine sparked memories of endless days on the streets, playing, walking, dreaming, seeing the flyers go overhead, and believing that some day she would be flying one herself. Another memory surfaced, too, one that was so old she could barely grasp it. She was standing on a street like this one, watching collectors, just like these, while she waited for someone. She could remember feeling anxious, impatient.

Could she have been waiting for her dad to come home from work?

Or she might have been waiting for the ice cream man. In summer, the heat got up to 125°F. Ice cream was one of TradeTown's best industries.

Le bought some ice cream for the little ones, while An waited impatiently. "I've got to hurry, Le," she said, trying not to show her eagerness to get away from her friends and her family forever.

"I know," said Le, looking harried as her youngest dropped his cone on the sidewalk and began to wail. Le picked up what was left of it and stuffed it into his hands. He looked at it in confusion for a moment, then began to eat it again.

Now An couldn't help hurrying. She ran right down the middle of the main drag. Poor Le hustled after her with her brood in tow, a living, moving, squalling symbol of everything An was trying to get away from.

Mom had been right about those caravans. It had been hard to get in. There were always lots of guys hanging around, waiting hopefully for the master. An had a couple of advantages over the guys, though. For one, she never, *ever* did drugs or alcohol.

It would be nice if *two* was the fact that she was smart and learned fast. But in reality, *two* was the fact that she was beautiful. The men liked having her around, to rest their goggled eyes on.

Not that she ever let any of them get anywhere with her.

Up ahead, on a huge dusty lot, she spotted familiar animals and men. She slowed down.

"Is that it?" panted Le. "Is that your—your group?"

"Yes," An said, and was ashamed by how satisfied she sounded. She wiped the silly eagerness off of her face, both for Le's sake and her own.

She had spent so much energy making the men think

she was an ice cube. It wouldn't do to arrive with a puppy-dog look on her face. Puppy dogs were much too much fun to tease.

"We'd better say good-bye here," she told Le, and then hugged her best friend, crying babies and all. Her vest rustled as all of the papers she had stuffed into the inside pockets—the letters of recommendation and the map—were practically squeezed out of their hiding place. The moment she entered that embrace, she knew it would be their last.

"I'll think about you, always," she whispered to Le. "Especially when things get tough."

"Me, too," Le managed to choke. "Always."

Then they parted, looked into each other's eyes one last time, seeing more sadness than hope in each other. Le hustled her brood back up the street without a second glance back.

An went to report for duty.

"You're late," said Master Rego, consulting his expensive chronometer.

"I had to say good-bye to my—family," said An.

Rego snorted. "This is not what I expect from you."

"This time I won't be coming back to TradeTown."

He raised a grizzled eyebrow. "Don't curse this trip with careless words. Maybe none of us will be coming back, eh?"

"But the rest of you *want* to come back."

"And you don't. Well, I've heard that plenty of times before. Maybe you'll get your wish and make it to the Star Port. But be careful what you wish for, it might come true. Come on and get to work, girl."

They finished packing up the caravan in less than half an hour. It boasted thirty camels and ten horses, specially engineered creatures with matted fur to protect their skin and nictating membranes that protected their eyes the way An's goggles protected hers.

There were four armored vehicles, too, another sort of protection altogether. An wished it could be six or seven vehicles; but the damned things were so expensive to buy and maintain, they were lucky to have as many as they did.

We should be able to fly this stuff out of here. If I want to visit the Star Port, I should be able to hop on a flyer, or a high-speed train, like we see on the vid networks.

If you asked Rego why things were so tough, he would have laughed and said, "What do you think this is, girl, Celestine, the Pearl Of The Outer Worlds? Be glad this is Storm, because Celestine is *dead*. Celestine was as pretty as Earth, and it was killed by the Vorns; but Storm is too ugly to kill. Storm was born hard and it'll die hard."

And then he might have cursed the Vorns, and so might his men, just for good measure.

Because the Vorns really had killed Celestine, the one planet among the Outer Worlds that had rivaled Earth. But the Vorns hadn't had as much luck on Storm. They hadn't attacked TradeTown for twenty years. An gazed north, the direction the flyer had gone, the direction in which she would be painfully making her way soon. She didn't look into the brightness that surrounded the sun—no one did that without special equipment. Instead, she looked toward the horizon, a place that had always symbolized hope to her. She wondered what was really behind the poverty and the isolation of her hometown.

Maybe I'll find out at the Star Port, she thought.

And maybe you'll wish you hadn't, said a small voice in the back of her mind, one that sounded a lot like her mom.

The caravan lurched off into the morning. This haul was mostly people, legal drugs, exotic spices, and various other odds and ends. There were some sealed, unmarked packages that An didn't ask about. Whatever they were, they would probably make up most of Rego's profit.

She got to ride in one of the armored vehicles on the first morning. She got to hold one of the rifles and look out a shoot hole until she had to pinch herself to keep from falling asleep. The heat and light were so dazzling, the caravan would stop and sleep through the hottest, brightest part of the afternoon. Then they would travel well into the night, with another sleep break of only a few hours. The pace was hard, but it was necessary in a place where you were either being chased by the heat, the storms, or even the Vorns.

When An felt herself nodding off, it helped to picture Vorn warriors lunging at her.

It helped a *lot*.

But they didn't see any Vorns on the way to Red Springs. They found their spoor, of course; they had done that on every other trip. Hardly anyone ever saw more than that these days.

"You hear what happened to Bently?" the guy riding next to An whispered, without looking away from his shoot hole.

"Who's Bently?" An whispered back. *Bently* wasn't a proper name for a person.

"Not who, what. Town ninety miles or so west of TradeTown."

"Didn't know there was *anything* west of TradeTown."

"Well, now there ain't. Vorns wiped it out. No survivors, what I hear. Shouldn't've been out there anyway, by themselves. Not out *there*."

An didn't want to believe him. That was like a story out of the old days, when the Vorns had been a real threat. That wasn't supposed to be happening anymore. And who was this guy? She didn't remember him from past caravans. What did he know, anyway?

But she couldn't resist asking him: "Was it a real small

town?" It had to have been a smaller town, there weren't enough Vorns to take out a place like TradeTown these days. That's what everyone said.

"Smaller than Red Springs, I guess," he said. "Maybe five thousand people or so. Why? You worried?"

An felt herself getting mad. She stifled the emotion, and tried to look nonchalant. "TradeTown has good defenses."

"Oh, yeah," he said. "But I'm glad I'm getting out of there."

An felt a terrible twinge. She had been running for other reasons. Was she getting out just in time?

No, things couldn't be that bad. The vid nets told people that there weren't any nests still intact on Storm, that all of the fertile Vorn queens had been killed. Sometimes warriors could ascend to queen form, especially in times of great stress, but there probably weren't any surviving males to fertilize them.

Right?

They're on their way out, An told herself, echoing what most other Humans on Storm were saying these days—those Humans who had never met Vorns in person.

That whole first day everything was boring, dusty, hot (though not as hot as it could be), and smelly. An was never sure who stank worse, men or camels. When their smell combined, it was truly memorable.

The men grinned at her, their teeth flashing under their dark goggles, their skin sun weathered where it was exposed. "This is your last trip, Anny?" they would say, giving her an unearned boost in status with that extra syllable. An didn't know how she would lengthen her name when the time came, but it probably wouldn't become *Anny*.

Some of the men tried to talk her out of leaving. Mostly, these were men who didn't know her as well as the others did. All they knew about her was that she was lovely, and they hadn't had a chance to try to score with her yet.

"Don't waste your time," Rego told them. "Our An is going places. She's not for the likes of you."

They advanced into the Badlands, kicking up dust until An was sure that anyone watching from a distance would have to use image enhancers to pick them out in the moving cloud.

Please don't let anyone be watching us from a distance, she prayed, feeling about ten times more nervous than she ever had on a caravan trip. She felt so odd this time around, it reminded her of the first time she had ever come out into the Badlands.

That time had been fun, when she looked back on it. But while it was happening to her, she had been scared. She had worked hard to hide that from the master, a fellow named Qiop who kept looking at her out of his one good eye and laughing. She could still see him sitting on his big, black horse, half-obscured by the dust, sweating and stinking in the impossible heat. Laughing and laughing at her.

There was nothing in the Badlands, that was what she had thought then. Most of it currently lay in the Yellow Zone, where the sand was still mostly yellow-white. Sometimes yellow dust filled the sky, and you couldn't tell where you were. The sun would turn into a broken egg yolk, a burning eye that could trick you into staring at it while you were trying to sort out where the horizon was.

Today, the lesser moon was up, too, looking like an afterimage of the sun.

Rego, of course, knew exactly where they were. He knew the name of every bush and tree, every bird and bug and lizard. He knew the tricks the life out there could play, the defenses they had. He could tell you which bushes had edible flowers, and what time of year it was safe to approach them. He knew which cactus contained hidden water, which tree had a poisonous thorn that could make you sick for days—or seeds that could bore into you until they germinated and spread tendrils throughout your nervous system.

Rego loved the desert. He guided them into the nothingness, hardly having to consult his locator at all. They rolled along forever, for twelve hours' worth of Storm's twenty-five-hour day. An felt like a zombie by the time the sun went down.

The beauty of the sunset roused her for a little while. It turned red, and shot purple and blue arms across the sky, like it was trying to drag itself back up again.

"Forget it," said An. "You're going *down*, you monster."

The sun slipped under the horizon, and the stars came out. Auroras flickered in the night sky, the one beautiful benefit of living on a planet that was bombarded by the radiation of a type-F sun. An sighed and closed her eyes, for just a moment. Her body rocked gently back and forth inside the armored vehicle.

Hours later, someone shook her awake and snarled, "You ain't sleeping while everyone else works!"

The rocking had stopped long ago. An put her rifle away and lent a hand with what was left of the work. But she didn't waste her time feeling guilty. Her reputation wasn't as important this time around.

She was really leaving.

It took almost a week to get to Red Springs. Absolutely nothing eventful happened, absolutely nothing went wrong.

Then, an hour outside of Red Springs, the sky turned a congested orange. Lightning flashed on the horizon, blasting the ground underneath it. Rego and his seniors studied the storm for a long moment from atop their horses.

"Superstorm," guessed Rego. "Ten days, at least."

An waited inside an armored vehicle, the same one she had been riding in all week, clutching the same rifle, and trying to stay awake. Now she held her breath, hoping that they would make a run for Red Springs instead of trying to erect an emergency shelter. She had lived through one Superstorm in an emergency shelter and she wasn't anxious to do it again. Besides, she had a creeping feeling in her gut, a fear that might have just been nervousness about venturing out on her own—or might have been something deeper, something instinctive.

"We can make it," Rego decided. "Let's run."

So they hurried the rest of the way to Red Springs. Though hurrying wasn't something camels normally liked to do, the sound of the howling storm at their heels was more than enough to goad them into their fastest pace.

An thought it might just be a trick of the wind through the shoot holes, but she could have sworn she heard another howling just underneath the wind. She strained to sort it out. It sent a chill up her spine.

"Do you hear that?" she asked the guy next to her.

"We'll get there in time," he answered, without looking away from his hole.

An squinted through her own shoot hole. Up ahead, she could see black towers looming out of the dust. The towers sat on top of bunkers: ugly, functional things that were practically the only sort of building you could find in Red Springs. The towers were there to keep the sand from burying the whole town. The tower tops were often the only things sticking above the sand after a Superstorm.

The bunkers were there because of the Vorns.

The caravan rolled straight toward those bunkers. By now, there was no way An could hear anything but the wind. She put her rifle back in its locker and scrambled out of the transport with everyone else, helping to hustle the still-loaded camels in through the storm doors. They would unload them once everything was locked down.

The sky had turned from orange to dark red-brown. An had to stop and gape at it for a moment. It was like a huge wave of dirty water, coming to slam itself down on them.

Someone squeezed her arm, tight, and she snapped out of her trance. Rego let her go, once he could see that she had gotten the message. She scurried in through the storm doors, and helped the men push them shut.

It was suddenly very quiet. An could barely hear the wind, anymore.

"Well," Rego said, wearily, "let's get the beasties unpacked."

Through the door, An heard the faintest howling, not quite like the wind, and she couldn't resist asking Rego something as they went back up the passage to the bunkers.

"Can Vorns survive outside in a Superstorm?"

"Oh, yeah, you bet they can. Are you kidding? Have you ever seen a Vorn? They're armored from jaw to clawtips. All the sand does is give their hides a nice polishing."

"I think they like the storms," said Egan, Rego's Second. "They think it's singing to them. You listen closely, girl, and sometimes you can hear them singing back."

An suppressed a shudder, along with a sneaking feeling that she had just received the worst possible omen.

The Superstorm lasted nine days. An thought she heard the howling of the not-wind for the first five. It made her wonder if she wouldn't be better off staying in Red Springs the rest of her life, inside the bunkers.

But by the time the weather had gentled, she was completely stir-crazy and couldn't wait to get into the open air again. She had to wait six extra hours for the sand-dozers to clear a path away from the bunker. She walked outside, closed her eyes to take a deep breath, and walked right into Rego.

"You'll be on a camel all the way to Desert Center," he said, without preamble.

"I guess I can stand that," said An.

"You're good with the animals. They like you."

"Uh-oh."

This was the way Rego spoke before assigning someone an unpleasant job, by telling them how qualified they were for it.

"I need you to herd," he said.

"That sounds easy," An said, suspiciously.

"I need you to herd the GodHeads."

An closed her eyes and took another deep breath. It wasn't just to calm down; this was the last bit of clean air she would smell for a while. Well, clean if you didn't count the camels and the stinking men, but even they were better than the smell of Godweed.

The GodHeads reeked of it, as if they had been ingesting it all their lives. When they had pounded on the emergency doors two hours into the storm, everyone had rushed to let in the poor souls who were trapped outside.

And everyone had groaned when they had seen who it was.

"The hellhounds are at our heels!" their leader had screeched as he came in, so they had hurried to close the doors again. GodHeads almost never spoke; when they did, it was to prophesize. The prophecy always came true, if you knew how to interpret it.

An had her own ideas about what the "hellhounds" were.

The GodHeads poked their heads out of the bunker, right on cue. Their leader speared An with his wild gaze, and she shivered. He didn't wear goggles; none of them did. The Godweed turned their eyes blue, which somehow kept them from going blind in the face of Storm's cruel sun. Those blue eyes stabbed at you from the middle of blasted faces.

"Don't let him get to you," said Rego. "Come on, let's hustle the troop out."

In another half hour, Rego's caravan was on its way again. They plowed through drifts of the red sand Red Springs was named for, then passed back into the Yellow Zone again. An tried to herd the GodHeads without getting too close to them. But this proved to be impossible. She had to move in closer.

She hoped that none of them would prophesize again. They looked at her, too often, with their wild, empty eyes.

Don't tell me anything bad, her eyes would plead back.

Their camels were slowly going crazy under them. An was sure it was the Godweed. She could smell it even through her protective veil, which she had tucked under her goggles so that it fell just below her chin. The smell wasn't exactly *bad*—it just made you want to get away from it. When she tried to analyze why, she couldn't put her finger on it.

An had learned something about Godweed in school. She had learned even more in the streets. Godweed only grew on Storm; a thorny bulb with pale yellow flowers that grew on leafy stalks from its center, it was pretty to look at in the spring. Chemically speaking, there was nothing remotely like it on any of the other settled planets; but that wasn't surprising. Storm was a rarity, a planet that was just far enough away from its type-F sun to allow life to have developed on its own, without the help of Human terraforming.

The plants of Storm were understandably odd. They had the most highly developed nervous systems of any plant life in the known galaxy, and they could adapt— mutate—at an amazing rate.

The drugs they produced tended to be potent and bizarre.

Godweed was a fine example. It was a hybrid spawned by the marriage of a native plant and bioengineering bacteria that had been designed to make the plant life of Storm a little less lethal.

Well, it was a nice try, An thought to herself, trying to watch the GodHeads without meeting any of their stares.

The drug Godweed produced wasn't classified as a neurotoxin—exactly. It wasn't listed as a psychoactive drug, either. Some neurologists who had tried it, themselves, said it might be a neurotransmitter, which was funny considering that it came from a plant. Even a plant from Storm. What did a plant with no brain need with a neurotransmitter? And how come a Human brain could use it?

While An was busy mulling that over, a camel bolted under a GodHead. This time An had to chase it well away from the caravan and then back again. *Maybe the Human brain* can't *use it,* she thought to herself in exasperation. *Maybe that's why the GodHeads are so hard to take.*

It wasn't a fun drug, that was for sure. No one tried it for fun, more than once. But the GodHeads valued the visions it gave them. An had heard that even the Vorns wouldn't touch a GodHead who had ingested enough Godweed. So it was almost a comfort to have them along.

Almost.

One guy seemed to look at her more than the others did. He was the guy An had thought was their leader. But he never said anything to the others, never gave any orders. His camel bolted more than any of the others. Maybe he kept staring because he was horny. Could they get horny? Wasn't that against their religion? Not that religion had ever erased anybody's sex drive.

He's telling his camel to run, An thought to herself. There—it happened again. This time she watched his face. He wasn't surprised or startled by the camel's sudden movement. He was looking right at *her*.

The camel had a harassed expression in its eyes. Its mouth was foaming as if it were being mercilessly goaded. But how was the GodHead doing it? An looked at the man's skinny flanks. He wasn't using his legs to goad the animal.

He's doing it with his sweat, An decided. *He's sending neurotransmitters from his brain to the camel's.*

She laughed wildly. It felt good to laugh that way. None of the GodHeads seemed insulted by her mirth. They turned their gaunt faces in her direction, attentively. If An stared at them hard enough, she could almost understand what was behind their blue eyes. Their filthy, tangled hair framed their faces like halos; they were glowing from within. She was even beginning to sort of like the smell.

"That's enough for you," said Rego, herding her camel away from the group and out into the open air.

"Huh?" said An. Egan had ridden in to take her place with the GodHeads. She felt a stab of dismay. "I was doing a good job!"

"You did a fine job, but I don't like the look on your face."

"What's wrong with my face?" An demanded, but she was starting to feel a little dizzy, now.

"You were getting the Godweed look."

"No!" An said, more in astonishment than disagreement.

"Oh, yes," said Rego. "I've seen it before. It can happen to anyone. You lasted longer than some people I've known."

An couldn't speak for a while. She and Rego rode well away from the GodHeads, back to where most of the pack animals were patiently clomping along. An caught herself looking at the unmarked packages, wondering if they contained Godweed.

"Will Egan be all right?" she asked Rego.

"Sure. We're only two hours from Desert Center."

"*Two Hours?* So we've been riding—*eight hours* today?"

"Just over." He looked at her, sideways. "Seemed like less?"

"Two or three hours. Couldn't have been more than that. Rego, I didn't even have a lunch break!"

"Yes you did. I saw you ride up to the wagon and get your share. I thought you were just preoccupied. I should have known better."

An's stomach felt full. It was almost time for supper, and she still felt like it wasn't even time for lunch yet. No wonder the GodHeads got so skinny.

And now, the sun was going down. An had to remind herself that it wasn't the middle of the day, but she couldn't quite convince herself.

"What are you going to do, tomorrow?" asked Rego.

An was confused for several moments, until she remembered that tomorrow she and the caravan would be diverging. They would be going east while she continued north, through the Empty Quarter.

"I've saved enough to pay the ferrymen for a ride on an armored vehicle," she lied.

Rego grunted. "Some say it's safer to walk than to trust those rats. I've heard tales that they'll throw people out if the Vorns get too near. Save their own hides."

An didn't go for the bait. "There haven't been any reports of Vorns in the Empty Quarter for—longer than I've been alive."

"No official reports," said Rego. "Out here, we have our own reports. You could run into them, An. Don't think you can't."

"Yes, sir."

"Those ferrymen, they've been known to rape women, too."

"Yes, sir."

"You've got your knife?"

She showed it to him. He nodded and said, "Good. But I wish you had a gun. I'd give you one of the rifles, but there are plenty who'd kill you for the rifle, what otherwise wouldn't give you a second glance."

"Thanks, anyway."

"Don't thank me. I'm wondering if I ever should have hired you in the first place. You should have stayed safe and sound at home with the babies."

Safe and sound except for the father of those babies, An thought to herself.

"But you've got luck," Rego said. "You could make it."

"Thank you," said An, and was glad he didn't know what she really planned to do. He might knock her out, tie her up, and drag her back home.

The sun set, bathing them in a red glow. Then they had an hour of magnificent starlight, with no city lights to dim the heavens. An looked up at the galaxy and felt her heart pounding like it never had before.

That's where I'm going, she promised herself. It didn't seem outrageous that she was sitting on a camel as she thought it.

In another hour, the greater moon rose and turned everything bright silver-blue. Everyone grew long shadows.

Dead ahead, a yellower light was glowing.

"Desert Center," called Rego, with irony. Desert Center wasn't anywhere near the center of the Badlands. That had been wishful thinking on the part of the survey team that had first mapped the area. Since then, no one had had the heart to change it.

It was almost pretty in the moonlight, with its tinted adobe buildings. But An had seen it in the light of day, and it was just a smaller, cheaper, more faded version of TradeTown.

Apparently the entire town was asleep, except for the watch; so they camped just inside the walls for the night. An only did work that kept her well away from the God-Heads. Rego didn't yell at her. In fact, he didn't seem to want to talk anymore.

That was good, because An was afraid he might guess the truth. What she really planned to do was hike across the Empty Quarter. She had been carefully studying maps for the past two years. She had a printout of the most recent mapping in her inside vest pocket. She had a pretty good locator, which had cost her half a year's pay. She knew where all the hostels were, and she knew how much she'd have to carry on her back to get to each one.

The armored ferries were just too expensive. If she had tried to save enough money to pay the ferrymen, she would have been twenty-five years old before she could leave TradeTown. *Twenty-five!* Her life would be practically over by then!

She couldn't wait. The time was ripe.

An rolled herself up in her sleeping bag and let out a long sigh. Nearby, she could hear some of them men talking quietly.

The GodHeads were sitting away from camp, staring out at the Desert. They probably wouldn't even sleep. When she woke again, they would still be gazing into the Empty Quarter.

What are they looking for? An wondered, half in fear and half in exasperation.

A shadowy image began to shamble forth from the back of her mind, to answer her question. But she was asleep before it could show its face.

Excitement woke An up just before dawn.

Rego was already awake, and so was Egan. An sat up and stretched, thinking that she might have a quiet cup of coffee with them before everyone else rose. After all, this might be the last time she would ever see them. Rego was the master who had hired An most often; he was the only one who had never even hinted that he wanted to sleep with her. She would miss him.

She got up, and froze.

The GodHead was standing right next to her. She could see the whites around his eyes, and his head was tilted back as if he were smelling her, translating the smell into information inside his brain, reading her.

He's going to prophesize, thought An with dread.

But he didn't speak for several moments. An shot a glance at Rego and Egan; they hadn't noticed anything was going on. She looked at the GodHead again and sent him a silent plea with her eyes.

Don't give me away. Please don't give me away.

And then he touched her. He reached out and put his hand on her arm. An was too amazed to cringe away. She was wearing her protective clothes, surely his sweat wouldn't penetrate them, wouldn't convey the chemical Godweed message into her nervous system.

No more than it had done so through the thick fur of the camels.

"I'll pray for you," whispered the GodHead, so only she could hear, and then he let her go, turned away.

An gaped at him. Was that a prophecy? What did it mean? Did she need to be prayed for? Was she in danger? Or was he just trying to tell her that he liked her, that he hoped for the best for her?

Dream on, said her mother's voice.

An's arm was tingling, but that was probably from the pressure of his grip. You couldn't turn into a GodHead just because one touched you. The camels sure hadn't. They were standing around, snorting and complaining like their old selves.

The sky lightened into a deceptively gentle glow. The local birds immediately began to twitter and argue, and the rest of the men woke up. An went to get her coffee. She felt an odd pain around her heart, and wished she could regain her lost excitement.

But this was the price you paid for leaving home, no matter how much you wanted to leave it.

"Shop around for a good ferryman," Rego told her. "Don't just pick the first guy you see."

He might as well have been talking about finding a good husband. "I will," promised An.

"Use your instincts," said Rego. "You've got good instincts. Don't let your dreams trick you out of using your common sense."

"Okay."

"You've been a good worker. You've got my letter of recommendation—?"

"Right here." An patted her vest.

"Take care of yourself, and keep working hard. You'll do better than most people from TradeTown."

"Thank you, sir."

Egan handed her some coins. An almost dropped them when she noticed one of them was a gold point instead of the usual silver.

"That's your pay plus a bonus," Egan said. "Good luck, kid."

"Thank you," An stuttered.

Rego and Egan nodded to her, then turned and walked away. They had said their good-byes, and she was free to leave now. She tucked her money into another hiding place in her vest, a place that was carefully padded to avoid jingling, and finished her coffee.

An said good-bye to a few more individuals, all of whom seemed to be too busy to talk very long. She was grateful for that, and she was sure they were, too. Caravaneers were not people who indulged in much sentiment. An left the camp and walked up the road a good distance before turning to look at them again.

They were leaving. An watched them melt into the yellow landscape, never realizing that this was the last time she would ever see anything like them again.

She found a supply store in the merchant's quarter and bought a thirty-pound portable water tank. She would have brought one with her, but Rego would have guessed her plan for sure, if he had seen it.

An strapped the tank to her backpack and then filled it from a public tap. It was heavy, but she could carry it if she paced herself. Her backpack was a good one—it distributed the weight tolerably.

Besides, pretty soon this pack is going to be lighter than you'd like! she told herself as she rode the public transport to the edge of town. In Desert Center, the public transport was a run-down old bus. Some old ladies, with hens tucked under each of their arms, stared at An. The hens stared, too. She couldn't tell what any of them were thinking.

An got off the bus before it could take her to the ferryman's quarter. She didn't want any of the ferrymen to see that she was setting out on foot, alone. They might wait until she got a respectable distance from town, then follow her. That would be an end to her adventure right there.

So An walked the long way around, even though she knew it would cost her several extra hours. She put some hills between her and the town before she angled back over in the direction she would ultimately need to go. She didn't see a soul, except for some hardy little brown birds who clung to bare bushes with tiny feet. They stared at her with their clever eyes, fully aware of what she was. These birds didn't like Human food; they had to outwit the smartest plants in the known galaxy to get their daily sustenance. They had to figure out new ways to outwit those plants when the old ways stopped working.

Just now, they might be wondering if An would be useful in any of their plans. She fervently hoped she wouldn't.

The ground was easy walking terrain, pretty flat once you were away from the hills. An knew she would have to keep well away from the tempting shade of what few trees there were; far enough away to avoid their extensive root systems, as well, which could trigger deadly seed storms if the vibration of her walking set them off. It bothered her that anyone would be able to see her from miles away.

But after she had been walking a few hours, she got used to the silence, the emptiness, the absolute aloneness of her new situation.

I like this place, she told herself, with premature confidence.

After noon, An found shelter among some rocks and sat for lunch. She checked her locator, and smiled with satisfaction. She was on course, now. She nibbled some trail rations and took a few sips from her water tube. According to the tank indicator, she had drunk about fourteen ounces of water all day. That probably wasn't enough, but it was only 85°F now, so maybe she didn't need that much—yet.

In about another hour, she would reach her first milepost, if she was really on the right course.

An rested for half an hour, then started off again. She felt tired, now; so she slowed her pace a little, but tried to keep it steady. Soon, the exercise perked her up. Her feet were doing all right in their walking shoes, and her legs were actually feeling great. She didn't stink too much yet—she had bathed daily at Red Springs, and it had only been a day and a half since her last shower.

Of course, by the time she reached the Star Port, she would stink to high heaven, but that was the least of her problems.

After an hour had gone by, and she didn't see the mile-

post, she checked her locator; then pulled out her map
and doubled-checked that. She hadn't made the speed she
had thought she would, but she still seemed to be on
course.

In another half hour, she saw the milepost up ahead,
just as she had expected. She stopped to inspect it—its
numbers were almost gone. No one had come by to maintain it in years. The ferrymen had made their own roads,
torn into the ground by their heavy wheels. They didn't
use the mileposts. But An could tell from looking at this
one that there was supposed to have been a highway built
through this area.

Why hadn't it been done? Had they run out of money?
An felt the most peculiar mix of sadness and nostalgia,
looking at the half-rubbed-out numbers. TradeTown was
like this. The Place That Almost Was.

Someone had scratched RU WAS HERE in what was left
of the paint on the base. An resisted the urge to scratch
AN WAS HERE TOO! She checked her locator, and started
off again. The first hostel was ten miles away. She hoped
she would make it by nightfall, but she was getting tired.
She had ridden horses and camels all day long, but she
had never walked all day with a heavy pack on her back.

When the sun started to go down, she was almost relieved. At least she could give up and rest for the night.
She checked her locator—the hostel ought to be four
miles farther down the road. It was time to camp.

A light breeze was blowing when the last of the light
faded and the first stars broke out on the horizon. An
didn't pay it any heed; it wasn't the sort of wind that pre-
ceded a Superstorm. Those always turned the sky orange
and the air dead before they hit. You had a couple of
hours of building pressure, until you felt like someone
had a vice on your head, and then *WHAM!*—the wind
would start to howl and the sand would start to fly.

Tonight there was just a gentle breeze and a girl who

was surprised by how much she liked the hugeness, the silence. An nibbled her trail rations and gazed up at the stars.

Who needs a fancy house when you have a ceiling like this? she wondered.

The lesser moon began to rise. It was bloodred while it sat on the horizon. People called it a bad moon when it was that color. But it was nice to look at.

A sound came over the hills, from far, far away. It was sort of a metallic sound, like the vibration of insect wings. An had been hearing it all day, from the bugs who seemed to be the only inhabitants of this part of the desert.

A lizard scuttled past An's foot. One second later, another lizard dug itself out of the sand, and scuttled after the first one. The underground society of the Badlands was coming out for the Night Life.

The sound came again, but it seemed a little closer.

You woke up your cousins, she told the bugs, settling back to sleep. *I hope the bugs don't make that noise all night long. Not that I would hear ... I'm so tired.*

The sound came again, from just over the nearest hill. It didn't sound so buglike now. It went:

"Vvvvvvvvvvvvvvvvooooooooooooooooooooorrrrrrrrr-rrrnnnnnnnnn ..."

An sat up. She had heard that sound once before. Everyone who lived in the Badlands heard it at least once in their lives. No one ever wanted to hear it twice.

An struggled into her pack. She took a moment to check her locator, then set out in the uncertain light. The greater moon would rise soon—that would help. For now, she just struggled forward, checking her locator from time to time, trying not to hurry so much that she would sweat a lot. If she sweated too much, the Vorn would latch on to her trail and follow it right to her.

She probably already has, An told herself, bitterly. But that was too frightening to think about.

She had a spurt of energy that propelled her through the first hour. Then her weariness came back, and she started to stumble. Her water pack felt like it weighed three hundred pounds, but she stubbornly refused to discard it. Out here, that would be even more certain death than the Vorn could give her.

Maybe she's gone, An hoped. She checked her locator again. She was still on course. She still had two miles to hike to the hostel. She was making lousy time.

And what are you going to do when you get there, anyway? Without a rifle. Hide? Barricade yourself?

Those were good questions, but not very helpful at the moment.

"Vvvvvvvvvvvvvvvooooooooooooooooooorrrrrrrrrr-rrrnnnnnnnnnnnnnnnnn ..." came the sound again; closer this time.

Is she trying to frighten me? An wondered. All the sound did was give her another energy spurt; it didn't paralyze her with fear. But maybe that was the idea. She would be exhausted soon. The Vorn was running her down, wearing her out. If she got to the hostel, she might not even have time to barricade the place....

Think about that later. Think about that later. Think about that later.

An made that her mantra, setting her pace by it, her head down as she plowed ahead. The greater moon came out, pushing her shadow far off ahead of her. She shivered, thinking the Vorn would be able to see her now.

Vorns don't use their eyes. They use their noses. Or whatever they have that lets them smell.

An saw the building up ahead. She didn't hear anything behind her now, but she could *feel* the Vorn coming. She turned and looked back the way she had come.

Nothing moved in the moonlight, seemingly for miles.

She's out there. She's coming.

The sight of the hostel gave An another spurt of energy. She was gasping as she hurried up to it. It looked strong and secure—she just might be able to keep the Vorn out of it.

At least for the first night.

Think about that later, think about that later, An chanted to herself, and then almost ran into the first trip wire.

Her eyes registered it before her memory could communicate with her legs. She almost stepped right into the outer perimeter of the grid. It was buried in the dust, but An could see the telltale ridges. She could see them, because Rego had taught her how to lay defenses like these. She had helped lay wires three times on this very journey.

"Hello!" she called. "Hello in there! I'm Human! Please, let me in!"

No one answered for several moments, and An couldn't resist the urge to look over her shoulder, again. Nothing was moving in the desert.

"Hello!" she called again, frantically.

A man poked his head out a window. All she could see of him in the silver light were his black hair and the glitter of his eyes. He must have discarded his goggles for the evening.

"Watch out for the wires!" he warned.

"I will! Can I come in?"

"Wait," he said. In another moment, the heavy door was activated, and it swung inward. He came out and waved. "We turned them off!" he called.

An hurried inside. He pulled the door shut behind her, and she turned to get her first good look at him.

He took her breath away. And it wasn't just his smell that did it, though it hinted that he might not have bathed in weeks. He was wearing a marine's survival uniform, something An had seen plenty of times in TradeTown. But his looked a lot smarter on him than most, because he was the handsomest man she had ever seen in her life; so handsome that she wondered if he was even from Storm. His looks were too elegant, too finely crafted for Storm.

That's what people probably said about my dad, An thought to herself in wonder.

His skin didn't have the golden cast An was used to seeing; it was more like coffee with cream in it. His hair was jet black, which was a common sight on Storm; but his eyes were just as black, not the amber or brown of the native Stormer. His face was molded differently, too. It was his cheekbones that made the biggest difference, and his jawline that was so clean you could almost cut yourself on it. His mouth was perfect. Yes, perfect; that was what An decided in that first moment, before she took a deep breath and blurted out the truth: "There's a Vorn on my trail," and watched the perfect mouth turn down in a frown.

She would see that same frown—possibly on that same face—again and again, years later. Jo's face.

"Male or female?" he asked.

"Uh—" An was surprised by the question. She had thought he would just kick her out again.

"Did it make the Vorn sound?" someone else asked, and An turned to find another marine. This one had the same skin color as the first, but his hair was blond and his eyes were blue. They weren't GodHead blue, but they gave her a start. "You know," he said, " 'Vvvvvooooorrrr . . .' "

"—Yes," said An.

"Female," said the blond, and he grinned at his dark-haired friend. "Crispy critters."

"Crisp—" An panted, "crispy—?"

"Can you act as bait?" asked the dark-haired one.

"That's what I've *been* doing," said An. "What do you mean?"

"Just sit over there and make a fire for your supper," he said, pointing to the center of the huge, main room with his chin. It had a fire pit, and they had already gathered materials for burning. "Pretend you don't know she's out there. We'll see if she can get through our grid without tripping it. See how good she is."

"Okay," An said, without much enthusiasm. He walked past her without listening; he and his buddy went to their gear, which didn't look that much more sophisticated than An's, if you didn't count the force rifles and the big ordinance packs. That seemed like a hell of a lot of stuff to carry.

But it proved to be worth its weight in gold points.

An shuffled over to the fire and lit it with numb fingers. "Should I sit with my back to the door?" she asked.

"If you're not too scared," said the blond-haired one.

An decided that she *was* too scared.

The black-haired one came over and patted her shoulder with his free hand. His gun was almost as long as he was tall. He didn't look much older than An, and neither did the blond. But they *acted* older. "We'll take care of you," he said. "I promise she won't lay a claw on you."

An's throat was suddenly too tight for a reply, so she just nodded. He gave her a last pat, and then he and his buddy hid themselves.

An fixed some tea. She tried to eat, but she couldn't choke anything down. About an hour went by, and she started to relax, wondering if the Vorn had lost her trail after all.

Then the locking mechanism on the door shorted out.

An gaped at the door, her mug suddenly loose in her hand. The door began to swing slowly inward. Outside was darkness, and An couldn't see anything moving. Something glittered, up high, perhaps seven feet off the ground. An squinted, leaning forward.

They were teeth, glittering in the darkness. They were

impossible fangs, nesting in an impossible face. It came forward into the light.

An dropped her mug.

My god. My god my god my god . . .

This was a warrior. When she slipped her huge bulk through the door, An could see that she was growing a fourth pair of limbs just behind her heavily armored head.

She's ascending, An thought to herself, almost calmly. *She's becoming a Queen.*

The Vorn was massive, at least twelve feet tall at the crown of her thorax, the highest part of her body. Her head hung at seven feet. She exposed her entire masticating system, dripping a slightly acidic saliva as she did so. She tasted the air.

An held her breath, sure that the Vorn would smell the two men.

The Vorn moved toward her, using only four of its major limbs. She was graceful, moving with a horrible delicacy, as if still suspecting trip wires.

An let out her breath in a painful rush and dragged in another one. Then another.

"Human," said the Vorn, in remarkably good Standard, "you smell delicious."

The marines opened fire on her when she was no less than ten feet from An. Her body jerked in a horrible jig as the projectiles hit her, penetrated her armor, and exploded inside. Her body began to smoke almost immediately; but they had to hit her a dozen times before she even started to slow down, and she never lost her monster grin, even as she was dying. She fell with her heavy snout pointed toward An, and just before the light went out of her vestigial eyes, she hissed, "Bitch!" almost plaintively.

An stared at the giant body, amazed to still be alive, dumbfounded by the crazy luck of the whole situation.

"All right!" the blond marine was crowing. "Bagged a *Queen.*"

"Almost a Queen," corrected the other. "She wasn't quite there."

Almost a Queen, An thought, and was overcome by an awful and completely unexpected wave of pity. A moment later, she was overwhelmed by another unpleasant wave, and rushed off to find a bathroom.

She found one that still functioned—sort of—at least enough to get the mess out of her sight. She voided from both ends, until she felt completely empty.

Afterward, she washed her face and rinsed her mouth, grateful that the sink still functioned properly, which meant that the water pump under the hostel was still working. She could replenish her tank while she was there.

The marines could have bathed, if they had really wanted to. But perhaps when you spent most of your time outdoors, in danger of being killed or running out of supplies, you had to suspend some of your civilized behavior.

When she got back to the main hall, the marines were butchering the Vorn.

That was a bit more suspension of civilized behavior than An was used to, even after growing up in Trade-Town. She couldn't decide whether or not she should be upset by the sight. Finally she decided to shrug it off.

"Want some?" the dark-haired one asked her.

"No, thank you." An dug out some dried fruit and nuts from her pack. Her stomach was tender, but still needed filling.

"She was going to eat *you*," remarked the blond one.

An shrugged. "I don't like Vorn meat."

"It's a lot like lobster," he said, but he didn't bother her about it again.

An tried not to watch what they were doing. They stripped the Vorn right down to her heavy, intricate skeleton, proving that she was not the giant insect she appeared to be. Without her armor, she looked more like a mammal.

But An didn't look too closely at the Vorn's inner organs. She wouldn't have been able to continue eating if she had.

After they had finished, the marines cooked some of the meat: what hadn't been spoiled by the exploding projectiles. They seemed relaxed, as if they hadn't just dispatched the most terrifying monster the known galaxy had to offer. They smiled at An in a friendly, nonthreatening manner. She hoped that their shared adventure would make her seem more like a comrade than a victim.

Once they had eaten, the men split the weapons and ornaments the Vorn had been wearing, some of which were quite impressive. She must have been a cunning old warrior.

"You've brought us good luck," the dark-haired one told An, and she smiled, pleased that he had chosen to look at the situation that way.

After that, the marines dragged the huge bulk outside, where the desert would strip it clean. They tinkered with the locking mechanism of the door, and even got it jury-rigged and functioning again; though they didn't seem too concerned about it.

"An ascending queen eats every other warrior within fifty miles," the dark-haired one told An. "She only spares the males, and the males aren't dangerous unless you attack *them* first."

An let out a sigh of relief when she heard that. The rest of her journey might be safer now. As she curled up for sleep a modest distance away from them, she heard their murmured conversation, which seemed to be about what they planned to do for the next few days. She was just drifting off to sleep when she heard the light-haired one say, "So, you want to fuck her?"

"She doesn't want it," said the dark-haired one.

"So? We saved her life. She owes us."

"She risked her life to make it right. I say we're even. Besides, we've got booty to trade, thanks to her."

"She's really fine. What's the harm in asking? Hey baby, you awake?"

An pretended to be asleep. It wasn't that she didn't find them attractive, especially the dark-haired one. He made her heart pound every time she looked at him. She was glad he hadn't grown up with her in TradeTown, or she would have been like Le by now, with three babies. Maybe even four.

She had never seen a man as beautiful as him. But she didn't want to make love to two men at once, and besides, she didn't have any birth control. She couldn't afford a pregnancy, now or maybe ever. She would have already had her fallopian tubes burned if she had had the money.

"She has too much class to act that way," said the dark-haired one. "She's the classiest woman I've ever met."

"Maybe she needs some romancing," suggested the other.

"Maybe *you* just need a bath. Ever think of that? You think she really wants a couple of stinking, sweaty marines?"

"Did you see her eyes? Like dark honey."

"Yeah, I saw them."

"Maybe she'll undo that braid for us. Can you imagine her on top of you, all that hair hanging down . . . ?"

"She would be over here by now if she was that damned grateful."

"Maybe she's shy."

"Maybe she's dangerous. You should have learned that by now. On this planet, things that attract you can kill you."

"I'm ready to die a happy man."

An heard a rustling. She tried to keep her body still without tensing it. When they came over, she was going to pretend that she had been asleep. But she had no idea what she would do after that.

She waited, but nothing happened. After several tense moments went by, she heard snoring. She ventured a peek at them.

They were asleep.

An let herself drift into her own dreams. The last coherent thought she had was, *I'm going to get my damned tubes burned just as soon as I can.*

In the morning, the marines were gone. They had left her some of the Vorn meat, which she ignored. The morning was clear and cool and the birds were singing. An had a feeling everything had just smoothed out for her. And it wasn't just wishful thinking. Her *instincts* told her.

You've got luck, Rego had said, a million years ago. *You could make it.*

When An was making her breakfast, she noticed a small package lying near the fire. It had been carefully wrapped. Surely the marines hadn't left it by accident; their lives depended on avoiding mistakes, big and small.

Was it a gift?

She unwrapped it. It was one of the Vorn's ceremonial daggers. It was beautiful, and would fetch a nice price at the spaceport. Her life would be a little easier because of it. Now she had the extra money Rego had given her *and* a Vorn souvenir to sell.

It wasn't a frivolous gift. She could still hear him saying that she was the classiest woman he had ever met. She liked to think that he was the one who had left it for her.

The dark-haired one. The one she might have met again, years later.

The one who might have been Jo.

An was dreaming.

She didn't know where she was in her life, at this point. She might have been back on Storm, still trying to get off. Or she might have been about to land on Cabar 4, twenty-five years later, to look for Early ruins.

Or she might have been even further along in her life, about to discover how things were going to end. She didn't know. She just dreamed, peacefully, not concerned about specifics.

She felt sand under her back. Maybe she was still on Storm, after all. She felt dry heat, felt a wind blowing over her body. It was a peaceful wind; but in the distance, she could hear a Superstorm howling.

Must be miles away, she told herself, deciding not to worry about it. She sighed, and tried to settle deeper into sleep.

"Hello!" said a friendly voice nearby.

An decided it was just part of the dream and ignored it.

"Hello!" the voice persisted. "Hello there!"

An opened her eyes. Overhead, there was a purple-blue haze, unlike any sky she had ever glimpsed.

"Are you awake now?" asked the voice.

An lifted her head. No one was near her. There was just more of that purple-blue haze, some sand underneath, and a lone plant that was growing near her foot. An took a closer look at the plant. On Storm, it wasn't a good idea to sleep next to plants.

This plant was a Godweed.

She recognized its fat, thorny base, the three yellow blooms that grew from leafy stalks at its center. As she was looking, the bloom in the middle looked up at her, as if it were a face. The other two blooms settled on the base, like a pair of hands resting on chubby hips.

"Are you awake?" asked the center bloom. "I hope I didn't startle you."

"I'm awake," An said.

"Good. I was hoping we had established enough contact with you for a message," said the center bloom. "I would like to ask you a favor."

"Okay," said An, hoping the favor would have nothing to do with the ingestion of Godweed.

"Will you deliver a message for us, when you get where you're going?"

"Where am I going?" asked An.

"You'll know when you get there," the plant assured her. "Will you ask them to come visit us?"

"Who?" asked An.

"The people who know everything," replied the plant.

"The people—oh, you mean the Earlies."

"The people who know everything. We would like to speak with them, but we can't leave Storm. We change too much when we try to grow on other planets, and we lose our intelligence."

An felt a stab of fear. "Are you trying to take over the galaxy?"

"No! Not at all, we just would like to find a way to keep ourselves from wasting away like we do, from being outcasts. And we'd like to visit other people, to talk."

"But those people you want to talk to are dead," said An. "The Earlies are dead."

"To you they're dead," said the center bloom. "But time passes differently for us. For us, they're still alive."

"Oh," said An, deciding to humor the Godweed. After all, it was a plant, and everyone knew how unpredictable plants could be. Sure, they looked friendly, but turn your back on one for half a second, and *WHAM!*

"We don't mean you any harm," the center bloom said, as if reading her thoughts. "Please just tell them we'd like to meet them. That's all. Okay?"

"Okay," said An, and then the purple-blue haze moved in and swallowed her up.

Afterward, she woke up again; but she woke up in a thousand different places, in a thousand different mornings, and she didn't remember that she had dreamed about the Godweed.

Not until near the end.

An looked at the simulation of Cabar 4 on her tactical screen. It was a type-M planet, with an oxygen-nitrogen atmosphere. Its mass and gravity were slightly greater than Earth Normal. It had one moon, almost the size of a planetoid, with a huge chunk blown out of it from some past collision.

Or perhaps the moon had been blasted by some *un*natural accident. Perhaps a mining accident, or incident of an ancient war. No one really knew if the Earlies had been inclined toward war. An suspected they had not. War would have interfered with the exchange of information they had seemed to value so much.

Green, red, blue, and amber lines showed her two large land masses, one in the northern hemisphere and one in the southern, with hundreds of islands sprinkled around each. Both land masses were green with dense rain forests; even the northern polar cap had a touch of green around its edges.

It was just the sort of planet the Earlies had loved. No EggHead would have been able to look at it without drooling.

An could have seen the real planet swinging below her through a view window if she cared to open the shutter, but she was happier looking at readouts. Soon she would begin descent. She would have done it already, if her thoughts hadn't been so muddled.

Jo must have assumed that she would be killed when her Egg popped open, so he apparently hadn't bothered to sabotage anything else.

Except for the emergency masks. That was interesting. Had he really believed that she would be alert enough to grab something on the way out of her Egg? That she would be able to stay conscious long enough to haul herself back in, and that she would then use the emergency tanks? She couldn't believe she had done it, herself. But Jo was a thorough man. He would have fought for his own life, so he must have expected that she would, too.

Did he picture the whole thing in his mind? How did he feel when he saw her dying that way?

She knew why he had done it; that was what kept twisting the knife in her. He had been an EggHead for twenty-five years, earning enough to be free and control his own destiny, but never moving up, never earning enough for the *real* ship he wanted. Eggs were nothing more than closets with jump engines; you had to be crazy, reckless, desperate to prospect in one.

You had to be broke. You had to be an Outer Worlder.

She knew how he felt about it. She felt the same way.

It was a gamble trying to decide what should be spent for supplies, for pleasures, for the rejuve treatments that kept you young in a job where you couldn't afford to be older and slower. An had just gotten a rejuve treatment herself. She had gambled and used some of her advance money from Iknaton Inc., the same people who had paid for her RNA drip.

"I need a rejuve, too," she had told the agent, when she was negotiating the contract. "My neural systems are going to need to be in top condition for the drip."

He had barely deigned to raise his lovely, sculpted eyes as he said, "We don't pay for rejuves."

"Right," An had said, knowing from his tone that it would have been useless to persist. She hadn't wanted to push the argument too far; this was a plum contract, the sort that was the fulfillment of years of hard work and reputation building. Iknaton was on Karnak, an Inner World, and they didn't soil their atmosphere with Outer Worlders who weren't very, very useful.

"I'm sure you'll find that once you've completed this assignment, your memory and linguistic upgrades will enable you to procure even more lucrative contracts in the future," the agent said, unnecessarily.

"Yes," An said, wondering how many rejuves he had had himself. He looked no more than seventeen, and he was obviously a big fan of face and body sculpting as well. Every executive she had glimpsed so far at Iknaton Inc. was the same way. Pretty predators. The technology that could be deciphered from Early glyphs had made them one of the most powerful companies going.

And now she was going to help them get more of it.

"This wouldn't have been possible ten years ago, you know," he continued. "RNA stock for Early glyph linguists was extremely rare. Now that some more of them have died"—He finally raised his eyes to look straight into hers, giving her a beautiful and dreadful smile—"who knows? Our cloning technology is vastly improved. We may not even need linguists, anymore."

"Except for the dead ones," An said, in her most neutral tone.

"In a sense, you'll be a linguist yourself soon," he said, losing interest in her face and returning to his screen and the contract.

An didn't tell him that she had doubts about the RNA drip. Offering to get one had been a desperate bid. She had never received one before. It was hard to believe that you could learn a language that way, even though people had been doing it for centuries.

Besides, the Early glyphs weren't just a language. They were pure information, precious information, offering a technology advanced far beyond anything current civilizations had achieved. Iknaton Inc. wasn't the only company that was willing to pay top dollar to someone who could find Early ruins. But then the EggHeads who located those ruins always had to step aside while the linguists came in and earned twice as much for translating the glyphs.

"We can't pay you as much as we could a licensed linguist, of course," said the agent.

"That's understood," said An. That was how she had clinched the deal in the first place, by undercutting union prices and eliminating the expensive middle man.

"An advance is unusual in these cases," he said. "But, of course you must have a rejuve." He fluttered his lashes. "To get your *neurons* in top shape."

"Of course."

"And you understand that you must bring us usable information, or you will be in debt to us, at thirty-eight percent interest, annually."

"You know my credentials," said An.

"Of course, we do," he had said, and then he had presented her with the signature pad.

An had signed, knowing full well that she might end up in debt to Iknaton Inc., that she might find nothing on Cabar 4. Knowing, also, that the drip could go terribly wrong and render her psychotic, as it did in three out of a hundred cases.

But she had been looking forward to seeing what Jo's expression would be when he saw her again, looking twenty-five when she was really forty. You allowed yourself those little indulgences sometimes when you were an EggHead.

Disappointment was piling up on top of her grief. She should have been paralyzed with it. But instead, her hands were busily programming ENTRY AND DESCENT. A noise was teasing at the edge of her concentration; when she held still for a moment to listen, it stopped, and she realized she had been humming.

"What's going on here?" she asked herself. She took several deep breaths to calm the beating of her heart, and tried to analyze her emotions. But they defied analysis. She was in the worst emotional pain she could ever remember feeling. It was as if a loved one had died. Yet, at the same time, she was full of happy anticipation at the sight of the Cabar system; and that wonderful sense of being on the verge of discovery had her heart beating, her hands dancing across the control boards. In another moment, she was humming again.

It was that damned RNA drip. She had suspected it would turn out to be more complicated than they had told her. She wasn't psychotic though; she couldn't be. She wasn't hearing voices or having visual disturbances.

So far.

Sober up, she warned herself. She took another deep breath, then fired into the upper atmosphere and let the Egg go into freefall. She felt the elevator drop in her stomach and the restraint webbing tighten over her body.

Why fight it? she asked herself. Why dwell on the suffering? This was a crazy way to be feeling, but she had work to do. A good EggHead always goes with the flow. Just now, her tiny habitat was plummeting to the hard,

hard ground. The gravity was 1.2 normal, so the drag on the Egg could not be regarded whimsically.

An fired side jets until the Egg was in proper position, then fired her landers. The floor came up and slapped her body through the padding of her bed/chair; but it felt right. It felt like it was supposed to. She switched on a tactical screen over her head and watched herself maneuvering toward the driest area she could find in the interior of the large southern land mass.

A warning klaxon sounded. But it wasn't a system failure; a quick glance at the tactical screen showed her a flashing, amber *X*, not far from her own landing sight.

Someone was already there.

Jo? Of course it would be him. He had invaded her Egg and seen her travel plans. He had known where she was going, and he had guessed why. Of course, he had decided to get the jump on her.

"Why didn't you just do that in the first place, you bastard!" she said through gritted teeth. "I could have forgiven you for that! Hell, I would have tried that myself, if you had been the one with the hunch!"

It was too late to change plans, she was committed to the landing. She only had enough thrusting fuel to get in and out once, so this was it. If Jo was anywhere near his Egg, he had probably heard an alarm to warn him of an incoming craft. If not—she might be able to avoid him.

Within a hundred feet of the ground, An opened the shutter after all. She wanted to see what she was landing on, and whether or not anyone was waiting for her. But she laughed at herself when she saw the dense, wet tangle beneath her. If anyone was waiting, she wouldn't be able to see them until she was standing outside and two feet away from them.

The Egg burned its way through the foliage. An let it burn a little longer. If she tried to sit right down, steam from superheated water might blow her poor Egg right back out to kingdom come. When she finally eased down, the Egg settled on its landing gear with barely a bump. An quickly shut everything down.

Moisture was already condensing on the view window. There was no fire from the landing, and when An looked at her ship on tactical, she was amused to note that it was only slightly hotter than the forest surrounding her. She had forgotten how hot Cabar 4 was. Thirty-two degrees Celsius, ninety percent humidity. Hot and damp, just like the Earlies always seemed to like it. She popped the hatch and let the atmosphere come in and wrap sticky tendrils around her.

Noise poured in with the damp air. Most of it was from insects, but she also heard the shrieks of creatures who seemed to be stuck halfway between avians and saurians. An breathed in the microbe-rich air and prayed that her inoculations would work better this time than they had the last. She had been sick with flulike symptoms for days.

And it had been worth it.

Her brain was buzzing with joy.

How wonderful it had been. She had stood on the planet by herself, feeling the huge loneliness. But she hadn't been alone, really. The Earlies had been there once, and their ruins still lived under the jungle somewhere. She had been sure of it then, she was even more so now.

You're not alone.

It must be the RNA drip again. It was trying to warn her about Jo, about the Earlies, about—

There was something else—

An pulled on her survival pack and clambered out of the Egg. She moved a little awkwardly in the gravity after spending almost two days weightless, Real Time; but she ignored the weakness. She sealed the egg back up again, and looked around. Big leaves dangled in front of her nose, throbbing with life. A bright red worm was busily eating one. Its poisonous coloring reminded her to pull on her safety gloves.

Jo would certainly try to kill her again. He was such a thorough man. He would look her right in the eye and blow her all over the landscape. He was just like the men from TradeTown after all, the men who made you pregnant, beat you up, abandoned you. Killed you.

The grief was overwhelming.

An ducked as a shrieking bird-lizard swooped over her head, warning her out of its nesting territory.

She grinned with joy, yet the tears flowed down her cheeks.

"Crazy," she said, "crazy, crazy, crazy!" Her thoughts were like the screaming, darting creatures of the jungle.

Stop it. Get back to work.

"Stop pushing me around," she told herself. "I have a right to be crazy." But she got to work immediately, pulling foliage over her egg. Soon it would begin to grow that way by itself, until she would need a locator beam to find it again.

The plant life here wasn't as dangerous as the stuff back on Storm, but it was every bit as tenacious.

An found the locator on the front of her left tibia and pressed in the code that would activate it. It began to vibrate pleasantly, telling her that her Egg was nearby. As she walked away from it, the vibration changed to a pulse, slowing gradually as the space between her and her Egg increased, but never stopping completely.

If only her RNA drip could do the same thing for her, give her a nice jolt as she got close to Early ruins. But she was expecting too much from a chemical implant. After all, what it really was supposed to do was complex enough. She would be able to read the Early glyphs. She had brought a mini-corder with one hundred hours of recording time on it, so she could babble information as it came to her.

But would it be enough?

"Each glyph is crammed with information," Dr. Mohamonero had told her, back on Omsk. "One glyph alone might contain enough information to keep a Human scientist busy for a lifetime."

Dr. Mohamonero, with his high-class name and his scholarly demeanor. But he had done his best to prepare her. His belief in the RNA drip had helped her to believe in it.

Now if she could only find some glyphs and try it out.

"You may be tempted to record everything the glyphs tell you," Dr. Mohamonero had warned her. "You might find yourself standing in one spot, babbling. You must be disciplined, and let go of any nontechnological information, just let it slip past you."

"I think I can do that," An had said.

"Do you?" He had grinned, but not unsympathetically. "You might be surprised."

No more surprises, An pleaded to the cosmos as she pushed her way through the rain forest. But that was always a useless plea, so she gave it up and just concentrated on making progress, stopping occasionally to make notations on her mapper.

Two hours had passed that way before she got the first warning, a throbbing on her eardrum that didn't quite register as sound.

An tried to peek around the dense foliage, but she still couldn't see more than a few feet in front of her. She leaned against a wall of ferns, hoping to ease her way through; but they gave suddenly, and she fell flat on her face into a clear area.

She looked up and found six giants standing not more than ten feet from her. Their gray skin made them look like shadows in the rain forest. Gray was the color of their clothing as well—thin, layered cloth that would have been armor if it had been made out of stronger stuff. It was almost like the protective clothing An had worn when she was growing up on Storm. It covered them from their necks to their wrists, and all the way down to their safety boots. They were speaking among themselves in a low rumble that barely registered in her lower range of perception.

They were X'GBri, only a slightly more welcome sight than a Vorn Queen would have been. She had seen plenty like them in the Spacer Districts on Outer Worlds that tolerated them. She definitely didn't want to see them *here*.

Their speech was making her eardrum flutter; she still could not quite "hear" them. Usually they spoke in booming tones designed to inspire respect and fear. Fortunately, none of them was looking at An.

She got up as quietly as she could and started to ease her way back through the wall of ferns. But they rustled just during a lull in conversation, and the lone woman in the group glanced over at An before she could disappear.

The woman cried, "Human! Come here!"

An didn't reply; she continued to push her way through the forest, hoping to lose them in the dense foliage. But in another moment, a giant hand reached through the leaves and seized her. She was dragged back out into the open.

The woman was standing with her hands on her hips, waiting. She was a little shorter than the males, only about seven feet tall. Her irises were a light gray compared to their dark violet; so light that they almost disappeared within the light blue of her eyeballs.

"Come here, Human," she demanded.

The man who had fetched An gave her a little shove, but she ignored him and the woman both.

So the woman came to An. She closed her fingers around An's neck and squeezed slightly, not enough to choke, just enough to increase An's nervousness two hundred percent. But An kept her face calm, her body relaxed. It was her only hope.

The woman studied An, her face alight with interest. X'GBri facial expressions always looked exaggerated to An, because their features were so large, their faces so mobile. Annoyance looked like rage, pleasure like madness. The Human amygdala, the organ in the brain responsible for interpreting facial expressions, responded to X'GBri faces with anxiety and confusion.

"You're an EggHead," said the woman in perfect Standard.

"Yes," said An. EggHeads could be found prospecting all over the known galaxy, so she knew she wasn't an oddity.

"You're surprised to see us," said the woman.

"I'm always surprised to see X'GBris," An said, truthfully. She didn't mention that she was especially so, in this case. She had thought the amber X on her tactical screen had been Jo's ship, not theirs. Had they chased Jo off the planet?

Had they killed him?

The man who had captured An was now touching her, an expression of avid curiosity on his face. This was typical of X'GBri, who were not known for respecting the privacy and rights of others. He stripped off her pack, her mapper, and mini-corder, dropping them like trash.

He spoke a word in the low-thrumming tone and pointed to her eyes. The others leaned closer, looking at them. "Tiger-eyes," he said, obviously for An's benefit, since tigers were of Earthly origin. An's irises were amber, the primary opposite of his own. He liked that.

His hands explored her breasts, and she tensed, knowing there was nothing she could do about it, especially not with the woman's hand still around her throat.

"Why do you tie your hair this way?" he enquired,

wrapping An's braid around his hand and lifting it to sniff.

"To keep it out of my face."

He clicked his teeth together, a sound that might have indicated amusement or simply mild interest. His own hair was blue-black, long and thick, of a texture that seemed almost capable of movement on its own. She cringed when a strand of it brushed her cheek like a serpent, tasting her.

The others were closing in, too. But An just became calmer, trying to radiate stillness from the inside out. The X'GBri loved conflict; she couldn't give it to them.

But when his hand slipped between her legs, An pushed it away and said, "No."

It was the wrong thing to say. His face became very still. It was a frightening phenomenon to observe, all of the life draining out of that mobile face, the purple eyes turning to glass.

Crazy, thought An. *Crazy eyes.*

He was giving off an intense odor now. The hairs on the back of An's neck stood up. "No?" he enquired, as if amazed at his good luck. "No, little female?"

He pushed the X'GBri woman out of the way. She let go of An's neck without protest, with an air of amused resignation.

The man finished wrapping An's braid around his hand, then unzipped the front of her flightsuit. As he slipped his hand inside, he leaned down and licked her neck, tasting her emotions.

"You're not afraid," he said. "I wonder what it will take to make you afraid."

His companions clicked their teeth in anticipation, like a hoard of insects devouring the rain forest. The sound made An want to scream.

X'GBris had some mammalian characteristics. The females had the same secondary sexual characteristics as

Human females: breasts that were round even when there was no milk in them. Their vaginas served the same purpose, though their vulvas had protective features that Human females lacked.

Male X'GBri could act very much like male Humans under certain circumstances.

Still, An didn't know what they would do. They might simply strip her and examine her. They might torture her, or treat her gently. They might want to have sex with her, or simply play with her. They might get bored and just walk away from her, threatening her not to come near them again.

They might kill her. They might have killed Jo. What would they have done to him? She tried not to picture him going through the same humiliating examination she was now undergoing. Her brain obliged by showing her scenes of possible death.

Stop thinking about him! Worry about yourself!

The male licked her again and again. His throat and chest were vibrating with contentment; almost a purr, but not nearly as friendly.

Then a voice An knew called to them, "Get your damned paws off her, GNno!"

An stiffened.

"Jo," said GNno, looking more surprised by An's reaction than by Jo's arrival. He licked her again and said, "What's this?

"Jo," asked the X'GBri woman, "why do you care about this female?"

"She's my mate," snarled Jo.

An couldn't resist craning her head around to look at Jo. There he was, tall and dark, his body lean and muscular, his hair cropped right next to his skull, like the hair of every EggHead in the business except for An. She had seen that look of rage on his face before; she was glad he was looking at GNno, not at her.

"Well," the woman was saying, "then you only have to fight GNno instead of all five of us. How lucky for you!"

"Are you afraid I'm going to kill your little man?" GNno asked An, licking her cheek. "Poor thing. When I'm finished with him, I'll take you with me. You're interesting."

GNno handed An to the other men, who held her as if she were a skittish cat.

Jo was stripping off his pack and removing instruments from his flightsuit. He unstrapped his gun. He had never even made a move to draw it; it seemed irrelevant. It might as well have not even been there.

He was meticulous and thorough, but An could see that he was moving automatically, not even thinking about the things he was dropping on the ground. He was left with just his flightsuit, but Jo's flightsuit had been chosen as carefully as everything else he owned. GNno wouldn't be able to take handholds of it, as he had done with An's.

Jo approached GNno. An shivered as she watched the rage and tension in his body. She had seen him move that way before, under similar circumstances.

GNno was smiling, with teeth that were angled inward so that prey could not escape once he bit into it. He would have been smiling no matter who attacked him. But he wasn't taking Jo seriously. His body was too relaxed.

An let out one tortured breath and dragged in another one.

Jo didn't hesitate. He went straight into GNno, who looked like he was inclined to simply tolerate the feeble Human blows until he tired of them and swatted Jo away. But Jo was made of tougher stuff than most, and he clawed, jabbed, kicked, and punched pressure points with murderous fury, without the slightest hesitation. Most people would have held back out of squeamishness, if not for mercy or honor. But Jo was not squeamish.

Like a sociopath, thought An, and she shivered. But some traitorous part of herself was proud, too, and excited. Nearby, the X'GBri woman had begun to purr, and An could not quite tell just whom the woman was favoring with her glances.

GNno grunted with pain and surprise. He fell back from Jo's attack, frowning, rubbing sore places.

"You're worth fighting," GNno said, and would have said more if Jo had allowed him. But Jo was already back at him again. GNno lost his lethargy in a horrifying instant, and began connecting strange blows to Jo's body, seeming to stab at him with all of his fingertips, as if they were blades. An saw agony blossom on Jo's face. But unlike GNno, Jo was not surprised by the pain. He merely used it as a goad.

An could see GNno was becoming very annoyed. He continued the fight out of sheer pleasure of conflict, but Jo was connecting with too many pressure points, and GNno was beginning to have to battle his own instincts to end the threat to his body. He finally seized Jo, forcing his arms flat against his torso, and lifted him bodily into the air. As if in slow motion, An saw GNno lifting Jo within reach of his powerful teeth. He was going to bite Jo's throat out.

"No!" An screamed with all of her might, but she had not even opened her mouth when Jo curled and brought his feet together, lifting them and slamming both of his reinforced heels into GNno's chin. GNno's head snapped back, and he dropped Jo, who rolled away. GNno fell over and struck the ground like a felled tree.

Jo stood back, ready to attack again. But GNno only managed to climb to his knees before he had to stop and shake the stars out of his head. He blinked, and seemed to have trouble finding Jo.

"You never could have done that without my help," GNno accused.

"Thank you," snarled Jo.

GNno bared his teeth, not really smiling, but looking pleased anyway. "Where are you?" he asked politely.

"Over here, motherfucker," said Jo.

"I never fucked my mother," said GNno. "But it wasn't for lack of trying."

He lunged at Jo, but he was just guessing at the location. Jo dodged easily aside and slammed both of his fists down on the base of GNno's skull.

GNno didn't get up this time.

The X'GBri woman strolled over to them and looked down at GNno. "He won't wake up for several minutes," she announced. "I suppose that means you qualify as the winner."

"Thank you, TTra," said Jo.

"You're welcome, Jo," said TTra, and she snapped her fingers at An's jailers. An felt the pressure fall away from her arms and legs. Pins and needles started to stab where the circulation was returning.

Jo was picking up his pack, his equipment. An did the same, trying not to look at anyone as she did so. She had no idea what she was going to do next.

Jo took her arm, led her away from the X'GBri.

"Don't follow us, TTra," he warned.

TTra clicked her teeth at him.

In another moment, they were out of sight behind the foliage. Jo still had hold of An's arm, and didn't seem inclined to let go.

"My mapper," said An, as she realized she had no idea where they were.

"I've got it mapped, already," said Jo. "I've been all over this area, trying to avoid TTra and her mates. I think they followed me from Mythos."

An choked. "What were you doing on Mythos?"

"Looking for you."

Tears wanted to come into her eyes, but she wouldn't

let them. She was even sorry she had asked the question. She shouldn't remind him that he had failed to kill her. But why would he have looked for her on Mythos? That was where she had been before here. And before that, Omsk, for the RNA drip. Had he been there, as well? And *why*? It was driving her insane.

She decided to take a risk. "Couldn't we talk it over?" she asked. "Why do you have to kill me?"

He stopped so abruptly she bumped into him. She wished she hadn't looked right into his face at that particular moment; but it was too late, she was trapped. His expression paralyzed her. She had never seen one like it on his face, before. He might as well have been an X'GBri with a face like that.

"I hoped you would live," he said.

"You hoped I would live." An repeated words that seemed devoid of meaning.

But apparently to Jo they meant everything. She was dizzy, trying to understand what was written in his face, a mass of conflicting emotions that made her wonder if she hadn't been wrong, if someone *else* had tried to kill her, and Jo had tried to stop it. . . .

"I wanted to undo the damage," he was saying. "I chased you all along your route, but I kept missing you, I was always just a little too late."

But then: "I regretted it, An, even while I was doing it. I hated—I hate—"

He did it. He really tried to kill me. My lover, my Jo.

"I didn't mean it," he was saying. "I didn't want it. I can't stand it." His voice sounded like gravel passing over his raw, bloody throat. Every word hurt him. What was forcing the words out hurt even more.

An had imagined all sorts of awful scenarios that might unfold once Jo realized she was still alive. But somehow, none of them were as bad as what was really happening, the anguish in his voice, the pain in his face. It would

have been better if he had laughed at her, told her to go
to hell. Why couldn't he do that? Why did she have to
watch him suffer, too?

"Did you at least get something out of it?" she wondered. "Or was it all for nothing?"

Jo seized her arms, bruising the bruised places again,
but she hardly felt it. The pain was small compared to
what was inside her head and inside her chest.

"It was for nothing!" he was crying. "No matter what,
it was for nothing!"

Her throat shut tight. Her face couldn't muster an intel-
ligible expression; the muscles went slack. Dead calm
was flowing into her, pumping into her muscles, directed
by numbing chemicals from her overwrought brain. It
was just like she had felt with GNno.

No, it was worse. Far worse.

Jo watched the life slipping out of her face, and resignation filled his own. Whatever he had been trying to tell
her, he had failed. Finally, he let go of her arms. "Come
on," he said, wearily. "We need to put space between
them and us."

But An didn't follow him. He turned around when he
missed her, but she just shook her head, and turned to go
in the opposite direction.

She had gone two steps when a clicking erupted from
the trees. The almost-insect sound made her skin crawl.
She turned again, sadly, and rejoined her old lover, who
led her away through the trees.

They didn't speak again for the rest of that long, exhausting day. To An it seemed like an endless series of
starts and stops, and she would stand like a dumb animal
while Jo consulted his own, far more sophisticated mapper. She had felt a twinge of curiosity when she had first
seen it; how had Jo managed to afford such an expensive

and advanced piece of equipment? It was one of the models based on Early technology, she was sure of it.

But after a few hours, she no longer cared where or how he had gotten it. She no longer cared about anything at all.

There was just the endless, green, wet stuff to plow through; the wild, poisonous color of blossoms; the heat that made her body throb and her brain sleepy; and the occasional sound of clicking, or of subvocalized X'GBri speech, teasing her eardrum. She laughed at one point, and called, "If you're so fond of us, why don't you just join us? Don't be shy!"

Jo had laughed, too, with the same edge of insanity in his voice. But he had taken her arm again, and pulled her along, away from their mutual enemies, and eventually the terrain had begun to change, to become cooler, rockier, less dense. By the time the sun was low in the sky, Jo was no longer consulting his mapper or that other piece of equipment that An had decided was some kind of sensor. He no longer seemed to feel that the X'GBri were following them.

An's instincts told her the same thing. She felt a numb sort of relief.

Something else, too. A happy, chirping, buzzing sort of thing.

Not again, she scolded her brain. *Not now.* But the feeling continued, and she was forced to look around for the cause.

It was the terrain. Early ruins were near. At one time there must have been warm, pooled water in the rocks. The Earlies had loved that sort of thing.

"Careful," she whispered to Jo. "We're about to find what they suspect we're really looking for."

Jo frowned, consulted his sensor again, and started off in another direction. Soon they were climbing in and out of crevices.

"The X'GBri hate to climb," he confided. "They're too impatient."

The sun was sitting on the horizon when he called a halt and consulted the sensor again.

"They've been gone for hours," he said, and unstrapped his pack.

An eased her sore body to the ground, barely pausing to slip off her own pack. She watched him while he uncurled a compressed sleeping bag and pulled out some food. "Have you got enough to eat?" he asked An.

She nodded, made herself pull out her own supplies. The sleeping bag felt good under her sore bottom. But as she chewed the food, she barely tasted it.

She was sitting near him, but not as near as she once would have. Back on the Egg, when she had first discovered his betrayal, she had wanted to ask him why he had been willing to forget that: the closeness, the kisses, the heat, and the laughter. And if he could forget it, why hadn't he simply shot her? Stabbed her? Or a million other things?

Now she didn't want to know.

She was trying not to look at him, but her eyes kept creeping back toward him in horrified fascination. He was staring at her, his fine features drawn by joy and anguish, a combination that made him look as if he had been stunned by a riot prod.

His brain is just as mixed up as mine is, she thought, and marveled at how handsome he could look in that condition. It was as if he had been stripped to the bare essentials, revealing the hand of the celestial artist who had molded his wonderful form. He looked no more than thirty, but then she had never seen him look older than that.

"You look beautiful," he said, and An suddenly remembered her own rejuve treatments, how she had wanted to please him. Now she didn't want that at all. The tone of his voice frightened her. She looked away again.

"I'm not asking you to forgive me," he said.

"No," she agreed.

"But you have to trust me now, An. You don't have any choice. TTra knows damned well that we're looking for Early ruins. They'll just follow us until we find what they want."

An nodded. She was in an impossible situation; she had invested everything in this latest venture, and it had all gone to hell. She took a sip of water to undo the lump in her throat.

Her canteen went flying as Jo knocked her over and pulled himself on top of her.

"No!" she screamed, "Jo, I want to live! Don't—!"

But he was kissing her, not killing her. He kissed her hard, and his mouth was salty. She realized, with shock, that he was crying. In fifteen years, she had never seen him do that.

He held her face in his hands and pressed his forehead against hers. "I killed you," he sobbed. "I killed you and I couldn't fix it. I got my ship, An, the one I've always wanted. I got it not more than two days after you left. I tried to go after you and undo the damage, but you disappeared on Omsk, and I left too late, and you were always just one jump ahead ..."

"Then why did you have to do it?" she managed to croak.

"You know why."

"I want you to say it," she said, though she really didn't.

"I never trusted you, An. Never." He pulled back and looked at her face, pale and still in his hands. His eyes said, *Who are you?* a question she had seen thousands of times behind his glances. He was haunted, completely torn by his emotions. She began to pity him, and she hated the feeling.

He said, "I saw you in my dreams, every time I tried to close my eyes. I'll never let go of you again, An. I love you."

Those words were even more shocking than his tears. She had never expected to hear them from him. Every year she had been away from him, she had known she might never see him again. EggHeads didn't form connections like that; it was too painful when they fell apart. But maybe Jo was tired of being an EggHead. God knew, An was.

He said, "You're alive. I can touch you and hold you." He kissed her again. This time she tasted sex on his lips; he wanted to make love. She couldn't push him off of her. So she asked him a question instead.

"Why did you plan it that particular way, Jo? Why not poison me, or shoot me? Why not plant a bomb on my Egg?"

He shuddered as if she had struck him a terrible blow. But he answered, his voice low and strained.

"I didn't want to do that to your body. I didn't want to watch you die, either. I knew I couldn't stand that. And I couldn't stand to think of you burning or—coming apart—"

Horror was dawning on his face, as if he himself were just now learning of his betrayal. He looked at her sideways, as if that could help him to see inside her.

"I could never tell what you really wanted, An. I could never tell if you were just—jerking me. I didn't know if you loved me or if you were just waiting to shoot me in the back."

He pushed himself away from her, but took her hands and kissed her palms before sitting again, a respectable distance away from her.

"Twenty-five years in an Egg. That's why I really did it. You know what I'm talking about."

The horrible thing was, she did know. She had felt that paranoid herself, even about Jo. She'd had thoughts about killing rivals, though she had never acted on them.

But she never would have tried to harm Jo.

She watched him. His face was closed again, almost back to its old expression. How many years had she watched him this way? How many times had she seduced him, like a lamb taming a lion? Every single time she had been with him.

He had made love like a battering ram unless she finessed him into more gentle, pleasing rhythms. She had been the one who tended to seek him out, to demand things of him that he really had trouble giving.

Of course he had snapped. He had tried to trust, but he had been forced past his limits. And now he was suffering for what he had done to her, she could see that. He would have to live with the fact that he had tried to kill what he loved most in life.

He saw the way she was looking at him. "You think I'm crazy," he accused.

"You're acting—" she said, but then was afraid to finish the sentence. "The pressure—"

"What pressure?" he snarled. "What fucking pressure? Is that what you think happened? Am I that kind of fucking weakling?"

"No," she said, then shut her mouth when she recognized what she was doing. What she had seen a thousand other women doing back on Storm, trying to soothe a man who was getting ready to hit them. Only succeeding in getting them angrier. She shut her mouth and kept it shut while he ranted.

"You don't know me! You don't know a fucking thing! You think this is the kind of thing you can just look at and say, *Oh, poor baby, he couldn't take the pressure—*"

An stopped listening. He kept yelling, but he seemed to be losing coherency as time went on. She didn't look at him or show any other emotion. She just let the weariness sink into every fiber of her muscles, into her very bones.

"—You think you've been out here a long time? You don't fucking know the meaning of the word! You don't fucking have a clue—!"

She was glad he was screaming that way. It helped her to kiss a childish dream good-bye. Just like every other woman in her family had been forced to do, before her.

"—How many times do I have to die before I make it all right, before it all goes away—?"

An felt almost comforted by the knowledge that so many had gone before her. And now she knew why so many of them had stayed with their men. That was what she was going to have to do, too. She couldn't imagine how she was going to accomplish what she had set out to do on Cabar 4 without Jo's help. Yes, he might betray her again.

But next to what had happened in her Egg, any other betrayal would seem trivial.

"I'm fucking tired of all this fucking shit and those goddamm motherfuckers running me down and drying me out and taking every goddamn thing a man could ever care about and shitting on it—!!"

No, she didn't care what happened anymore. She was an EggHead, she was going with the flow. If they succeeded, they would be rich, able to do whatever they wanted to do in the future. Before, she had hoped they might do it together. Now all of the pleasure had gone out of her future, leaving a cold, empty place, worse than any loneliness she had ever felt in the Egg.

Silence woke her from her reverie. Jo had finished his rant. He looked ashamed, now.

"I'm sorry," he croaked.

In a matter of seconds the old Jo had come back, banishing the crazy man. He was gazing at her again, like he still couldn't believe she was there, like she was a ghost.

"Don't yell at me, anymore," she told him. No, she *ordered* him. The old Jo would understand what she was saying.

"I won't," he agreed, and she could see that he meant it. He would rather die than lose control like that again.

An nodded, and tried to look away. But the hunger in his eyes was horrifying, and she couldn't, no matter how much she told herself it was dangerous to keep looking.

She kept looking. Her mind emptied until there was nothing in it at all.

Just the void and Jo's eyes.

An could remember what it felt like to be full of youthful energy and hope. That was how she had felt on the morning when she had first glimpsed the Star Port, after struggling across the Badlands of Storm for three weeks.

She had been seeing the city lights since the night before, shining on the horizon. She had been able to see ships taking off for the past three days, the burn of their rockets and the vapor trails they left on their way up. It had made her feel wonderful—she was on the right track. But she had been surprised by how many ships took off every day. She tried to count them, but she had lost count somewhere around fifty-three.

And then the morning came when she could see it sprawling on the plain. Even the port was ten times bigger than TradeTown had been. The city that had grown next to it was twenty times bigger. Neither of them looked anything like the cities of the Badlands. They soared and glittered. Their covered streets had no holes in them. People could walk underneath with naked faces.

An consulted her locator and saw, with satisfaction, that she had followed the map almost exactly. She had deviated slightly near a red zone, which had shifted red sand far west in the last SuperStorm and confused her. But that had been the only time.

"Hurray for me," she said with a parched throat. She had used the last sips of her water the night before. Since then, Tempter plants had tried to lure her with the sounds of dripping or trickling water. An knew perfectly well that she wasn't equipped to do battle with Tempters, that they would whip her with paralyzing stingers, and then send their roots into her flesh while she lay there, helpless.

But the sounds had tormented her so. She had made it to the Star Port just in time.

An started walking toward the city. There were no roads out of the desert from her side, they all led out the other side. She walked in the sand for most of the day, the city growing gradually larger in her field of vision, tantalizing her even more than the Tempters had. She hoped there would be a drinking fountain, somewhere, soon.

You're almost there. You can make it.

Some time in the late afternoon, when the sound of distant, firing rockets had long since become a familiar companion, she put her feet on pavement. It was the very beginning of a road leading inside. The sand lapped up on it, as if it would like to devour it. During SuperStorms it probably did, but then workers would come out and blow it back where it belonged.

Maybe I'll get a job like that, An thought, as she followed the pavement. It was leading more toward the port section than the city; but An hoped it would take her to someone who could give her a drink of water.

The idea of blowing sand for a living wasn't too appealing, but it would be a start. From there, who knows?

Yeah, who knows? Not me, that's for sure.

It was funny, but now she was having doubts, getting cold feet as it were—though her feet were pretty hot and tired at that moment. Hot and tired and swollen, and wouldn't she just love to get off them for a whole day? Get off them and sip cold drinks, sit in an air-conditioned room. . . .

Would she be able to afford an air-conditioned room? Where should she go first? What should she do when she got there? She hadn't allowed herself to worry about that stuff in the Empty Quarter. She had used all her energy to get across. But now, plans had to be made.

Only she couldn't seem to think about anything but water.

Get a drink of water first, she decided. *Then worry about what comes next. Like, maybe another drink of water!*

She plodded along for another hour before she picked her head up and saw the vehicle approaching her. She stopped dead, wondering what to do. There was a man driving, and he was looking right at her. He was wearing some kind of uniform.

Was she not supposed to be on the road? Maybe it was government property. But then, weren't all roads government property?

He slowed his vehicle down and pulled up next to her. It was a two-seater jeep, and it was littered with debris from his lunch. All he had to protect his face and eyes were a cap and some sunglasses. He stared at her in amazement for several minutes, taking in her dusty appearance; then stared out into the Empty Quarter.

"Where the hell did you come from?" he asked.

An pointed out into the desert.

"You walked all the way out here? From where?"

"TradeTown," croaked An.

His mouth dropped open. Obviously, he knew where that was. An shifted from foot to foot, wondering if she should ask for water, ask for a ride. But suddenly she was too shy to do either.

He didn't look like a bad sort. He might have been thirty, and he had the dark-brown face of a man who walked around in nothing but a cap most of the time. His eyes were brown, too, and altogether ordinary. He had a patch on his sleeve that had the Star Port insignia on it. An admired it.

He shook himself and started digging around in some things on the floor of the jeep. He pulled out a bottle of water and handed it to An.

She was so grateful, her hands shook. But she was able to get the top up and the water into her mouth without too much trouble.

"How old are you?" he asked.

"Nineteen," lied An.

"And you walked all the way here."

"Worked a caravan all the way to Desert Center."

"Jezuz Christ."

An was trying to take little sips. He was still looking at her like he couldn't believe she really existed.

"You need a job?" he asked, suddenly.

"Yes," An said, hoping that what he had in mind had nothing to do with sex.

"I know a guy you should talk to," he said. "Want to get in?"

An did get in. She pulled off her pack and her empty water tank, and stuffed it in with the clutter, then stuffed herself in, too. She couldn't walk another step, and this fellow seemed all right. Her instincts said so.

Of course, her instincts may have been influenced by

her aching feet. But the deed was done, she was in the jeep. He turned it around, and headed back toward the port.

"Anyone who could walk through the Empty Quarter is someone we need to hire," he said, making An feel proud of herself—and very hopeful. "How did you know where you were going?" he asked.

"Used a map."

"Jezuz. You have a locator?"

"Yes."

"And you walked with that tank on your back. I can't believe it. When did you run out of water?"

"Last night."

"You are one lucky kid."

An flinched at the sound of the word *kid*. She hoped he believed her about her age. If they knew she was fifteen, she wouldn't get a job, equivalency diploma or no.

"What's your name?" he asked.

"An. Yours?"

"Ro. I've worked for the Port Services for ten years. They've got pretty good benefits if you don't care too much about getting rich. You worked caravans?"

"Yeah."

"Handling animals and stuff?"

"Yeah."

"How long did you do that before you walked here?"

"Four years."

"God, you must have been a baby when you started."

An hoped he wouldn't figure out just how much of a baby. But he didn't ask. He was driving her past fields of parked ships now, and her jaw fell open as she looked at them. All those years she had pretended she would fly one, and now here they were. They were all sizes, shapes, and makes. They even drove past a couple that were the size of skyscrapers; but they were parked faraway, in special areas.

"I can start today," she said, suddenly remembering that he was there.

He laughed.

"I think you'd better rest today. You look like you're ready to fall over."

She was. In fact, she couldn't decide if she wanted to fall asleep or if she wanted to keep staring at the sights. Star Port was super-high-tech compared to TradeTown; she saw almost no adobe. She saw metal, glass, smooth surfaces made out of stuff she didn't even recognize.

She saw transients and drug addicts, too; but she didn't recognize them as such. Not yet. She still hadn't found out that Star Port had an unemployment rate of sixty percent. She still didn't know how lucky she was to have met Ro.

"You get SuperStorms up here?" she asked.

"Oh, yeah. Mostly out of the Yellow Zone. Bet you couldn't tell, huh?"

"TradeTown is pretty yellow, too."

"I know. I was born there."

An smiled, pleased to meet a countryman.

"My folks brought me here," he said. "And we sure as hell didn't walk! But I've heard of people who did. I guess my brother walks a lot."

"He works caravans?"

"He's a GodHead."

An shut up. She didn't know what to say that wouldn't either sound offensive or patronizing. That was a horrible thing, having a brother who was a GodHead. She sneaked a peek at him; he didn't seem that upset about it.

"That's how come I was out here to pick you up," he was saying. "Premonitions run in my family. I had a feeling someone was coming. I didn't think you'd be coming from so far away, but—usually I try to pay attention to my feelings. Poor thing, you looked like you couldn't walk another step."

Don't prophesize for me, An silently pleaded. But that was silly. Ro was helping her out. Being paranoid had become too much of a habit in the Empty Quarter.

They drove past countless buildings. The port was built like a giant wheel, with buildings and roads radiating out from the hub of the Control Center and fields in between them. There were vast fields surrounding the southern side; that was the side An had come in from. That's where they had seen the biggest ships.

Now they were headed for a building not far from the Control Center.

"You'll have to take the first thing that's available, before you get what you want," Ro told her. "Okay?"

"You bet!"

"Even janitorial. That's not a bad job. You get to see the inside of the Control Center, places you wouldn't be able to go if you were higher up."

An nodded sagely, without the slightest idea of what he was talking about. He pulled into an employees' parking lot—a lot that required a parking fee, even though he was driving a company vehicle. An frowned at that. It was the very first of a series of unpleasant surprises.

Ro took her arm as they went into the building. It didn't have any identifying signs or numbers, and the door they went through was around the side. It said MAINTE in faded letters. The NANCE part of the word had been peeled off.

An walked into a wall of cool air. It made her feel faint with relief.

"Could I have another drink of water?" she asked Ro, who steered her past a cooler for a few sips out of a paper cup, before taking her into an office. It contained a desk with a screen on it, a few chairs, and a middle-aged man with a wide, pleasant face. He looked up from the screen as they came in and fixed An with a sharp stare that made her think of Master Rego. He even had grizzled eyebrows like Rego.

"Yes?" he enquired, making An's knees turn to water.

"Have a job applicant for you, Geo," said Ro.

Geo turned his intimidating stare on Ro, whose only re-action was to grin in triumph.

"This is why you drove out Fifty-ninth Avenue?" Geo asked him.

"Yep. She walked right out of the Empty Quarter."

Geo's eyes widened. He stared at An again, this time seeing her pack, her empty water tank, her dirty face and clothes in a different light.

"You *walked*?" he said. "From *where*?"

"Just from Desert Center, sir," said An.

Geo's mouth didn't drop open. Instead, he merely asked, "Why?"

"I want a job, sir."

Geo looked at Ro again. "I should know better than to doubt one of those feelings of yours."

The two men laughed, and Ro pulled up a chair. An wondered if she should, too; but she was afraid to move.

"Where am I supposed to find a job for this girl?" Geo asked, and An's heart sank.

"Anyone who would walk here all the way from Desert Center to get a job *deserves* a damned job," said Ro. "Make one up for her."

"Oh, yeah, I have that power all right. Maybe I should just give her mine."

"You'll find something."

"There isn't anything, Ro, not right now. I suppose I could look at the bulletin board, but I doubt anything has come up since this morning."

An dug frantically in the inner pocket of her vest and pulled out a packet of papers. "I have recommendations, sir," she pleaded, and stuck them under his nose.

Geo looked at the papers. He took them from her, gingerly, and unfolded them. They were stained with sweat. An cringed when she saw how tawdry they looked. And to think she was handing *paper* to a man who was sitting in front of a *screen,* who probably never even touched paper all day long!

He unfolded the first one and studied it for a long time. An wondered if it was Rego's letter. She hoped so, that was the best one of all.

Geo looked at her over the top of the paper. "This is your map," he said.

"Oh—I'm sorry. I didn't know it was on top." An stuck her hand out for the map, but he didn't hand it over.

"Ro, come look at this," he said. Ro got up and bent over Geo's shoulder. The two of them traced An's trail with their fingertips.

"Says here," said Geo, " 'Vorn Queen.' What does that mean?"

"I ran into a Vorn at the first hostel," said An. "I thought I'd better mark the location and give it to the authorities when I got here."

"Geez, look how far back that was," whispered Ro.

"She was a *Queen?*" asked Geo.

An blushed. "Not exactly. She was ascending."

"And you *survived?*"

"Some marines helped me."

He didn't comment on that. An wished he hadn't found the map, hadn't seen the notation about the Queen. It made her look like a liar or a braggart.

Geo handed the map to Ro, who took it back to his chair and studied it some more. "Okay," Geo said, turning to his screen. "Job."

An tried not to hold her breath while he searched. It was taking a long time, she would have passed out if she hadn't made herself breathe.

"Do you mind if I keep this?" Ro asked her.

"Huh?"

"The map. As a souvenir?"

An had meant to keep it herself, but something about the way he looked as he was asking made her say, "Yes, keep it. But we have to tell the authorities—"

"I'll tell 'em," said Geo. "How about janitorial?"

"Sounds fine," said An.

"Position opened up fifteen minutes ago." Geo glanced at Ro, who was still absorbed in the map. "Just about the time you walked in this office."

"I'll take it," said An.

"Huh. Can you start today?"

"Yes."

Geo laughed. "You'll start tomorrow."

"Okay."

"Report here, six A.M. Got a place, yet?"

"I'll take her out to Desert Sands," said Ro. "My shift is almost up."

"Right," said Geo, and gave An a wink. "Most of us live there. It's close, and you can ride the bus to work every day."

"Great," said An, and now she finally did sit down, falling into the chair like a load of wet laundry.

The Vorn dagger fetched a hundred points, gold. An was astonished at the price—the clerk and the manager had had an excited, lengthy conversation before purchasing it from her. She had worried that they would try to cheat her; the people in the last five shops had sniffed at it, and offered twenty points, silver.

But this had been the dagger of an ascending Queen, and An felt that she should honor the old warrior's memory with a decent price.

The clerk and the manager of the last shop were also the only ones who had treated An with respect, and who had asked An where she had gotten the dagger. She told them the truth, and was treated with information in return.

"This piece is prewar!" the manager told her excitedly. "It must be a thousand years old! It must have been passed from warrior to warrior as they fought and killed each other. Can you imagine!"

An could imagine.

"Look," said the clerk, and showed her a glyph that was traced on the bottom of the hilt. It shifted under her eyes, and she had to squint to focus on it. But squinting didn't help.

"Ah, hah," said the clerk, "it's moving, isn't it. That's an Early glyph!"

An frowned. "On a Vorn dagger?"

"Yes, curious, isn't it? A warrior wouldn't have cared about it, herself. The females don't use their eyes for much. A male must have carved it there. I've only seen one other like it, and that was in the Smithsonian back on *Earth*."

An's eyes widened. Earth was the hub of the Inner Worlds—to think that she had something that would interest *Earthers*.

"This is a very rare piece," said the manager, "a very important one. We're so pleased you brought it to us! Please think of us the next time you come across a piece like this!"

"I certainly will," An promised, taking the one hundred points, gold, which would pay her rent for the next year. She thanked them, and ran out to catch the noon bus back to work.

Had the marines had the slightest idea how valuable the dagger was? She hoped that the rest of the booty had been equally valuable. They had saved her life, and they deserved the good luck.

How wonderful! Enough money to pay rent for a year! Things were going so well, and Geo was happy with her work. She might be able to move up to a job with Security soon. Janitorial wasn't bad, but it was hard on her back sometimes. And there were all sorts of fees you had to pay, just for the honor of being allowed to work; all sorts of taxes. She needed the higher pay.

An hopped on the bus that would swing her past the Lunch District. She still had a chance to grab a sandwich before getting back to work. She was only halfway through a ten-hour shift; she would need the fuel.

She loved the big, clean buses. They were cooled by nano, not by coolant and blower like at An's apartment. They were silent and had such a smooth ride. You could get anywhere you wanted inside the city in minutes.

And the most interesting people rode the bus. People from everywhere; people from nowhere. People with skin the color of the blackest sand; people who looked bleached white. Most people were An's color—some variation of brown. Most people had dark hair and eyes; but some had white hair or gold hair—even *red* hair. And sometimes it was even their natural color.

And then there were the aliens.

Usually An only saw X'GBris, but sometimes she would see someone from a race she didn't know. The very first day An had rode the bus with Ro, to look at Desert Sands Apartments, she had seen someone with green skin and scales; a slender person with graceful, cat-like movements who looked at everybody with huge pink eyes that didn't seem to have pupils.

"Where is that person from?" An had asked Ro.

"Nowhere Humans have ever been before," he remarked, enigmatically, but couldn't tell her what the race was.

Today, there were X'GBris on the bus again. They were the same people An had been seeing all week, a group of young males. She was careful to avoid looking directly at them. Their exaggerated expressions always embarrassed her.

One fellow got off at the Lunch District, along with

An. She watched him out of the corner of her eye. He was more interested in the fruit bars than in the sandwich joints. She lost sight of him after a few minutes.

She bought a sub and went to the park to eat. She strolled around with a naked face, not even needing sunglasses under the durable, flexible UV screens that covered the city. Having a bare face felt so wonderful.

There was a spot she had discovered, down by the artificial brook, where hardly anyone went. There was a carefully tended zen garden, with subtle blendings of red, black, yellow, blue, and white sand. It sort of reminded her of home.

She was sitting on a low rock when she saw the X'GBri again. He had come down to the brook with a bag of oranges. He looked at her once with curiosity, but seemed to only consider her one of the sights. He turned his attention back to the brook once he got bored with her. He crouched by the water, his gray clothing throwing off unexpected highlights of silver and purple.

X'GBri always seemed to wear some shade of gray. An wondered why that was. Their own UV protection? Or was it something only X'GBris would really understand? Some sort of display taboo?

She couldn't help staring at him as he ate the oranges. He popped them into his mouth, whole, and dug his teeth into them, then worked them back into his throat to the point where he could swallow them. He unhooked his jaws, and the muscles of his neck then carried them down his throat. The cloth around his neck stretched to accommodate the passing bulk.

I'm glad he's not eating meat today, thought An.

A child came wandering along the bank of the brook. An wondered why he wasn't in school. He couldn't have been more than nine. He was throwing rocks at the water, trying to hit the fish without much success. He saw the X'GBri eating the oranges, and went over to watch.

An didn't like the city children. They were mean, rude, and openly contemptuous. They were destructive and arrogant. Back home, in TradeTown, you got some measure of respect just for having made it to adulthood. In Star Port, the children would come right up to an adult and call her *bitch* or *stupid*.

Sometimes, at the terminals, child passengers would harass An or the other custodians. Geo and Ro could scare them off with one word; but An was still learning the trick.

The X'GBri didn't seem to mind that the child was watching him.

"How do you *do* that?" An heard the child asking.

The X'GBri showed him, unhooking his jaws and forcing the orange down his gullet. The kid was extremely impressed.

An looked away, resting her eyes on the zen garden for a while. She wished she had a place where she could make one for herself. At Desert Sands Apartments, you only had a few feet around your front door where you could put things. Maybe some day she could move into a better place, if she worked hard enough. Maybe she would become middle class, and have a house.

She wondered why Geo and Ro still lived at Desert Sands. Maybe they were saving up.

She heard giggling and a strange clicking sound. The child was now rough-housing with the X'GBri. That didn't surprise An; city children always seemed to express themselves by kicking and punching. The X'GBri didn't seem to mind, though; he was playing with the kid, grinning and clicking his teeth like it was all good clean fun. Maybe X'GBri children were kind of rough, too.

The kid leapt at the X'GBri, screeching like a karate master. The X'GBri grabbed for him, smiling, enjoying himself. His big hand closed around the child's neck.

The child went limp.

At first An didn't quite get it. The kid was just hanging there, not moving, and the X'GBri was looking at him with a blank face.

"Hey," An started to shout, meaning to say, *you'd better drop him before he chokes*.

The X'GBri's face twisted into a tragedy mask. He dropped the limp child.

The child was dead. His neck was broken.

An stood up. She thought about going over to help. Then the X'GBri looked at her. He had forgotten she was there. He had forgotten someone was there to see what he had done. He looked at her like a snake looks at a rat.

An turned and ran with all her might; but he caught up to her in just a few steps. He dragged her to the ground and held her tight. He put his big hand on the top of her head and made her look into his tragedy mask of a face.

"It was an accident!" he choked.

"I know," An said, and started to cry. "I know!"

"You mustn't tell anyone!" he said, holding her fast with those big hands, lying over her with a body that felt like it was made of concrete.

"I promise," said An. "I won't tell anybody."

He licked her cheek, and An squeaked with horror. She thought he was making a pass at her. But he did it again, and this time it was more like tasting than licking.

They can taste your emotions, An remembered. *They can tell if you're lying.* But she didn't even know if she was lying, herself, so how could he?

He got up slowly, and backed away from her. She watched him go, her heart banging in her chest. She got to her feet and almost fell again, because her knees were shaking so badly. He turned and walked away, calmly, without any evident tension or fear. He didn't look around, didn't come back. He just disappeared.

Now what? wondered An.

She turned to look for the child, but she was out of

sight of him, now. She couldn't make herself go back to where he was lying. So she went back to the bus stop, instead. She would think about what to do on the way back to work. *Probably call the police. Probably at least tell them I saw a body by the brook.*

It really was an accident, she thought, as she sat down on the bus. So what should she tell the police? At least there weren't any X'GBri there to make her nervous.

The doors closed after the last passenger got on, and the bus started to glide off; then it suddenly stopped again. An's eyes fastened on the door, premonition lifting the hairs on the back of her neck.

Six X'GBri males got on the bus. The last one was the one who had killed the boy. They all stood in the aisle and looked at the other passengers until they saw An.

They stared at her for the rest of the ride, but didn't try to come closer.

When An got off, she had to pass right by them. She had to brush against their bodies. They looked down the back of her neck as she passed them, into her eyes, and right into her brain. Once she had passed them, they followed her.

An started crying again. She was walking toward the local terminal, which only handled flyers and didn't have a lot of foot traffic outside of it. *Why didn't I go to the main terminal? That place is packed with people.*

She could hear the sound of their heels on the pavement, behind her. Some Human men walked by, flyer pilots in colorful flightsuits; but An didn't know them, and they didn't seem to give a damn about what was happening to her.

Inside the terminal, there was a corridor that had several doors branching off of it. They would be able to take her into any one of those doors and do—what they were going to do.

There were monitors *outside* the building; someone might see An's dilemma.

But only if she made a big fuss *right now*.

An made herself stop and turn to face them. They stopped, too. They stared at her, intently.

"What do you want?" An tried to shout, and was mortified when the sound came out as a pitiful squeak.

"It was an accident," said the killer.

"I *know* that! I was there, remember? I *know* it was an accident."

He frowned. The others did the same.

"What do you want me to do?" An asked, with sudden inspiration. "Just tell me!"

"Wait," he said. "Until I can negotiate."

"Okay." But An wasn't really sure if she would wait or not. If she waited too long, she could be in big trouble.

"Promise," he demanded.

"I promise."

He was giving her that snake look, again. He didn't know whether to believe her. She hoped he wouldn't lick her; that was more than she could stand. She *would* wait. She had promised—it had been an accident—she didn't feel right, lying to him.

But she didn't feel good about *not* telling, either.

"Do the right thing," she pleaded. "Please, do the right thing."

His face twisted. An's stomach turned, right along with it.

The X'GBri walked away from her without another word.

Once again, An was surprised to be alive and unmolested. Once again, her knees almost dumped her on the pavement.

But the moment passed, and she was able to walk again. She went into the terminal, where her job awaited her, and kept busy for the rest of the day. When she allowed herself to think, it was to hope that things would be taken care of *soon*.

But even she was surprised by just *how* soon.

The first sign was Geo. He popped his head into the corridor An was cleaning. She was sweeping her vacuum nozzle over every inch of the walls, ceiling, and floor to remove the dust and sand people brought in with them. It was near quitting time, and she was so tired she had almost forgotten about the death she had witnessed only five hours before.

Almost, but not quite; so when she saw the look on Geo's face, she had no doubt what it was about. Her stomach turned again. She switched off the vacuum unit and put it down.

"Someone wants to see you," he said.

"The police?" choked An.

His eyes narrowed. "What?"

"Is it—is it the police?" An said, mentally kicking herself. "Or is it—who is it—?"

Geo came into the corridor and shut the pressure door behind him. "An, are you in trouble?"

"Sort of," she said.

"What did you do?"

"I didn't! I saw something."

"You witnessed something?"

"Something really bad."

"What did you see, An?"

"I can't tell you. Not yet. They're—they're negotiating."

Surprisingly, Geo nodded. "That makes sense. I've got the Port Commander in my office, with some X'GBris. They must be pretty powerful individuals, because they're bossing the commander around like he's a lieutenant."

"Oh God," An said, suddenly too frightened to move.

Geo studied her for several moments before saying, "I

don't think you're going to be dragged out of here, kid. I think they want to talk. I think they want to hear something in particular from you. Are you up to it?"

"I know what they want to hear," she said. "I'm ready to tell them, I guess." And then her feet started to move, as if she really *was* ready, as if she actually had courage.

Geo put his hand on her shoulder and kept it there, all the way up to his office. That helped a lot. An tried to think about what she would say to the X'GBris, but every time she thought about what had happened, she could see the kid hanging limp in the X'GBri's hand, and she would start to shake. So she cleared her mind instead.

That was a skill that would come in handy, in the years to come.

There were twenty-two people crowded into Geo's office. There was the Port Commander, who was wearing an extremely simple and extremely expensive suit. There were twenty X'GBri males, varying in age from very young to mature, and there was one X'GBri woman.

She was the one who commanded the most attention. She was the one who spoke first.

"You saw," she said to An, without preamble.

"Yes," said An.

No one spoke for several moments. Geo stood just behind An, which should have made her feel better; but An was too awed by the woman.

She had *twenty* mates!

Unlike most of her friends back home, An had been an avid watcher of the educational vids. They had helped her in school, and they had fueled her dreams. She knew a little about X'GBri society. She knew that all X'GBri women had multiple mates; but few of them ever had more than ten.

A woman who had twenty was extremely powerful. This one was so powerful, the Port Commander hadn't yet dared to speak a word.

The X'GBri woman let her face fold into a frown. She was older, but An couldn't tell exactly how old. She was just beginning to learn that a person's apparent age meant nothing, not with the rejuve treatments people could get. The X'GBri woman's air of confidence and authority was what gave her away.

Otherwise, there was no telling how old she was.

"There was an unfortunate accident," the woman said. "We are extremely grieved. The one who had the accident is a favored mate, very young, and fond of children. He would never harm a child, deliberately."

She paused, to watch An's reaction. The words were the truth, or probably the truth; but the woman's tone was giving An a second message. A threatening one.

"Our own young do not have weak necks," said the woman. "Our necks are almost unbreakable. To play by grabbing the throat is quite common."

"Oh," said An.

"I would be very grieved to lose this one," said the X'GBri woman, her eyes searing into An's. "One tragedy is enough, why compound it with another?"

"Yes, ma'am."

"Remuneration has been offered to the family of the child, and they have accepted it. Only one thing remains."

She paused, and showed An the tips of her sharp teeth.

"You must tell the truth," she said, "before the Port Commander."

"Yes, ma'am," said An. She turned to the Port Commander, and told him the whole story, from beginning to the point where An had realized the child was dead. But she left out the chase that had occurred afterward. That seemed wise.

"So, it really was an accident?" asked the commander, and his tone also implied that he wanted her to say it was. An was glad that she really believed it. At that moment she would have been intimidated enough to lie, and she would have had to live with it afterward.

"It was," she said. "He just didn't know his own strength. The child was very over-excited, and the man—" She glanced at the X'GBri in question, saw once again the look of tragedy on his face. She wished she hadn't, because then she started to cry.

"The man looked very shocked," she managed to say. "He looked . . . looked horrified."

"Thank you," said the commander. "You've cleared it up for us."

No one else had anything to say, so Geo took An out of the room. He led her down to the cafeteria, saying comforting things to her as they went. He made her sit down for supper, and then he and Ro and some other workers kept her company while she choked it down.

"Can you believe the parents wouldn't press charges?" Ro asked. "Just because they got some money?"

"Yes," An said, and that was the last thing she said for the rest of the evening.

"They killed a child, you know," An said.

"Huh?" Jo replied. He hadn't been listening. He was dividing his attention between his mapper and his fancy sensor, trying to decide if they had been in this particular spot before, this wet, hot spot on Cabar 4, its air thick with pollen, bugs, and smells.

"The X'GBris," An said.

"They're not around at the moment," Jo assured her.

An had to think for a long moment before she understood what he was talking about. *Do I have a fever?* she wondered, and felt her forehead. But that wasn't very helpful. Of course, it was hot and sweaty. Every inch of her body was.

And why had she been thinking about the dead child? That was years ago. She had met lots of X'GBris since then. Of course, she had never been in this situation before, being chased this way, being hounded.

Yes, I have. He chased me. He said, "It was an accident!" and I thought he was going to kill me because of what I had seen.

She could still see that snake look on his face, the look of a predator who was about to sink his teeth in.

"I hate it when people look at me that way," An said.

This time Jo looked up. He touched her face, but his hand was hotter than her skin. "You okay?" he asked. "An?"

"No," she said, "I'm confused. I feel—confused."

"Have some water." He took out his water pouch and made her drink from it. The water was warm, but cooler than her throat was at least. But it had an unhappy side effect.

"I have to pee," said An.

"So pee. We'll watch the butterflies."

The butterflies would come and settle on any pool of urine or sweat. They were wonderful creatures, with lovely coral-pink wings, or deep blood rose, or sometimes even a delicate shade of yellow, just the sort of color you might like a bouquet of roses to be. Once An had awakened in the middle of the night to see millions of blue butterflies in the light of Cabar's blasted moon. But she might have dreamed that.

Everything seemed a dream, now. The gorgeous colors, the animals that were always watching you, the green plants that seemed to want to grow right over you if you stayed in one place too long. If you looked at the butter-flies closely, you got a shock. They weren't insects at all, but creatures that looked like fragile lizards. But they were warm to the touch, and they had tiny beaks and long, pink tongues that darted out and lapped up the urine or the sweat, or the nectar inside the flowers.

Which smelled a little like sweat, now that An thought of it. The odor of the flowers was kind of musky.

The sex smell, she thought. *After all, the blossoms are sex organs. . . .*

Funny that she had sex on her mind. She and Jo hadn't made love in the two weeks they had been on Cabar 4. He hadn't tried since the first night, and now An found her-self wanting him at odd times, watching the sweat glide down his naked back when he peeled down his flightsuit, seeing the look of concentration on his handsome face, feeling his strong body near hers as they stumbled through the rain forest together.

Stop thinking about it, she told herself, and then a mo-ment later wondered what it was she was supposed to stop thinking about. Her mind had already lost its grip on the memory.

Anyway, she had to pee. She did so, with a minimum of fuss and trouble, like the seasoned lady prospector she truly was.

"We need to talk about the future," Jo said, sounding as if it was the last thing he wanted to do. An didn't answer him; that required too much thinking. She hoped he would carry most of the conversation by himself.

But then he said, "Should we give up, An? Do you want to leave?"

She felt an urgent twinge in the pit of her stomach. "No," she said. "The Early ruins are here."

"Where?" he said.

An just shook her head. She looked around, as if she

could spot the hidden city right then and there, when she
hadn't been able to find anything after days of searching.

He was right. They were wearing themselves out, and
for what?

"I'll be in debt," she said sadly. She hadn't been in debt
for such a long time.

"I'll pay your debt," said Jo.

An hardly heard him. She still didn't know how much
money he had. The fancy sensor should have given her a
clue, but she was too numb to see the bigger picture.

All she could see was forest. It was scandalous to have
so many plants in so small a space!

"My reputation will be ruined," An said. "They bought
me a drip and everything . . ."

"Let's stick around for a few more days, then," said Jo.
"Why not?"

An nodded. That was a good idea. She was so glad he
was there with her. They worked so well together.

"How come we never worked together before, Jo?" she
asked. "We make a good team."

"Let's move south," he said.

So they got up and started walking again.

Some time later, Jo seemed certain that they were back
in familiar territory. The thick forest had grown a little
less dense, and there was more pooled water in the area.
"We're going in circles," Jo said. But An didn't want to
leave. She remembered it, too—or the part of her mind
enhanced by the drip did, because it was singing to her.

*Earlies lived here! Earlies, who knew the secrets of the
universe. . . .*

"We're close," she whispered. "We're so close."

"You've said that a hundred times."

Jo was looking at his sensor again. He was frowning.
An admired him for a while without speaking. Her brain
was buzzing, dumping all sorts of happy chemicals into

her system. Maybe that's why she didn't want to leave. Maybe she was becoming addicted to these feelings.

"Company," said Jo.

An shrugged. At this point, she didn't care anymore if the X'GBris caught up with them. It might even be nice to have people to talk to for a change, someone besides each other. Especially with the heavy burden that lay between them, a burden that was made all the harder by the intimacy that was also growing between them, the comradeship.

Maybe that's why I really don't want to leave, An thought. *Maybe that's why he doesn't want to leave, either. Once we leave, will we have any reason to ever be together again?*

"Listen . . ." Jo said.

All An could hear was the sound of the forest: the buzzing insects, the screeching bird-o-saurs, the hissing . . .

The *hissing*?

It sounded poisonous, angry. Once An was aware of it, she also became aware of the growing alarm it caused in her. She pressed herself against Jo, trying to push him along with her, away from the sound, but he held her tight and whispered, "Shhh. Don't move . . ."

Now the hissing was punctuated by roars and shrieks, the sounds of large, dangerous animals. *Enraged* animals. An's knees began to shake, and Jo had to hold her tighter. But he didn't seem frightened. He listened, intently.

"What is it?" An whispered. "Some kind of mating challenge?"

"Sort of," he whispered back. "It's the X'GBris."

Knowing that the sound was coming from intelligent creatures only frightened An more. "Let's get out of here," she pleaded.

But Jo wouldn't let her move. "If they hear us, in their excited state, there's no telling what they'll do to us."

He said that in all seriousness, but still he made no move to draw his gun. Why were guns so irrelevant when it came to the X'GBris? An was beginning to wish she could just shoot them all and be done with them. But Jo was the one with restraint. That was funny. Very, very funny.

Something crashed and thrashed very close to them, and the hissing almost seemed to be coming from right over their heads. An pressed her face against Jo's chest and prayed. She didn't believe in God, so she prayed to the Earlies, instead.

Don't let me die before I find you. Don't let me . . .

The thrashing retreated several paces, as if someone were chasing someone else. More shrieks and hisses sounded.

"It's a status battle," Jo whispered into An's ear. "Someone must have challenged GNno." He stroked her hair, and pressed a small kiss against her forehead.

An knew without question that Jo was enjoying the moment, protecting her, and comforting her. She also knew that she needed him. Every shriek made her hair stand on end. Maybe it was instinctive: Males who heard the sound might become excited, ready for a fight. Females might become apprehensive, waiting for their security to be rearranged.

Or maybe An was just a coward. She couldn't stop shaking, even after the sounds went away.

"Maybe we should go back to camp, now," said Jo. He let go of her slowly, as if testing to see if she could stand on her own. She could, but he held on just a little bit longer anyway.

"It's scary, the first time you hear it," he said. "You should *see* it. That's really something."

"I'm sure it is," An said weakly. She accepted some water from him, carefully avoiding his eyes. If he pressed the intimacy too far, she might end up making love with him. That would be just one more tender memory to hurt her when they parted forever.

"Let's go," she said, when she was ready to walk again, and they made their way cautiously through the trees. As they left the area behind, An felt a stab of homesickness.

Her artificial memories didn't want to leave. They wanted to stay, to find Early ruins.

Tomorrow, she promised them, and left them behind.

They slept among the crevices again, the place where the X'GBris hadn't the patience to climb. An managed to go to sleep without getting any closer to Jo, without encouraging him. He had become his closed self again, and would only steal occasional, haunted glances in her direction. She could feel those glances as though they were hands.

She could even feel them in her sleep.

She felt them now. She was aware of him, in the room with her. He was waiting for her to speak to him. But she was standing, not lying down, and how did they end up indoors? They were outside, on the rocks; she was sleeping. And Jo . . .

"Have you forgotten me so soon?"

An opened her eyes and was disoriented by what she saw. She was surrounded on all sides by giant view windows. On the other side of the windows, a SuperStorm was raging, a swirling mass of red and yellow sand. She was inside the old control tower at the Star Port, on Storm. It was still fully functional, but had been shut down because its technology was only compatible with the *planned* colony, not with the one that had eventually developed on Storm.

It was too high-tech for Storm.

"The only reason we're allowed in here is because you're a janitor," Jo was saying. But when An turned her head, it wasn't Jo in the control tower with her. It was Ro. He was standing on the other side of the central console.

"You!" she said, shocked and surprised. Ro had disappeared two years ago.

No, wait, it was over *twenty* years ago. He had simply vanished, as if he had walked out into the desert the same way An had walked in. She had had nightmares for months, imagining him with wild, GodHead hair, consulting her map as he made his way into oblivion.

"I'm so glad to see you," she told him.

He smiled at her. He didn't look a year older. Well, neither did she, thanks to the rejuves. "I knew you would want to see this place," he said. "And tomorrow you start your new job . . ."

An was finally moving up to Security, finally getting away from Janitorial. It had taken three long years. It shouldn't have taken that long. The pay raises had been meager, and most of her supervisors—with the notable exception of Geo—seemed indifferent to An's hard work, to her talents, her intelligence, her drive.

In short, they didn't give a damn.

Her new raise was an extra point an hour, silver. Of course, there was a raise in the taxes she paid out of it, as well, so An was more bitter about it than happy. And now Ro was showing her this marvelous tower, the one that would have been if things had been better.

"Why did you have to show me?" she asked him. "It was such torment to see how lousy things turned out to be."

"It prodded you out of here, didn't it?" Ro said. "It lit the fire. You still have important things to do, An. Look."

He moved to the central console and touched its smooth, blank surface. A keyboard appeared in multicolored, glowing lines. It wasn't quite like any keyboard An had seen before. It didn't have letters and numbers. It had glyphs.

Early glyphs.

Ro played his fingers lightly across the keyboard. "Want to see what TradeTown would have looked like?" he asked her.

"Yes."

A three-dimensional map of the planned TradeTown appeared on the surface of the console. It started out as a simple series of roads, including a superhighway that led in and out of town; then grew from its major structures, flyer port, star port, government buildings; then schools, libraries, coliseums, parks; and finally businesses and homes.

"Look," Ro said, pointing behind An, at the windows. An turned and looked.

There was TradeTown, the way it would have looked from its own star port control tower. It glittered, it shown, it was high-tech and beautiful.

"This was the device they used to attract investors," Ro said. "They could show you more than just three-dimensional maps; they could make you feel like you were really there."

An gaped at the dream town. She couldn't get her fill of looking at it, her heart soared at the sight of it; yet there was another side of the feeling, too. It was a side that was rapidly overtaking the feeling of pleasure. It was a side that game show contestants knew when they were shown everything they *could* have won if they hadn't made the wrong choice, given the wrong answer, guessed the wrong box.

"Red Springs," said Ro, showing her a resort town without one black fortress tower to scar it. "Desert Center." A place of lovely, graceful, tinted buildings, with landing pads on its roofs for the personal flyers that everyone was supposed to have.

"Star Port," said Ro, and showed her a super city, a

place that made the real thing look like a slum. "This is what cities look like on the Inner Worlds."

"Why—" An said, and was embarrassed to realize that tears were flowing down her cheeks. "Why can't we . . . have that?"

"The Vorn wars?" Ro asked. "Do you suppose that can really be the answer?"

"I guess," said An.

"Yes, most do," said Ro, still behind her, his voice turning oddly rough. "But why do you suppose we aren't allowed high technology? Why are our entertainment 'nets' a mockery of what Nets can really be? Why must we use message drones instead of the sophisticated intra-world Nets the Inner Worlders have? Why are our weapons second rate? Why aren't we allowed the cutting edge of Earth technology?"

"They say—"

"They say the Vorns would steal that technology. Right. Yet, we would have won the war by now, if we had it. An—*we would have won the war.*"

An wiped her face and tried to make her voice sound like she wasn't crying at all. "Why wouldn't they want us . . . to . . . to have stuff? Why would they treat us that way?"

"Because we would have had power. Because we could have negotiated with them from that powerful position. There are those that say that the rich cannot get richer if they are fair to their associates. Or their employees. Do you understand?"

"Sure," An said. "I guess so."

"An, look at me."

But An didn't want to turn around. Ro's voice had changed too much. She would see the truth about what had happened to him. But her feet were turning anyway; she couldn't make them stop. She turned, and saw the real Ro.

His mass of filthy hair framed his face like a halo. But his eyes weren't GodHead eyes, they were the eyes of her old friend.

"Is it so terrible?" he asked her, his voice roughened by thirst and GodWeed. "Some of us are *called,* An."

"You're addicts," An said, without emotion. She had known, all along, that this had been his fate. She just hadn't wanted to admit it.

"Yes. We're addicted to the truth. We see the future. We see your future, An."

"Don't prophesize for me."

"I must. You can make TradeTown what it should have been, An. You have a fate awaiting you, out among the stars."

"You've got to be kidding. I'm a janitor!"

"You *were* a janitor. Look at yourself, now."

An looked down, expecting to see her work coveralls. Instead, she had on her flightsuit. It was darkened by sweat, and smelled of Cabar 4.

"Find the Earlies," said Ro. "Look at the glyphs."

"I'm trying! I'm going crazy with trying!"

"Keep going crazy," said Ro, but he didn't smile. He meant it. He looked at her with his old, sane eyes, in the middle of his filthy, half-starved face. How could he be so reasonable when he was a GodHead?

"Is this how you seem to each other?" she asked him.

"Yes," he said.

Behind him, the SuperStorm was raging again. The three-dimensional map had sunk back into the surface of the table, which had darkened to its original, fathomless black. An could smell something in the room, something familiar.

GodWeed.

"Ro, is this a dream?"

"Yes," he said. "And no."

An tried to touch the central console, but her hands

went right through it. "Is it the GodWeed?" she asked him.

"Some day, GodWeed may form the basis of a communication Net that will eventually make the Nets of the Inner Worlds seem primitive," said Ro, then smiled with gnarled teeth. "But for the time being, there are still a few bugs to work out of the system. . . ."

"For instance?" An prodded.

"For instance, the obvious physical side effects. And then there's the time distortion. For me, it's twenty years earlier than it is for you. I'm sorry I couldn't speak to you then, An; but on the other hand, you wouldn't have understood back then."

He pointed to the view windows. "Look," he said.

An looked. The dream TradeTown was out there again, glittering in the sunlight. It was gold and red, it warmed her skin.

The sunlight.

"What's—what's wrong with the sun?" An asked. This had to be a dream, because Storm's sun was type-F. This sun was a benign G, like Earth's sun.

"This is something even the city planners couldn't imagine," Ro said. "When you get where you're going, you'll understand. Ask the Earlies, *How do you terraform a planet with a type-F sun?* They'll tell you, *You don't terraform. You solaform.*"

"Solaform?" An blinked in the golden light.

"You change the sun," said Ro.

Of course, thought the adult An, far away in time and space. *No wonder Early ruins are always on planets with type-G suns.*

"How do you know so much about Earlies?" An demanded.

"I don't know enough," said Ro. "That's where you come in, An. Go where you have to go. Do what you have to do. Then we'll talk again."

He started to fade.

"Good-bye!" An cried. "I never got to tell you good-bye!"

"Don't worry," he said. "I know." And just before he faded completely, he managed to tell her one more thing.

"My brother says to tell you he's still praying for you."

"Thank you," said An. But he was already gone.

After three years as a janitor at Star Port, An was promoted to a security position. Her new job involved screening passengers from incoming and outgoing flights for weapons, explosives, illegal drugs, and a wide range of detectable parasites. Despite its importance, it was not a job that required a great deal of training; consequently, it didn't pay much more than a janitorial position had. It paid the bills, and that was all.

Ro disappeared shortly after her promotion. One day he had taken An to the defunct control tower and shown her the plans for the Storm that could have been. An had been depressed by the sight, but Ro had been oddly optimistic.

"That Storm could still be built," he said. "Things could change, An. I have a feeling they've already started to."

And then he had vanished.

Geo had gotten permission to break into Ro's apartment after he hadn't been seen for three days. Everything had been left behind. An had asked Geo to look for her map. He never found it.

"You think he went into the Empty Quarter?" Geo asked her.

"I don't know," she answered, and thought she was telling the truth.

She had nightmares for several months, and then she tried to move on. Work kept her busy, but she envied the people on the outgoing flights. She hoped that one day she would move far enough up the ladder to go "out" herself. She saw all sorts of people; mostly wealthy people or people with government jobs. She saw all sorts of people with rejuves. She wondered if she shouldn't save up for a rejuve herself.

Wouldn't that be odd, going back to TradeTown to visit and looking younger than everyone else? Her mother would be elderly, by then. Maybe she should save up for her mom, too.

"Hey, Mom," she would say, "have a rejuve!"

"Why?" her mother would answer. "So I can work for twenty more years in the poultry plant?"

Two more years went by. The raises were pitiful, and An began to admit to herself that she was trapped in a dead end. She was clever, everyone had always said so. But the Company didn't care for clever people. It liked obedient people.

Her blue-collar job wasn't going to get her out of the ghetto. If she wanted to get ahead, she would have to take some risks.

"Risks?" scoffed Geo, his wide, brown face crinkling with dismay. "Jeez, An, what're you gonna do? Join the marines?"

"Yes," she said.

He paled. Geo was forty-five, old enough to be her father, and he acted like one.

"Don't do it, An. Please don't do it. Not the marines, sweetheart."

"Space/air wouldn't take me. You have to be a college graduate to be in space/air."

Geo took her by the shoulders and regarded her in silence for a moment. She quailed a little under his stare, and she could feel people staring from the nearby tables of the Company cafeteria.

"I got across the wasteland by myself, Geo," she reminded him. "I found a job in a town where there's fifty percent unemployment. I have luck on my side."

She wished she hadn't said that last part, because his face got so sad.

"That's what my boy Lo said, just before *he* joined the marines. An, you know how Teo and me got our boy back? We got him in a box the size of a hat."

An had a quick, searing memory of the Vorn warrior who had tried to eat her. She saw the double rows of teeth. "Geo, I'm so sorry."

"They don't have to send kids out after those guerrillas, goddammit. People've been trying to tell them that for years. But most marine officers are InWorlders, An; they think us OutWorlders are a dime a dozen."

An didn't know what a dime was, but she got the point. "I'm not aiming for infantry, Geo, I was hoping for a desk job."

"You and every other recruit."

"I have to do something! I can't stay here for the rest of my life!"

"What's so bad about here?" Geo let her go and picked up the rest of his sandwich, as if to use it as an example. See? Look at this great sandwich! Bet you can't get a sandwich like this offworld.

He took a big bite and chewed, considering what he would say next. An waited politely. Geo was a good man, and she never ignored his advice.

Usually never.

"This is the secret of the universe," he said. "This is

the meaning of life, and I'm gonna tell it to you. Most of us go thirty, forty years before we see it, and it's right under our noses." Geo looked into An's eyes, and his own were shining. "Being with your loved ones, having a roof over your head, and food on the table. Having a vote, having a library where you can go and read other people's ideas. Getting up in the morning and looking at the red sunrise on the big, black mountains west of the port, looking at the stars at night and wondering about them.

"That's what makes life worth living."

An sighed. She understood what he was saying, but her eyes were still full of TradeTown. She was still desperate to get away from it.

"You could get off this planet, An, and you might even find a nicer one. But you're gonna miss this dry, sandy place. This place has a beauty all its own, and your heart is gonna want it back."

"It's not the place, Geo," said An, struggling for the words. "It's—it's the situation."

"Which would go from bad to worse in the marines."

"But the Vorn war is dying out! They haven't sent new troops out our way for ten years!"

"There's enough of it left to kill you, sweetheart. Believe it. Those Vorns are the toughest motherfuckers you'll ever want to lay eyes on. When they're stranded, they fight to the death."

Suddenly some man An didn't even know leaned over and tapped her on the shoulder. When she turned to look at him, he said, "That's right, kid. They wanna fight to the death and all you want is a job that pays more money. That's why kids like you get killed out there every day."

The other men at his table were all staring at her, grimly backing up their friend. An blushed all the way to her toes.

Geo pulled her gently back. But he said, "He's right.

Let's think about it a while, okay? I might have some ideas for you."

"Okay," An mumbled, grateful to have escaped from the conversation.

Geo didn't say another word about it all day. She bade him good-bye in the afternoon, and started walking to the bus stop.

It was another hot, dusty day, the kind where you had to buy a tall, cold drink to take along with you so you wouldn't faint before you got where you were going. The Star Port was nicer to look at than TradeTown; though it hadn't turned out to be the paradise she had imagined it would be. It was too crowded. Everyone looked busy, tired, angry, or happy, depending on what kind of day they were having. Just about everyone wore light fabrics for comfort; but the upper-class teenagers were walking around in the latest fashions from offworld, colors so dark they looked almost black, in fabrics that clung like a second skin.

An couldn't help envying them.

Those kids were driving around in their own transports, aiming around the throngs of pedestrians, bicyclers, and buses like they were an unfair annoyance. These were the kids who went to college, who even got into space/air if they wanted.

An walked past a window with new clothes in it. The mannikin was slimmer than An, but she knew she would look good in the outfit. In fact, she knew she would look great. That's why she'd gotten other offers over the years, alternate methods of getting offworld. One man had approached her while she was looking in a window like this one, and he'd gotten straight to the point.

"God, you're a beautiful girl. Have you ever thought of becoming a fancy girl?"

"No," said An.

"Why the hell not? Elegant, classy ones like you are

rare. Hell, you look like a damned princess. Guys would pay their last dollar to watch someone like you. You can dance, right?"

"Yes, but—"

"The money is good. My agent fee is ten percent. And with rejuve, you wouldn't have to retire for another eighty years. By then, you would have some nice investments, savings—"

"Sounds great," agreed An, "but there's just one little problem."

"There's no problem, kid, it's easy. Just take off your clothes and move that lovely little body."

"That's the problem," said An. "I don't want to dance naked for a bunch of goons."

"Oh," said the man. "Okay." And he went away.

Fancy girls must be a "dime a dozen" too.

An walked past the marine recruiting office. It was packed with young, unemployed people, as usual. The line led out the front door and around the corner, where the posters started.

The posters were full of young, healthy, strong, capable men and women. And *proud*. Their eyes practically glowed with pride.

QI DID SOMETHING EXCITING THIS WEEKEND said the first one, showing a typical, middle-class young man in casual clothes, looking like someone had just told him he had become a millionaire.

HE SAVED THE WORLD said the next poster, showing Qi with a military haircut, in a high-tech uniform, shouldering an anti-aircraft gun.

Lots of other posters showed people doing interesting things with interesting equipment. But An couldn't find even one that showed a Vorn warrior.

Bet that would shorten this line up, she thought, as she tried to stroll past the office. But then she had passed the poster that had first caught her eye.

AFTER TWO YEARS, YOU'LL QUALIFY FOR A FIRST-RATE
COLLEGE EDUCATION.

The kind of education that got the good jobs. The kind
that got you those extra, status-indicating syllables in
your name, the kind that got you respect, security, and the
power to control your life. So you had to risk everything
you had for two years to get it. What else was there? A
sixty-hour work week for the rest of your life.

An got in line.

Two hours later, she was standing in front of the recruiter. He had been looking down at his recorder when
she stepped up, as if he was so bored by typing in the sta-
tistics of pathetic losers, he couldn't be bothered to look
up anymore.

An stared at him. She didn't say a word. She had
watched the last fellow make a fool of himself with his
overeager questions and his impatience. But the last fellow had been over two meters tall and built like a tank.
The recruiter had ignored everything he said, simply
looked him up and down and passed him on.

The recruiter was young, handsome, like an older version of one of the posters. His looked rugged, fit, and like
he'd seen a lot. An felt a stab of fear, but put it aside.

He glanced up at her, then looked again. An's heart
started to pound.

"Miss," he said, "you may not meet our physical re-
quirements."

"I hiked across the Empty Quarter by myself," she said.
"From TradeTown."

His eyebrows twitched up. Good. He knew where that
was and what that meant.

"All right," he said. He took her name, age (which this
time was her true one), ID number, and printed out a
form. "Take this through the red door."

"Thank you," An said.

He looked right into her eyes and she took the form

from him. He looked like he didn't know if he was helping her or not. He looked like he was sorry he couldn't be sure.

An went through the red door.

The men and women were put into separate dressing rooms, where they were directed to strip and were issued T-shirts and shorts. An was encouraged that hers didn't hang on her too much. Perhaps she wasn't a weakling after all.

She was weighed and measured. She was two millimeters under the minimum height requirement. "You're a little underweight for your height, too," said the doctor.

"Maybe," said the boy behind her in line, "but that lean meat is *quality*."

"Shut up, recruit," said the doctor. In the same tone of voice he told An, "If you don't pass the preliminary trials, you won't qualify."

"Yes, sir," she said, and got in another line.

She passed the stress test with flying colors. Running had always been easy for her. She also passed a stamina test, a climbing test, and a jumping test. Her hand-eye coordination proved superior.

But she failed the bench press and freestanding weight trials.

As she moved on to the pull-up bars, she saw the handsome recruiter standing with a group of other officers. They were watching her. She averted her eyes.

A small woman with nut-brown skin and breasts as large and firm as cantaloupes was doing chin-ups while a recruiter counted. The minimum was ten. The woman passed easily.

"Eleven," the other recruits counted enthusiastically, cheering the woman on. "Twelve! Thirteen! Fourteen! Fifteen!" And on and on, until she passed thirty. She could have done even more, but the recruiter finally said, "All right, all right, pass on. We haven't got all day."

Everyone applauded the woman as she marched on to the next trial.

If she can do that many, I should be able to do at least ten, An thought hopefully. *I'm slim. I don't have much weight to lift.*

But the guy ahead of her, who was taller and more muscular, had to struggle to get through his ten. He didn't try for any extra. He was passed on, and then it was An's turn.

Her heart sank. But she gave it her all.

She struggled to do the first chin-up. About three quarters of the way up, she knew she wasn't going to make it. But she froze there, too stubborn to let go.

"Come on, baby," one of the other recruits called. "You can make it."

But she couldn't make it. She tried until her muscles were cramping, and the spasms forced her hands off the bars.

"Fail," said the recruiter.

An made herself walk away with her chin up. But it wasn't easy.

After the trials, she waited with the other recruits to see if her name would be called. No one talked or joked now. Everyone was too nervous.

The nut-brown woman was called. The tall, muscular guy who had chinned before An was called.

An was not called.

As she left the building, the handsome recruiter called after her. She stopped and waited for him.

"Do you know what they would have done first?" he asked her. She shook her head. She didn't trust herself to speak with so many tears behind her eyes, just waiting to fall at the slightest sign of weakness.

"They would have cut that long, silky hair," he said. "Right down to your scalp. You probably would have looked great, with that face of yours, but it would have been a shame."

An nodded.

"Do you have a job, An?"

She nodded, again.

"Good. I never would have forgiven myself if you had made it. I mean—" His eyes faltered for a moment. They were amber with spokes of green in them. Looking at them made An feel a little better. "I mean, I would have been worried sick about you. But I would have bent over backward to find you something if you had been unemployed."

"Why?" An said, her voice just above a whisper.

Those amber eyes held steady now. "Because you're beautiful," he said. "Because it took guts to get across the Empty Quarter, and then to come to this recruiting station and give it your best shot."

"Thank you," said An.

They stood in silence for a moment, until An felt the tears coming back. She said, "Well," and started to edge away.

"Can I take you to dinner tonight?" he asked.

An hesitated for a moment. "Tomorrow?" she said.

"Great. Seven okay? I'll pick you up at your apartment."

"I'll give you my address—"

He laughed. "I made an extra copy of your application."

"Oh," said An, embarrassed and glad.

"My name is Javici," he said.

An quailed a little at the sound of the extra syllables. "You're—you must have been—"

"An Inner Worlder," he said, and pointed to the bars on his shoulders "But I earned *these* the usual way. The hard way."

An nodded. "See you tomorrow," she said, and waved

at him as she walked away. He was watching her, so she managed not to cry, even when she passed the poster that talked about college.

Geo called An off parasite duty a half hour early the next morning. "I want to show you something," he told her. They got into a jeep and drove out onto the landing fields.

An watched the tugs towing a ship the size of a cathedral across a field the size of a small city. "What do you suppose a ship that size costs?" she wondered.

"If all of us on this planet got together and sold our souls to the highest bidder, we still wouldn't have enough money to buy that ship," said Geo.

"Who does, then?"

"I don't know. One of the big companies, I guess."

An was beginning to feel depressed again. She hadn't told Geo about her failed attempt to join the marines. She hadn't been sure if he would be sympathetic or if he would simply be disappointed in her.

They were driving past the larger prospecting vessels now. Geo sealed the top over the jeep and accelerated until the ships were a blur zooming past. Then he slowed down again, and drove An past some smaller vehicles. These ships probably wouldn't have housed a crew of more than five or six.

An hour later, the ships were still getting smaller. "What next?" An said with a laugh. "Space scooters?"

Geo didn't laugh with her. He just kept driving until he turned a corner.

An saw the Eggs.

They had one jump engine and two rear thrusters, plus some smaller, maneuvering jets. One of them was open, and an EggHead was crawling around inside. Her living space was about the same size as An's double bed.

An felt like laughing again, but didn't want to be rude

to the EggHead. "People live in those things?" she whispered to Geo. "For months on end? That's crazy!"

"That's a wise observation," he said. "I should drive you away from here and slap you silly if you ever ask to come back."

An gave a sidelong look. "Why did you bring me here?"

"I think this is your way out."

"What?"

Geo looked at her, speculatively. "You tried to join the marines yesterday."

"You followed me!"

"No. Javici tried to call you at work today. You were on parasite duty, so I took a message. He can't make it tonight. He's shipping out."

"Oh." An was too dazed and embarrassed to be upset yet. "So, you naturally asked him who he was. . . ."

"He was very impressed with you. He said you have nerve. Well, I think you do, too."

"But an *Egg*?"

"I was an EggHead."

An looked at Geo again. He was a solid man, large and comfortable looking. A family man, a father.

She glanced at the lean woman who was climbing around in the Egg. She looked like she was made of wire, muscle, and bone. Her face was set in a permanent, introspective scowl.

Geo's face was like the afternoon sun. But when the EggHead glanced over at them, Geo gave her a hand signal, which she recognized and returned.

"But—" said An.

"I had to come home again, An. Maybe you will, too. But you can earn one hundred thousand gold points on just one job if you get a good contract. That's *gold* points, not the measly silver ones you're earning here. Eggs cost fifty grand gold, and people usually work under contract for the manufacturer for a year or two to pay off the debt. But that's good, because you learn the ropes that way. And afterward, you're free to go anywhere you can reach on your own earnings."

He turned and gave An a wistful look. "That's twenty known worlds and who knows how many that are off the maps completely."

An gaped at the Eggs. It seemed ridiculous. It seemed impossible. Crazy!

"I can't do it!" she said.

A year later, she was paying off her debt and signing ownership papers for her Egg.

In twenty years An had never gone home, never seen Mom, Le, or Ro, never seen Geo or Javici again. But she was still jumping in that same Egg.

Javici might have been her lover instead of Jo. Geo might have given her away at her wedding. Had they ever sent drone messages to her old address? Had they collected and piled up there over the years? There would be no place else for them to go; certainly not to her new address: Cabar 4, Avenue of the Endless Jungle.

"They're back again," remarked Jo, pausing to regard his sensor.

An didn't even nod. For two weeks and two days, that was how it had gone. Jo and she stumbling through vegetation or climbing wearily over rocks; Jo looking at his sensor, and saying, "They're back. They're gone. They're back. They're gone." It was all the same to An, now.

Yet her brain continued to chirp happily at the sight of certain places, singing, *It's here somewhere, it's here somewhere, tra-la tra-la!*

Oh, shut up, An thought, wearily.

They stopped to eat, sitting with their heads together so they could talk quietly.

"If we weren't still hanging around, TTra and GNno wouldn't be either," said Jo. "They think we're sure there's something here." He paused to chew for a long moment, then said, "Are we?"

"Yes," said An.

"How can you know that?"

"My drip."

He was quiet for a long moment. An could feel him studying her, even though he wasn't looking at her.

"An," he said, finally, "something could have gone wrong with your drip."

"I have a feeling it didn't."

Jo shifted, easing his sore muscles. Last night, when they had found a pool in the rocks to bathe in, An had seen vicious bruises on his ribs, fading marks from GNno's fingers. The sight had broken her heart, but she had offered no comfort.

"They wouldn't let us leave now, even if we wanted to," said Jo.

"Do you want to leave—without me?" The thought was disturbing. She would be alone with the X'GBris. Yet at the same time, it might be for the best. . . .

"No," said Jo, without hesitation.

An looked around her. They had been back and forth so many times, yet things still did not look familiar. Plants grew so quickly here, and every time she and Jo passed through, they pulled vines and branches into new positions, where they promptly began to root and grow again. She consulted her mapper.

"We're not far from my Egg," she remarked.

She wondered if she ought to look in on it. But that was a foolish impulse. She didn't want the X'GBris to find it. Her locator would keep her in touch.

Her locator.

Where was the pulse?

She kept still for a moment. When had the pulse stopped? It wasn't supposed to do that, it was supposed to keep going, even half a planet away. But there was nothing, not the slightest touch.

She consulted her mapper again. "Jo," she choked.

He froze at the tone in her voice.

"My Egg."

He waited for her to say more. But she couldn't. She got up, and he followed her.

An had to use her mapper to find what was left of the Egg. They must have destroyed it only a few days ago. She could see what was left of the jump engine. Jump juice had leaked out and burned a huge hole in the ground. Vegetation had tried to grow over it, but had failed.

A few of her meager belongings could still be seen scattered about, but they were quickly disappearing. An didn't touch them.

"An."

She almost lost control at the sound of compassion in Jo's voice. She couldn't look him in the face. Somehow, having him see her Egg in this condition, having him witness what was left of it, with bits of her life cruelly discarded and scattered around as if they were nothing, she was nothing, made her feel ashamed.

"An, please. My ship is still intact. I want you to come with me."

"No room," she choked. "Two people can't squeeze into an Egg."

"Not an Egg. I sold my Egg. Remember? I have a ship now."

She couldn't answer, couldn't think, couldn't move. Twenty years. She had thought she would go crazy inside that Egg. She had wanted to move on to better things, to sell it, be rid of it.

She started to cry.

Jo put his arms around her and pulled her close. She buried her face in his neck and cried her heart out.

After a long time, she came up for air. He still held her, but that's what she wanted. He pressed his forehead against hers and said, "I'm sorry."

Funny, he hadn't said that when he had tried to kill her. Just when her Egg had died.

"Let's go away from here," she whispered. "I don't want them to find us here."

She let him lead her away.

When they were well away from the wreckage, An thought of something. "How about your ship?" she whispered. "Is it still okay?"

"It's okay," said Jo. "They don't have the technology to find it."

An prayed that he was right. The idea of being stranded here, with only the X'GBri to help them off, was more than even her tumbled brain could stand.

It's here somewhere! it sang, oblivious to her grief.

Shut up, she told it again.

In the morning, blue light poured into their rocky grotto, and the birds instantly burst into song. An opened her eyes and beheld the face of her lover. His eyes were still closed. For the moment, he was at peace; when he woke the lines of pain would fill his face again, and his eyes would be haunted with regret.

And frustration. And exhaustion.

Mine, too, An was sure. She gazed at blue morning and wished desperately for something to happen today, anything, for an end to the fruitless search.

Soon, Jo had opened his eyes. They looked at each other for a moment. For that moment, An felt none of the hurt and betrayal, none of the suspicion that she ought to be feeling.

"Today," she pleaded. "Please, Jo."

"Today," he promised, though he had no business doing so.

They splashed in the rocky pool, fed themselves, checked their equipment, and started off.

"No sign of our friends," Jo said, inspecting his sensor.

They walked down the same forest path they had traveled every day for fifteen days. "Let's—" said Jo, and then fell through the ground to his waist.

"An!" he cried, and tried to warn her off the path. But she had taken an involuntary step toward him, and her weight on the path widened the hole.

They fell through together.

An was surprised to bounce a little as they landed, falling on moss. There was a moment of terrible silence, when she couldn't hear or see anything. Then Jo said, "You okay?"

"Yes. Can you see?"

"Wait a moment."

An waited. Slowly, her eyes adjusted to the light. The outline of buildings began to appear in the dimness. Here and there, shafts of light stabbed through the tangled growth overhead and illuminated subtle colors, which were overlaid by something else, something that moved and shifted, something that seemed to cover every inch of every surface. Someone who had never seen anything like them before might have thought they were insects. But An had seen them before, on other ruins.

They were glyphs.

An's brain did not greet them happily, as she had thought it would. It waited, quietly.

"Now what?" she asked.

"Let's look around," said Jo, his voice subdued by awe and relief.

An looked up at the hole. Sunlight was falling through, but no X'GBri heads were peering after it. Jo was already walking into the dim shadows. She followed him.

Underneath their feet, the moss was soft and springy. An tread carefully, wondering if there was yet another cavity beneath this seemingly solid footing, another city beneath this one.

But the Earlies would not have built on such unsteady ground. They were master builders; their cities showed no sign of wear or erosion, even after centuries. An had walked among other Early ruins that were not ruined. And now there was *this* city. It was no larger than TradeTown. Early cities were never large; they had been more autonomous than Human societies were.

The dim light made it hard to find the overgrown roadways. But the glyphs called. They even called to Jo; he led An among them, down what appeared to be a main street. She followed, her mind at peace, her eyes darting everywhere.

Not here, she thought as she looked at one group of glyphs or another. *Not these. Not yet.* The main road twisted, turned into a maze, just as they both expected, just as Early roads always did. The business of information had been more important to Earlies than the business of getting to places in a straight line.

An didn't feel lost at all. She looked into empty windows and doorways, saw odd overlaid images of glyphs in her mind, of information overlapping information. This was what it must be like to be inside a Net, to see the actual information as it was really stored.

Perhaps this was even what it was like to be inside a brain.

As usual, there was no sign of recognizable technology. As usual, that was just an illusion.

Before long, Jo had given up trying to lead and was following her. "How about this big building?" he asked, but she shook her head.

"That's not the one."

"What do you mean 'not the one?' There are glyphs inside all of these buildings." He stopped and went closer to one of the walls. The surface shifted under his eyes. "There are glyphs *everywhere*." He moved closer, and the glyphs changed shape, became other glyphs. Yes, they were Early glyphs all right, seeming to wiggle as if they were alive.

An *saw* them, but she was able to let them slide by without *reading* them. They were like a silent crowd among which she had not yet spotted a particular face. Jo hurried after her. She could hear his footsteps. In her mind, she could hear other steps as well, but not the kind made by human feet.

She hurried along the road, which called to her memories more than her own hometown had ever done. It would have confused her if she had allowed herself to think about it. If she had tried to place the memories with an event in her own life, she would have been shuffling back and forth in her files, looking, looking. She let herself stay on automatic pilot and stayed the willing passenger. Her feet went up the main road, down a side street to the left, a place of charming curves and twists.

There was a little building at the end of the street, right in the middle, as if it had been the purpose for the street in the first place. An went in the arched door, Jo following close behind.

There were glyphs all over the main room. But to An, they all seemed to flow into arrows, which pointed to a small archway to their right. An moved toward the archway with a feeling of joyous and terrified anticipation. She stepped through and let her eyes rest on the wall immediately opposite her.

Her mind seemed to turn off, like a screen gone blank.

INFECTION

An had been afraid of Omsk.

She didn't even know where it was. It was just a code you punched into your navigational systems. When you came out of jump again, you would find an artificial planetoid waiting, a dark, menacing circle on your tactical screen, with no features to distinguish it except for red letters at the bottom of your screen:

OMSK;SECURITY LOCK;NO ACCESS

Conceivably, there were ways to find out where the code was taking you; but people who tried to do that ended up in Heavy Prisons if they were caught. An had never been inclined to take that particular risk. Just going to Omsk was bad enough.

It was the place where criminals, monsters, and dissidents were *reprogrammed*. It was the place where mentally ill people went to have their illnesses pushed, burned, dripped out of their brains.

She supposed, for some, it was a place of hope. But if that was the case, why were the guards in her Egg even before she was out of the deepsleep cycle? They must have scooped her up right out of jump, and she had gotten a bad scare when hands had touched her when she hadn't expected anyone.

They had been featureless, sexless people inside black security suits. There had been five of them. Two had pulled her upright while another shined a retinal scan right into her newly opened eye. It had gone obligingly wide with shock, and she had screamed.

"An," said the discreetly distorted voice of the scan man, confirming her identity rather than greeting her. "Come with us."

She had been frightened again when she had seen that her Egg was open and darkness lay beyond it. But it was the darkness of a parking bay, not the void. They had helped her out gently enough. They didn't push or grab, and they walked at a comfortable pace. But An felt as if her every movement were being monitored.

"This is a voluntary RNA drip, you know," she said. "I'm not a criminal."

"We prefer not to know your business," said another distorted voice.

An didn't speak to them again. They led her down a series of cool, neutrally lit hallways and stopped in front of a lift.

"Go in there," said a voice.

An went. They stood with their face plates pointed toward her until the doors shut them away from her sight. An felt an upward motion. As she went up, the gravity decreased, until she had to use hand and foot holds to move around.

I'm on a ship, An reminded herself, with wonder. It was spinning an artificial gravity. She had moved up to the center of the spin, where a transport bubble was waiting for her. As soon as she seated herself in the bubble and strapped herself in, she felt more at home.

But the good feeling died as soon as she saw Omsk beneath her, still a black, featureless sphere, even under the naked eye. She felt acceleration, was pushed back into the smothering protection of her seat. The black sphere swelled, zoomed up to swallow her whole.

And then she had met the doctor.

"Mohamonero," he said, shaking her hand.

She had never heard so many syllables. He was tall, coffee colored, with blue-black hair cut close to his scalp.

He had almond eyes, a wide, mobile mouth, a softly hooked nose. She found herself wishing he were not so good looking.

He looked young, no older than twenty-five. But Omsk was also a place where you could get rejuves, if you were fabulously wealthy. An was settling for Mythos, with its cheaper rejuves, this time.

Mohamonero had examined her, seemed happy with what he discovered, and packed her off to predrip, where she had floated for a time in nothingness.

She had dreamed that someone was looking for her.

Then Mohamonero had come to fetch her again. He had smiled at the sight of her face. "You've had rejuve a few times, haven't you?" he had said. "You seem too self-assured for your age. Some people have managed to live three hundred years or more. You might just make that."

"I don't care whether I do nor not," she had remarked.

He laughed. "You sound just like Kokoboro. I could never get him in to get his rejuves, he was too busy scrambling after his glyphs."

"Kokoboro?"

"Your donor."

"You knew him?"

"Oh, yes. He was my good friend. This was arranged between us years ago. He wanted everything to be used; his bones are in our forensic department, his liver is floating in a vial at our university. But it was the idea of the drip that pleased him the most. He said it was a form of immortality."

An had never given the donor a second thought. She had been afraid to. She had been afraid it would come from the brain of some poor dissident, raped from its owner.

"I'm glad to know it was—from a friend," she said.

"He left a message for you."

"For *me*?"

"For the recipient. It's rather long, you probably won't have time to see the whole thing. But you can watch it while you wait."

"Thank you," said An.

Mohamonero left her alone with the viewer. She had thought she detected a shine in his eyes as he left the room.

Good, she had thought. *Doctors should be compassionate.*

An pushed the START square on the bottom of the screen. Up popped the image of a man who was as old as Mohamonero was young, as stout as he was slender, as light as he was dark. The only thing they had in common was their almond eyes. Kokoboro's were sparkling with humor.

"Help!" he cried. "It's all a mistake! These fiends are holding me prisoner!"

An blinked.

"Hah-hah!" said Kokoboro. "Just kidding. Please forgive me, whoever you are, but I've always been an impetuous fellow.

"So. Who are you? Are you male or female? I've always wondered what it would have been like to be female. I won't really find out, you see, but it's fun to imagine what life will be like for my recipient once my memories are implanted.

"You'll be getting my knowledge of Early glyphs, which, I don't mind telling you, is considerable. I wonder, will you get my intuition, too? Is that the sort of thing that can be transplanted along with one's experience? I've always had a feeling for Early glyphs, a great sympathy. How I wish I could have met them!

"You must either be an archeologist, an anthropologist, or a prospector. Really, I suspect they're all the same thing. But whatever your goals are, I must tell you a secret. I think the Earlies wanted us to read their glyphs!

"How could they know others would follow them? The answer is: How could they not know? If the Earlies had one great passion, it was to pass on information. You'll understand once you take your first Kokoboro-enhanced look at the glyphs, but perhaps you already suspect, eh? You've seen them? You've seen the way they shift when you change position and become yet another set of information? It's the nature of reality, to shift and change like that, the nature of truth.

"I suspect the Earlies saw truth as a constantly moving, metamorphosing creature; they have a glyph that means *information,* and it looks like some sort of amphibian. When you first approach it, it's in the egg stage, and it progresses all the way to an adult stage as you get closer—then shifts back again. Beautiful!

"Of course, we're not seeing the glyphs as they really should be seen. We lack the receptors. Earlies must have been able to process an enormous amount of sensory input. Perhaps they didn't need the filters we have in our brains to sift out information overload. Can you imagine? Seeing *everything,* hearing *everything.* What would drive us mad was normal to them.

"Somehow, for the last thirty years, I've found myself being guided in certain directions. I suspect the Early glyphs work a sort of programming on observers; at least on Humans. When I began my career, I used to look at *everything,* just *everything* I laid eyes on. It was a feast! Sometimes I suspected you could gain a lifetime of information from just *one glyph. What sort of mind could invent a written language like this?* I asked myself. And is there more than that? Did they have other ways of passing on information that I haven't detected yet, oriented as I am toward the visual cortex? Would the Vorns perceive the Early ruins differently, perhaps through their sense of smell? What would the X'GBri learn by tasting them? I confess, I am the only living Human ever allowed to study Early ruins on X'GBri and Vorn planets; yet I don't know the answer to that question.

"Perhaps you will find out. I'm so glad I'll be with you when you do. Whether you do or not, I hope someday you'll make the same contribution that I have, and become an RNA donor. I suspect that this is the only way Humans will ever approach Earlies in their capacity to pass on information. What a fitting tribute to my life's work!

"Ah, I'm beginning to get sappy. I am sorry. I am dying of a degenerative nerve disease, you see; and somehow, instead of thinking of my past, I can't help but project myself into the future. I thank you for that opportunity. You are my immortality. And for that reason, I can't help passing one more secret on to you. Really, it's more of a hunch; but lately my hunches have proven to be quite perceptive—no pun intended.

"Listen carefully now; this is important. I suspect that the Earlies are—"

The picture froze as Dr. Mohamonero came back into the room. "It's time," he said.

"May I listen to this again, when I'm finished?"

"I don't see why not. You should be up and around almost immediately."

An followed him out of the room.

She hadn't been up and around immediately, or even shortly. She had been unconscious for an inordinate amount of time, worrying her doctors very much. By the time she had regained consciousness, she had forgotten completely about Kokoboro's last secret. She had been so relieved to be thinking normally, she couldn't think about anything else.

"Don't be surprised if you can't read the glyphs right away," Mohamonero was telling her now. "Information of this complexity, not to mention this volume, can take any-where from a few days to several weeks to be assimilated properly. It would be easier for you to learn a language."

"I thought that's what I was doing."

He laughed. "The Early language is a whole category unto itself. You'll see."

She had seen. By the time she left Omsk, she had only been able to read some of the "simpler" glyphs. But Mohamonero had been pleased, so she had been fairly confident.

"Mo," she said, as they turned the last corner. He hadn't even raised an eyebrow at the shortening of his name. "Will you be a donor after you die?"

"Yes," he said. "I wouldn't have it any other way."

"Like your friend, Ko."

Mohamonero smiled wistfully, and An relaxed. She felt she could trust him now.

"Am I done?" An asked. "Is it over?"

"Are you?" answered a harsh voice. "Is it?"

She opened her eyes, and saw the wall of Early glyphs, felt the damp heat of Cabar 4. But why was it so dim? Oh, yes, they had fallen through the forest floor.

And here were the glyphs she had spent so much money, pain, and time trying to read. Here they were, and they meant nothing to her. They were just scratches on stone. Something had happened to her brain; she could feel that. But whatever it was, it wasn't comprehension. It wasn't understanding.

"Oh, Jo"—she sighed—"I've failed."

"You tried, baby," said Jo, from somewhere behind her.

There were gray shadows in the room, pressing close and looming over her. A shiver crept up her back. She forced herself to turn her head and look over her shoulder.

Of course, there was GNno. He wasn't smiling now; his face was a classical tragedy mask. Beyond him, TTra and her other mates were standing with Jo, not holding him, but keeping him their prisoner, nonetheless.

"You can't read the glyphs," said GNno.

"No."

GNno licked her cheek. "Yes, it's true. You are defeated." He looked at the wall again, cocked his head at it. But he didn't understand it any better than An did.

"We might as well kill you now," he said reasonably.

"You're jumping to conclusions, GNno," TTra said. An could have sworn that she was disappointed, too, though she couldn't quite say what gave her that impression. TTra was smiling, apparently enjoying herself. She touched Jo's chin with a sharp fingertip.

"What do you propose?" she asked him.

"I'll fight," said Jo. He seemed almost happy for the opportunity.

"All five this time," she warned him.

"Yes," said Jo.

"No!" said An.

"Yes," TTra said, sighing, "one a day, I think. He'll have a chance to recover in between."

"For our lives," snapped Jo. "You will release us, alive, and allow us to leave."

"For your lives?" GNno laughed. "Not just for fun? You don't know how to live, Jo. I'm disappointed in you."

"Goddammit!" An balled up her fist and struck GNno on his chin. His mouth was open at that moment, so he made a sort of popping noise as she struck him. Beyond that, the only other response she got from him was mild surprise, which only made her angrier.

"We will *not* fight you, and you will not kill us! Who do you think you are, anyway? You're a bunch of damned scavengers who can't do anything on your own! You've been following us around like we had the secrets of the universe in our hands—well, go find your own damned secrets! Do your own work! What are you, feeble-minded?"

GNno's tragedy mask frowned with puzzlement. "What are you implying?" he asked.

An let her breath out in an explosion, not quite a laugh. "*Implying?* I'm *saying,* GNno, I'm *stating* that you are a bunch of worthless thieves."

"That's an insult," he said.

An looked at him through narrowed eyes.

"You earned the right to travel by yourselves," he said. "You earned nothing more. You are an ill-mannered woman."

"Truth hurts," said An, and was rewarded with a flustered silence from him. She turned to TTra.

"You have harassed us for weeks, you've done nothing to help us. Now we've lost our shirts on this project, and you have the ruins, TTra. Get off our backs!"

"We have nothing," said TTra. "We have no translator with us. We will get no more than a salvage fee from this planet, and we'll have to fight for that. We are satisfied with the challenge, and Jo is satisfied. If you are not satisfied, it is because you cannot be pleased."

She was still smiling, but An could see the frustration and disappointment there, too, as if it were glowing under the X'GBri woman's skin. TTra was close to an outburst.

"I want the fight," said Jo, and he really meant it. He had been pushed past the limits of tolerance, of patience, even of sanity. His haunted eyes pleaded with hers. "For our lives," he added.

He wanted this. He wanted the fight, he wanted the pain. It was his punishment for himself, his release. He wasn't ready to escape, yet.

Men were such strange creatures.

"Jo," An said, then stopped, on the edge of tears.

"Who will go first?" TTra asked, politely.

"Me," said GNno. An looked at him, suspiciously.

He wants to get it over with, she thought. But he was smiling, he was behaving the same way he had the other time. X'GBris loved to fight, they were never afraid.

Not afraid. Sorry. He's sorry.

GNno was sorry. But he took Jo out into the street and beat him unconscious. Afterward, he carried Jo back into the small building and placed him in the little room, next to An. She cradled Jo's head in her arms.

"I win," said GNno. "Four to go."

He handed An a pouch of water, and left the room.

An was trapped in a loop.

It started in the special glyph room, the place where her mind had gone blank and left her with nothing to tell, no Early secrets to give Iknaton Inc, or the X'GBris, or Jo.

It also ended in that room. An would think, *Why did I come in here again? Wasn't I just in here?* Then she would wander out, find Jo in a stupor; rifle through both of their packs looking for meds to inject him with, find nothing but painkillers, think, *I'd better not give him one, I might have done it already;* wander out again looking for TTra, thinking to talk her out of the other fights; find GNno or one of the others, instead; think *They wouldn't understand;* come back into the little house to get a drink of water, pick up the water pouch, try to drink and find it dry, think, *There must be a way to make water come in the house, somewhere;* and wander into the special room, hoping to make enough sense out of the glyphs to get what she needed.

Think, Why did I come in here again? Wasn't I just in here?

Enough things changed as she went 'round and 'round to make her *aware* that she was going 'round and 'round. For instance, sometimes when she looked at the glyphs on the walls, they were obscured by throbbing red lights. Sometimes they would turn purple on top of the red background, and An would get a strange buzzing inside her skull, or her eardrums would flutter.

And she got thirstier and thirstier.

And the X'GBri's were starting to look at her funny, wondering why she kept coming outside, staring at them blankly, then going back in again.

Wasn't I just out here? What was I trying to do again?

Eventually An became aware that she was in a loop. She even started wanting to get out of it. But it was a tricky loop. It would tell her, *Go into this next room, that will lead you out.* And she would be looking for those damned meds again. *Go outside, talk to TTra.* And the X'GBris would stare and frown. *Go inside and get a drink. . . .*

An didn't know when she finally formed a strategy to break out. It happened unconsciously. That was the trick, because every time she tried to focus on some conscious intention, she would get stuck deeper in the loop: Go *here,* do *that,* go *here* again. It was instinct that finally got her off the hook.

But there was a price to pay.

An forced her body off course, through an unfamiliar door. Her body tried to resist the change, and she bumped into the door jamb. Her vision exploded with colors, turning everything neon, making everything around her glow so intensely that An lost all sense of meaning in what she saw, all sense of definition. At that same instant, a voice started screaming in her ear:

> What an EggHead, You're an EggHead,
> La-la-la la la la laaaaaaaahhhhh!
> What an EggHead, you're an EggHead,
> La-la-la la la la laaaaaaaaaahhhhhhhhh!

An shook her head, trying to find the obnoxious singer, but then the voice multiplied into several voices, a whole choir singing a song from a musical vid so old, only fragments of it remained for modern viewers. An never could remember the rest of the words to that song. It had always driven her crazy.

"Stop it," An told them, but her voice was completely drowned out. She stumbled down some steps and out into the open, but couldn't see where she was going in the neon landscape, the strobing, crazy light.

And then, suddenly, the colors vanished, and An saw the thing. It was coming toward her with a bloody face, its skin peeled back to reveal dreadful dagger teeth, its arms and hands stunted versions of An's making it look like an impossible cross between a Human being and a Tyrannosaurus Rex. It was stalking toward An, baring its teeth at her, reaching out with those awful hands.

She screamed like a siren.

And the thing disappeared. An was left alone in a small courtyard, with the hot darkness all around her. The holes in the forest floor above her threw ineffectual stabs of light into the dark corners of the ruins.

"Shit," said An, and sat heavily on some steps. "Shit. What was *that* supposed to be? *Me?*"

She was exhausted, thoroughly wrung out. She understood what had happened. She had been caught in an obsessive-compulsive loop. You couldn't resist one of those without paying a heavy price. Your brain always punished you for not indulging its faulty wiring. In this case, her brain had shown her what she might become if she didn't obey its obsessive-compulsive urges.

An understood that because she was an EggHead. Egg-Heads were *checkers*. They checked systems over and over again, worrying that they had missed something, that something had gone wrong while they weren't looking. It was like having some button in your brain that said UH-OH, a button that was there for a perfectly good reason—except that it was stuck in the ON position. If it got stuck too often, you turned into an obsessive nut, someone who could never trust others to do anything right, someone who could never feel secure that they knew how things stood with their Egg.

Or with anything else.

Face it, it's more than that. Colors and voices. You're going psychotic, right here in the middle of this hot, wet mess; at the worst possible moment. But then, is there ever a good moment for it?

TTra entered the courtyard, cautiously. She studied An with an expression that was too alien to read. An wondered if TTra was having the same trouble with Human faces.

"You made an alarming noise," said TTra.

"I had an hallucination," admitted An.

"Really?" TTra sat opposite An, on another set of steps, perhaps more because she wanted to get a better look at An's face than because she needed to rest. "What did you see?"

"I don't even know," said An.

TTra sat perfectly still. An knew she was being mercilessly examined, but she was so relieved to have broken out of the loop, she didn't even care. She just rested, didn't even try to think.

"You're going insane," said TTra.

"Probably," An agreed.

"It must be the drip. I have heard that such results can occur. Have you been seeing bright colors?"

"Yes."

"Hearing voices?"

"Yes."

"What is it like?"

An thought about it for a moment. "Emotional," she said. "Painful. Exhilarating. Confusing." She thought for another moment.

"Devastating," she finally added.

"So you are destroyed," said TTra, and seemed satisfied with the idea. But her tone of voice didn't reveal whether it was malice that caused her to feel so. It could have been more like the satisfaction that comes with seeing the end of things, wrapping things up. "It makes for fine drama," she finally added, confusing the issue even further.

An didn't take it personally, anyway. It didn't matter.

"You shouldn't try to keep the men from fighting," TTra said, at last. "It isn't fair."

"It isn't fair, all right," said An.

"It's your own fault," said the X'GBri woman, her eyes like pools of purple ink in the semidarkness. "So why not enjoy it?"

"Enjoy it," An said numbly, without quite comprehending the concept.

"So he tried to kill you," said TTra, smiling a little. "Is that so bad? It can only add spice to your relationship."

"What are you going to do to us when you're through?" An wondered, thinking that now was the time to ask, when she couldn't get too upset about anything. But TTra wasn't giving any ground.

"I'll do what I'll do," she said. "What I deem suitable when the moment comes."

"Right," said An.

She would have gone back into the house then, but she

didn't dare. That might just start the loop again. TTra continued to stare at her, without restraint, without shame. An wondered, *Does she like me?* Then, *Does it matter?*

In that light, with her almost prehensile hair, TTra looked like a Medusa, like she could turn men to stone with her will. "How do you boss the men around?" An asked her. "They're bigger and stronger than you. They should be able to beat up on you."

TTra clicked her teeth. "And how would they agree who would go first? They must fight for the privilege. And while they are fighting, I am taking their lives into my hands. I am making them wonder who I love the most. It's simple. You should have tried it yourself, long ago."

"Really?" An asked. "You believe those tactics would work with Jo?"

Abruptly, TTra stopped clicking her teeth. She became very still. Her mouth started to tug down into a frown, but didn't quite make it. She stood, her body like some marvelous, deadly machine, and turned her back on An, walking out of the courtyard.

Just as she was leaving, she said, "No."

An rubbed her eyes, and wondered if she dared to go in again. She was thirsty. Maybe she should try to figure out how she could find water in the house.

She almost went into *that* room, again.

But at the last moment, she went to find Jo, lay down beside him and went to sleep.

Safe she assured herself as she dropped off. *Loop can't get me now.*

Dream on, said a voice, the one that always sounded like her mother.

An did dream, but not very lucidly; at least, not at first. She slept a long time. Next to her, a warm body stirred, and she snuggled closer. She scratched an itchy spot on her stomach, under her fur.

The nest was deliciously comfy. It was warm, and a breeze was making the tree branches sway, gently. An opened an eye and saw her mother's face near hers. It was covered in red-brown fur. Mother's wide mouth was open slightly—she was snoring. An shooed a fly away from her.

She caught sight of her own hand. The skin was dark, and her fur covered the back of her hand, thinning out just above her knuckles.

Mother opened her sleepy eyes, looking for An. She took An's little hand in her own and kissed it, then snuggled An closer.

"Oooo," she cooed to An.

"Oooo," An answered back.

There was plenty of food. In nearby trees, other family members were resting in their own afternoon nests. All danger was faraway, on the forest floor; but there was very little of that. An and her family were bigger than most of the predators, and smarter than all of them. They teamed up to fight enemies. But most of their time was spent lazily gathering the plentiful food, traveling here and there, taking afternoon naps.

An felt happiness, contentment. She couldn't remember ever having felt this way before. There might have been one time, perhaps when she was just a baby in her mother's arms. But her mother had quickly infected her with anxiety, perhaps even from the first few days.

This is mother, An corrected herself, feeling the furry mother beside her.

No, she said, after thinking for a long moment. *Wait. What is that other place? When is that other time?*

She was starting to wake up. The comfort of the nest was going away; there was a hard floor underneath her. Her muscles were cramped. She had been a burden to her real mother, who had always worried, who had spent days at a time in depressions so bleak and terrible that An had feared to approach her. An had fled to Le's house during those times. She had sometimes wondered if Mom would let her come home again.

But she really did remember a time when someone held her like this, loved her, and snuggled with her. The memories were dim, but they were there. Had Mom done that, before Dad left? Or had Dad been the one to hold her that way?

No, it couldn't have been him. If he had been the one, he never would have left her.

Come back, she told the furry mother in the cozy nest. *I want to stay here,* she told the warm world with the plentiful food. They were better than her real past. They filled an aching place in her she had hardly dared to acknowledge.

But they went away, breaking An's heart. When she woke, she was crying.

Jo staggered into the room.

"I won this one," he said, then fell to his knees.

An hurried over to help him. As she touched him, he groaned in pain.

An knelt beside him and gently undid his flightsuit. "What are you doing?" he asked, but he didn't resist. She peeled the fabric away from his chest and looked at the bruises. They covered every inch of him now. Some were light, but others were dark and awful.

"I was asleep," said An. "I'm so sorry."

"You don't like it," said Jo. "You always hated to watch me fight."

"I can't stand to see you hit."

"I thought you would like it this time. Because of what I did. What I have coming."

A drop of blood began to ooze from his nose. He wasn't aware of it; so when she undid her own suit and

pulled off her undershirt, he gazed at her with a dreadful
sort of hope in his eyes. She dabbed at the blood before
it could flow onto his lips.

"Water," she said, and left him holding the undershirt
to his noise.

But the water pouch was empty. There wasn't even a
mouthful for Jo.

"I'll get more," she promised her, and ran into another
room.

This was a big room, an important-seeming place, with
glyphs that flowed and made soothing shapes. An pressed
some of the glyphs and watched a large basin rise out of
the floor. She touched some more, and an animal came
out of the wall. It grabbed the side of the basin with stone
hands and extended its face over the edge. A tubelike pro-
boscis unrolled from its face, as if it were living matter
instead of stone, and a stream of water poured out of it.

An put her hands under the water. It was warm and felt
good on her skin.

How did you know how to do that? she wondered. She
had stared and stared at that damned wall when she was
stuck in the loop, and no good had seemed to come of it.
But it must have done her some good, after all. She must
have actually learned something from Kokoboro's drip.

Something more than what it was like to be psychotic.

She ran to get Jo. He was slumped in the same spot she
had left him. He was administering a stim to his arm.

"You didn't need a stim now," An said.

He tried to shake his head, winced at the motion.
"Painkiller," he said.

"Come have a bath," she urged, and started to help him
up.

"A bath," he said, as if the words had no meaning for
him. But he let her lead him into the large room—
important because it was a place for bathing. The Earlies
had dearly loved to bathe.

An undressed Jo and helped him into the water. She clenched her teeth at the sight of his poor, mottled skin. She rubbed him, gently, with her wadded-up undershirt. The pain was leaking from his face; perhaps the painkiller was doing its job.

The bruises were starting to fade.

An thought it was a trick of the light. The water must be bending it, making things look better than they were. She brought the cloth to his face and gently dabbed.

The bruises above the water were fading, too.

"Feels good," Jo said. "Feels so good."

"We'll do this every day," An said. "Until you feel better."

"I love you, baby," Jo said.

An dabbed at some bruises on the back of his neck. "I love you, too," she admitted. But she didn't tell him how much she wished she didn't.

An found it impossible to sleep that night. Every time she closed her eyes, glyphs went dancing through her mind. They wanted her to join them, come dancing along like she was part of an information conga line. An *wanted* to join them; but something was missing. She couldn't quite manage what was needed. She would grasp for the missing thing, and wake herself up in the process.

Then start over again.

Not another damned loop, she thought wearily, and decided to give up. If she was going to sleep again, it would only be if she passed out from exhaustion. And that was fine with her.

So she kept watch over Jo, instead. He was sleeping peacefully on his sleeping bag when GNno came to get An.

"Don't wake him," she hissed.

GNno frowned, but he didn't try to disturb Jo. He led her out of the little building and walked with her down the winding streets. He seemed almost familiar with them.

An wondered if he had been trying to do some decipher-
ing on his own. But if he had, he had failed; he led her to
a larger building, apparently thinking it was more important simply by virtue of its size.

"You wasted your time in a useless building," he said.
"That is what went wrong. I shall take you to a place of
importance, and you will possibly be able to give me
good information."

"Information about weapons? And ships, and better
sensors?" asked An.

"What else?"

"Theoretically, that sort of information could be
gleaned from any Early glyph. That's what I've heard. All
of their science, philosophy, technology was represented
in their language."

"If that were true," scoffed GNno, "we would know everything now."

An was amazed at his arrogance, his absolute belief in
what he was saying. His attitude was so typically X'GBri.
It was what made it so hard to deal with them—if you
didn't act the same way, they rolled right over you. If
you *did* act the same way, they took it as an invitation to
fight.

"Here," GNno said. "This large place. This must be important."

"It was," said An. "It was for public bathing and relax-
ing."

GNno clicked his teeth at her. "Nonsense," he said.

How do you know what it was for? An asked herself.
Then, *Show him! Make the water come!* Then, *Don't do
that! He might want to bathe with you!*

GNno thrust her up to one of the walls. She stared at it,
blankly.

"Well?" asked GNno.

An had been afraid to look at other glyphs since the ep-
isode with the wall—not to mention the exhausting loops

she kept finding herself trapped in lately. But when she looked at GNno's wall, she didn't feel too bad.

In fact, something was happening in her head. Something interesting, possibly even something that was an improvement. She still couldn't find anything to say about the glyphs, but she thought maybe she could pinpoint what was happening to her, if she had a moment to think about it.

"What does it say?" demanded GNno.

"Hold on," said An.

This feeling reminded her of something. Some activity was going on. *Something to do with information.*

"Can you read it?" said GNno.

"Hold on," said An.

Whirring, clicking. No—counting. Something was counting.

"Counting?" she asked aloud.

"What about counting? Is it a number system?"

"No," said An. "Wait."

Counting down, like a launch?

No. Counting *up.* Counting things up. Bits of something. Bits of information?

"Like a computer?" asked An.

"Is it a computer?" GNno demanded excitedly.

"No," said An. "In my head."

"In your head?" GNno seized her by her flightsuit and spun her around, then pushed her up against the wall so that her toes hung about a foot off the floor. He pushed his face into hers and said, "You know something! Tell me what you know!"

"I don't know what I know," said An.

"That's ridiculous! If you know something, you know it!"

"Haven't you ever forgotten that you knew something, then remembered it?"

"If you've forgotten, I can persuade you to remember!"

"You're not helping me at all!"

GNno let her down, slowly. "What do you mean *you don't know what you know?*"

This is impossible, An thought to herself. *Here I am, trying to go crazy, and people just keep asking me questions.*

"You never—know everything you—know, GNno," she said, struggling to voice what was happening to her, struggling with the desire to just forget it and let her brain count itself into a stupor.

But in another moment, the counting seemed to finish, and the words came in a rush: "Some things are in your subconscious, some are in your unconscious. The right side of your brain and the left side have to communicate through the corpus callosum, and maybe not everything gets through. That's the way it is in the Human brain, anyway."

"Our brains are better," said GNno.

"So you know everything you know."

"Of course."

"Do you ever talk to yourself?"

"What?"

"Inside your head. Do you ever think to yourself? In words?"

GNno loosened his hold on her clothes. He even stepped back a few inches. "Yes," he admitted.

"Who are you talking to when you talk to yourself?"

"Me!"

"Then why do you have to use words? Why do you have to use sentences?"

An was just guessing at that part. But it was a good guess. He was frowning, thinking about it; which made An feel good.

"Hah!" she said. "You're doing it now!"

"I am not!"

"You are. You know you are. Who are you really talking to, GNno? If you're talking to yourself, how come you don't already know what you're going to say?"

"I *do* know."

"Then why talk to yourself at all?"

"For entertainment purposes."

He clicked his teeth, in triumph. An tried not to laugh.

"I do that, too, sometimes," she said. "But lots of times I do it to get information from a part of my brain that's —less accessible. Sometimes it works, sometimes it doesn't."

GNno licked her cheek. She thought he did it rather hesitantly, as if he wasn't sure he wanted to know the truth.

"You're upset," he said. "You're worried about your lover."

"Yes."

"He beat CVvu today. You have a fifty-fifty chance, now."

An looked away. He was too close, and she didn't want him to know how she felt about that. In a rush, her new-found energy and confidence started to drain out of her.

"I'm tired, GNno," she said. "I want to sleep with Jo."

For a moment, she thought he would refuse her. But then he turned abruptly and pulled her from the room.

"We're wasting our time here," he said, as if it were all her fault. She stumbled alongside him like a reluctant child. "Your brain is too feeble for this work," he told her.

An wondered if he really knew just how true that was at the moment. But she couldn't help feeling stung by his attitude.

"Why can't you read the glyphs, GNno?"

"No drip."

"And no linguist? Not one expert among you?"

He didn't answer that until they were almost back to the little building at the end of the lane.

"They've disappeared," he said in a low voice.

"Who?" asked An. "All of them?"

"All of the X'GBri experts."

An gaped at him. He looked around, as if afraid that one of the others might hear him.

"They're dead?" she asked.

"No. They're gone. They have all gone somewhere. We don't know where."

That certainly explained why they had been following Jo and An around. It also gave An an idea.

"I might be able to read some glyphs," she told him. "I figured out how to make the bathtub work."

He grunted, following her line of thought. "That would be good," he said. "That would be—useful." He stared at her for a moment.

Uh-oh, thought An.

He almost looked like he was going to kiss her. Her nerves were jumping just like they would if she were with a Human man on some awkward first date, and he was dropping her off at her front door.

But in another moment, he turned away and left her there.

X'GBris don't kiss, said a little voice in her head. *They lick.*

Don't remind me, she said, and went in to find Jo.

An could feel Jo sleeping next to her. She had given him another bath, another treatment that seemed to ease his pain and fade his bruises.

But he had lost his third fight. Now he was waiting for his fourth.

An was waiting, too, dreading. She had watched the third fight. Jo was a tiger; but the third man, MJki, was a T-Rex. Watching the beating was awful. She had wept afterward, when Jo was asleep and there had been no one to watch. She had gone into the bathroom and let the stone creature pour water into her hands, splashing it onto her face until the tears went away.

Now she kept dreaming that they were coming to get Jo, and she couldn't wake up. She had to watch, she didn't want him to face them alone with no one on his side. She would drag herself up to wakefulness and find that it was still dark. Jo would be sleeping deeply and quietly, his face almost peaceful.

An would try to stay awake until dawn. She would sit with her back to a wall. But the other walls would start to chatter at her, the glyphs shifting about and clamoring in a friendly and energetic fashion. It was driving her mad. She had to close her eyes; and before she knew it, she was asleep again, sliding down the wall.

Please let morning come. Please let it be over. Please let Jo win.

GNno came in with two others, They woke Jo.

Wake me too! An tried to cry.

"No," GNno said. "You don't like it. You're taking all the fun out of it."

Wait!

But they left without her.

Wake me! Wake me!

Light filtered into the room. An could not wake. She could not even keep her mind on the subject; soon her thoughts were confused and senseless to her conscious mind.

To another part of her mind, they made perfect sense. *I must wake up* was still at the core of things, but everything that swirled around that core was changing, just like the Early glyphs changed while you were looking at them.

How hot it was in the room, and so dry. An was thirsty. That was bad, because there was no water. No food, either, for days and days, because Daddy had left with the girl and Mommy had no money. So they had turned the water off.

An opened her eyes. She was in her tiny room in the little box house. She was in her little bed. She had gone there, because the others had wanted to die alone. She was honoring their wishes.

Mike and John had gone begging to the neighbors, but An didn't try that. The neighbors always said no. They had just enough food and water for their own. They just acted like they couldn't see or hear you. They acted like you were already dead.

The whole planet was a desert, that's what Daddy had always said. He said people should never have come here, because when you stumble and fall, the desert soaks you up like a drop of water. One little, tiny drop that shouldn't even be there.

An got up and went into Carol's room. Carol was curled up on her bed. An had tried to talk to her a little while ago, but Carol wouldn't talk. Her eyes looked right through you; and her eyes were only half open anyway, so she might have been asleep. An watched to see if Carol's chest was moving up and down. She thought it was, sort of.

An didn't put her head on Carol's chest to listen to her heart. She was afraid that Carol would push her away. Or worse, that Carol wouldn't react at all.

Everyone had blamed An when she had come back without Daddy. He had taken her with him to the Star Port. They had met the girl there. An had never seen Daddy look so happy. He had stuffed a few credit notes into An's hand and had said, "Wait here." Then he had walked away, holding the girl's hand.

An had waited two days and almost two nights. She had finally wet her pants. She had been afraid to go to the bathroom, because Daddy would come back and he wouldn't be able to find her.

Some people had noticed An and taken her to the bathroom. They promised they would send for Daddy. They fed her and some men in uniforms had taken her home.

"He cleaned out the bank account," Mommy kept saying over and over. She wouldn't say anything else, and she wouldn't look at An.

Mommy was curled up in her own room, with the baby. The baby hadn't cried in a long time. That was good, because Mommy didn't pay attention to the baby anymore. It cried for a long time, and then it whimpered. Then it made these noises that An hated, these desperate little noises.

An didn't want to see Mommy.

David was lying with his mouth pressed to the pipe that went from the ground into the house. He had found out that even when the water was turned off, there was always a little bit in the pipe. If you were patient, you could get a few drops.

An didn't like David. He was two years older than her. He liked to push her and take her toys. When she had come home without Daddy, David had blamed her.

"It's *your* fault," he hissed at her for the first several days. "He didn't want you! You were too many kids!"

An was four years old, now. She was not a baby. She knew that they were dying. She was dying, too. She couldn't talk anymore, because her tongue felt big and funny.

"Daddy's coming back," she had tried to tell Mommy. "He said, 'Wait here.' He must be looking for me."

John had told her, "He's not coming back. He took you with him so we wouldn't know he was running away. So we wouldn't try to stop him."

"He cleaned out the bank account," Mommy said.

For some reason, Mommy had taken An with her to see Daddy's friend, Mr. Kyl. Mr. Kyl worked for the government. He was supposed to give poor people relief checks. He wouldn't give one to Mommy.

"John, Sr. told me about your secret bank account, Maggy," said Mr. Kyl, smugly. "You're not getting a penny out of this office."

Mommy tried to tell Mr. Kyl there was no secret bank account. He just grinned at her. An wanted to hit him, but she didn't dare. Mommy didn't like hitting.

Mommy begged Mr. Kyl on her knees. She was crying, too, but he just laughed. "You're a lousy actress, Maggy."

An made herself go into Mommy's room. She didn't look at the bed, where the awful noises had long since stopped. She went to the dresser and opened the bottom drawer. Under some fancy linen napkins she found the gun.

David had shown her the gun. Daddy had taught all the boys to load it. An hadn't believed that David knew how to load it, so he showed her.

The bullets were still in the gun.

"It's an antique," David had said proudly. "He's going to give it to me someday."

An took the gun. She went outside, past David and his pipe. She walked between the box houses, all dirty from the unadorned ground that rose all around you in clouds of dust every time something moved.

The ground felt good under An's bare feet. She walked to the main road, the one that led into town. She held the gun like a kitten, against her breast with both hands.

She was going to shoot Mr. Kyl in the heart. Just like she had seen in the vids. The bad guy always got shot in the heart. Or sometimes he fell out a window; but An didn't think she was big enough to push Mr. Kyl that hard.

Mr. Kyl thought Mommy had a secret bank account. Why had Daddy told him that? Daddy had laughed and smiled that last day. He had held the girl's hand.

Bastard, thought the adult An, back on Cabar 4.

Why did he want you all to die? someone asked her.

An couldn't answer with words. She thought about all the bitter complaints she had overheard from men when she was growing up.

"You'd better not get pregnant," one boyfriend had snarled at her, after kissing her for the first time.

"I'm not going to sleep with you," she had said back. "You think I'm crazy?"

He had answered with a look of pure hatred. The look had said: Prick-tease. Parasite. Lazy, dumb slut who spends my paycheck and makes brats who need to be fed so I can't get drunk once in a while because I've gotta spend all my money on *you!*

"I'm twelve years old, for chrissakes!" she had said then.

"If you're not gonna fuck me, then who needs you?" he had answered.

That's why, An told the voice.

But why are you so happy walking down the road with the gun in your hand? You like the feel of the warm ground under your feet. Why do you feel good while you're feeling bad?

An did feel good. She felt the same way she had when she had started her walk across the Empty Quarter, knowing she was going to change her life forever.

It's like the last day of school. The last day of a job you really hate.

She couldn't stay home and watch the others die. She was tired of being a witness. She was going to end this problem *herself.* Just her and the gun.

An walked for hours. She couldn't have done it if she hadn't known it was the end. Sometimes it seemed like she was hardly moving at all.

The ground got hotter, but her feet adapted to the heat. Her tongue got bigger. She was having torturous fantasies about water: pouring out of faucets, going over waterfalls, falling out of the sky. She thought she saw a giant water cooler. She shot a hole in the plastic and tried to suck the water out. But she didn't even believe it while she was doing it. So she kept walking.

Daddy was laughing at her. His face was smug, like Mr. Kyl's. He stuffed the bills in her hand and said, "Wait here."

The girl he was running away with was Carol's age.

Take that, you little parasites.

"You'd better not get pregnant," Daddy warned the girl.

An saw Mr. Kyl's office. Lots of people were going in and out, but they ignored An. She was already dead.

Mr. Kyl was standing by the water cooler. He was helping himself to a cup of cool water. An shot him before he could swallow.

The bullet hit him just above the groin. The pain was dreadful, awful—he had made sounds of agony until An wanted to weep out of pity, but she didn't have water for tears.

In the vids, people just fell down, neat and tidy. Then it was over.

This went on and on. People ran to help Mr. Kyl. Someone noticed An. He took her aside and took her gun away. Then he got her a cup of water.

"Just little sips," he warned her.

When she had finished the water, she told him about Daddy. She told it all mixed up, and sometimes she was sobbing so hard she could barely talk. But he understood everything. He believed her, and he gave her another cup of water.

He understands because he's seen it all before, said the adult An.

Your young ones aren't loved and cherished? asked the voice.

Some aren't.

How sad that your life was so hard.

It was, agreed An. *But that wasn't my life. I never knew people named* Maggy *or* David *or* Carol. *People haven't had names like that for centuries. And those things never happened to me.*

I know. I was just curious to know why you didn't want to leave the dream about the ape mother. So I made up a story out of your experiences and your fears.

But it was so real! Those people were real, they couldn't have been make-believe.

In a way, they were real.

I don't think my real father was as bad as the father in that dream. My mother was a lot like Maggy, *though. But who was the furry child in my other dream? With the furry mother, in the wonderful tree? I never lived in a tree.*

You didn't, said the voice, *but your ancestors did.*

Oh, said An, thinking it made perfect sense. But a moment later she woke up and said, "Huh?"

The voice was gone. An was wide awake, in a room full of light.

Jo's sleeping bag was empty.

An jumped up.

But Jo was already on his way back in. He was walking, and he was alone.

"Two-for-two," he said.

An helped him into the bathroom. She helped him strip, and got him into the tub.

"Are you reading them now?" he whispered to her, meaning the glyphs. He was very impressed with the trick of the bathtub.

"No," she answered, thinking that the truth was too complicated to tell.

She worried about the dream. She had been talking to herself as if she were talking to another person. That person had had special knowledge of her, but she hadn't recognized it as herself until she was awake.

She had heard of people having experiences like that, as if their brains were bicameral, separated to form a nonconscious mind. Those other voices seemed like the voices of gods to people who were in that state; or the voices of fairies. But whose had this voice been?

It hadn't sounded like a god. It hadn't sounded like a fairy. It hadn't sounded like Mom, the way her inner voices sometimes did.

In fact, the Mom voice was being strangely silent these days. It should have been telling An what a fool she was. But the new voice hadn't sounded anything like the Mom voice.

It hadn't *sounded* at all.

What if she started to hear this voice when she was awake? What was going to become of her? What if she had to watch Jo die? What if Jo tried to kill her again?

No wonder you're hearing voices.

An washed Jo with her undershirt. His body was beautiful, even under the bruises. She kept her eyes on it as she washed him, so he wouldn't look into her eyes.

She felt alert. She felt feverish without being hot. Kokoboro's drip had worked such a haphazard magic.

"I'm having blackouts," she confessed. "Like a drunk."

"I won't let anything happen to you," he said.

An was dismayed to feel the warmth rising inside her.

All the time when she was growing up, older women had warned her, "If a man hits you once, he's gonna hit you again. And again and again."

He never hit me. He just tried to kill me.

He was getting an erection. Her own body was responding. She hoped he wouldn't touch her or kiss her. She would give in if he did. She would be like those battered women, the ones everyone had pitied.

She wished she could look at it from the X'GBri point

of view. *So he tried to kill you. Is that so bad? It can only add spice to your relationship.*

And the Vorns wouldn't even understand her conflict. A Vorn female mates with a male—then she eats him. Very simple. What more do you need to know?

"I deserve to die for what I did to you," said Jo.

An didn't trust herself to answer.

"Every time they hit me, I think that's one more inch toward making it up to you. But it's not. I can't make it up. I should die."

An took a deep breath. "We deserve to live, Jo. Both of us."

"*You* deserve to live. That's why I'm going to win. I'll give your life back to you. That's something. It's not enough, but it's something."

"Jo, none of this . . ."

She almost said, *none of this had to happen.* But what good would that do? He knew it perfectly well. It was the core of his pain. And his suffering only made hers worse.

"GNno isn't going to get his paws on you," said Jo.

An felt an odd stab of pity for GNno. She had no idea where it came from.

"He wants to take you with him," Jo was saying. "He's got a surprise coming."

An washed Jo's face last. She looked bravely into his eyes. He wanted so badly for her to love him. But she did love him; that wasn't the problem at all.

He hated himself for what he had done. The scene of his betrayal and her near-death had replayed itself in his mind a thousand times, haunted his dreams, presenting itself for examination first thing every morning.

Why did he really do it? she wondered, watching his haunted eyes. *Just because he didn't trust me?*

That no longer seemed like such a logical answer. If he hadn't trusted her, why did he try to go back and undo his sabotage? And he had tried, she was sure of it. It was almost as if another man had done the deed, and Jo had been forced to watch.

Almost as if *his* mind was bicameral, too.

Did a god do it, Jo? Did a god come into your head and move your limbs, saying I must die? And when he left you again, did you guess who he really was?

Yes, he had guessed. So he had built a cage and put himself inside. She couldn't reach him there.

"Rest now," she told him. She helped him out of the basin. She watched him administer a painkiller. He got into his sleeping bag and closed his eyes.

"An," he sighed.

She went to him, but he was already asleep.

"Poor Jo," she said, gazing down at him.

Poor An, said the voice inside her head.

It was the night before the last fight, and An was asleep. But her mind was not dreaming. She felt the same way she had when she had talked to the other side of her mind. She decided to experiment, to see if she could make herself recognize herself.

Who are you? she asked the voice inside her head.

No one answered for a moment; but some colors flashed behind her eyes, and then the voice said, *Who, me?*

This was odd. This really did seem like another person. Something occurred to her:

Yes, you! Are you Kokoboro?

The RNA donor.

Yes. You weren't here before the drip. Are you an artifact?

You think I'm an artifact?

Yes. Don't you?

I don't know. That would be very disappointing. I thought I was you.

If you were me, wouldn't I know that I was you?

Maybe you don't know what you know. That's what you told GNno.

Right. Well, all I know is I got the drip and then you showed up.

That's not all you did. You did something else, too. Something important.

I got the drip, I almost got killed, I got bullied by X'GBris. . . .

You looked at the glyphs.

Someone put a hand over An's mouth.

An woke to find GNno was bending over her. It was his hand over her mouth. He looked meaningfully at Jo, who was still asleep, and then back at An. He took his hand away from her mouth and picked her up.

It was pitch black outside; very little light was filtering through the forest floor overhead. But GNno walked as if he could see exactly where he was going.

The insects and bird-o-saurs were whooping it up. An heard mating cries; or maybe it was GNno who was giving her that impression.

He took her deep inside a large building. *Not another confrontation with the glyphs,* thought An. But GNno set her down among some blankets. His nest.

"What are you doing?" asked An.

"Tomorrow is the last fight," said GNno.

"Yes?"

"Tomorrow you live or die. This is our last chance."

"For what?"

"Other choices."

He dropped down beside her. An cringed from him, but he didn't try to kiss or roll on top of her. Instead, he touched her feet.

There was another burst of color inside her head, but not as vivid as last time. Yet the voice seemed stronger:

Oh! it said. *That's nice.*

"Such little feet," said GNno. "Little feet, little hands, little face."

"You might hurt me," said An. But GNno smiled at that.

"I have control."

He stroked her feet with great care, then bent and started to lick her toes.

Oh! said the voice. *Oh, yes! That's wonderful! Oh, oh, oh . . . !*

Calm down, warned An, but she was feeling anything but calm. She could have resisted any other attempt at seduction; but her feet! No one had ever gone after her feet before.

You've been missing out! said the voice.

"You love this," said GNno. "I can taste it."

"Jo is my mate," said An.

"Don't make that excuse. TTra has five mates. You could, too."

"TTra wouldn't like it."

"TTra is first. You would be second."

"I'm not second with you," An guessed.

GNno engulfed her toes with his mouth, sucked, licked, and said, "No. You're not. But that's my problem."

He peered into her face. In the semidarkness, his eyes looked black, his pupils filled them from lid to lid.

What would he be like? An wondered.

"Do you know what the trouble is?" asked GNno. "You look too much like us. You should be like a Vorn. I wouldn't want to fuck a Vorn."

"They would eat you if you did."

He licked his lips. "You are small, like our children. We feel ashamed if we want you. But, in time, we see you as you are. We taste you. I'm going to lick you all over."

"No," said An.

Yes! said the voice.

"You have no choice," said GNno. "After I've tasted every inch of you, then you may say yes or no."

Great! said the voice.

"We can't make love, GNno."

Why not? asked the voice.

Because it's going to complicate my life too much.

"You may get on top," said GNno. "Slide your vagina over my penis at your own speed, and then establish the rhythm you want. I will let you ride me to your own satisfaction. I would like that very much."

Me too!

"GNno," said An, "I'm monogamous. I can only love one man at a time. I don't want to be second woman with five husbands."

He froze. An held her breath. He cupped her face in his hands, carefully.

"Then—a one night stand?" he suggested.

An thought about it. The voice did not interrupt her, but she could feel that it hoped she would say yes.

"GNno, remember what you said about shame? That's what I would feel if I had sex with you."

"Why?" he asked, as the tragedy mask settled over his features.

"Because you hurt Jo."

He didn't answer. He took her by the hand and led her out of the building. He took her back to the little house at the end of the lane and stood with her by the door. But he didn't want to let go of her hand.

"You're still afraid of him," said GNno.

An stared to deny it; but she couldn't.

"I still love him," she said. "I can't betray him."

"Then don't," said GNno. He let go of her hand and walked away. He was instantly lost in the darkness. An turned to go in, and was overcome by a wave of presentiment.

Jo is going to lose tomorrow.

Let's go make love to Jo, then, suggested the voice.

An tried to think up an excuse not to. *If he's awake,* she promised at last, knowing full well that he wouldn't be.

And of course, he wasn't.

Jo fought the last man at sunrise.

A short while later, An had to help him back into the little house. He was limping, badly, and he was temporarily blind in his left eye.

He had lost.

The last man was so low in the pecking order, no one had even bothered to tell An his name. She had hoped that this would mean he was the worst fighter. He might have been so; but Jo was exhausted by four previous fights, and this last man had an extra thing going for him. He was desperate. He couldn't let Jo win this fight, or his status would drop even further. He might have even been eliminated from TTra's entourage.

An wondered if she would have time to bathe Jo before they died.

They sat together on the edge of the basin in the bathroom. Jo took her hands.

"I'm sorry, baby," he said.

"You're my hero," An said, then could say no more without tempting the tears to come.

TTra found them there. She stood with her hands on her hips and studied them, frowning fiercely.

"How will you kill us?" asked An.

"Not so fast," said TTra. "Perhaps I'm not satisfied yet."

An moved closer to Jo, protectively. What more could they want of him? He was at the end of his endurance.

"You are two of a kind," TTra said. "Slim, dark elegant. I enjoy looking at you."

"Don't jerk us around, Tatty," Jo said.

An was surprised at the tone of his voice, the sound of

the pet name. Jo and TTra must have been at least a little more than friends. Now TTra was scowling at him.

"I haven't had my turn," she snapped. "I'm bigger than you, stronger. I can fight, too."

"You want a chance to beat me up?" asked Jo. "I didn't know you hated me that much."

"You are not fit for a regular fight. I have something else in mind." TTra stepped to the center of the room and held up her right hand. "Arm wrestling," she said. "Do you agree?"

Jo took a deep breath, and stood. He did so without An's help. An sat where she was, afraid that a word or breath from her might break the spell.

Jo stood opposite TTra and clasped her right hand. They looked long and hard into each other's eyes—in Jo's case, just one eye.

Please, thought An. *Please.*

Jo and TTra tensed, began to struggle against each other. All of their will and energies were directed into that point between them, where their hands clasped. Jo trembled with effort, but An could see his profile, the undamaged side of his face. It was hard and unyielding. He would rather die than give ground.

TTra seemed to be struggling with more than Jo. Her face wasn't nearly as unyielding. *She likes him,* thought An.

She liked him, but she wasn't giving up. She would see the fight through to the end.

An bowed her head. The moment she took her eyes off them, she heard a gasp.

TTra was leaning back slightly, her right hand pressed far to the right and down. Jo was leaning into her, the winner. He let go of her hand, and took a step back.

"A tie then," said TTra. "You have won your lives. Go now, leave us to our *prize.*" She indicated the room, her face a mask of contempt.

An helped Jo from the building. GNno and the others were waiting outside. They did not try to stop An and Jo from walking away. They only watched, silently, their eyes burning holes in the two Humans.

They knew, already, An thought wonderingly. But she cautioned herself against too much hope. X'GBri pride was hard to sort from X'GBri compassion. Anything could happen now.

The silent city passed on either side of them on the way back to the hole. But the silence wasn't absolute. The animals and insects buzzed and screeched as usual. And the buildings weren't really silent either. They made a noise An heard with her eyes.

"We've been here five days," Jo said, sounding so dazed that An wondered if she was only dreaming that he was speaking, "—and I'm still not sure what these ruins look like."

An laughed briefly and a little hysterically. What did Early buildings look like? They looked like a constantly chattering, singing collection of glyphs. The shape of the buildings were utterly unimportant. The buildings might not even be there at all.

She looked at them. Were they angular? Were they rounded and organic? But she couldn't decide. The glyphs were there. The glyphs were talking up a storm. The glyphs . . .

"What's wrong?" she heard Jo asking, from a great distance. "We have to keep moving, An, come on!"

"*I* was wrong," she mumbled.

"Look, TTra left a rope ladder. We'll have to climb."

"I can read them."

"Move your ass, girl. Up!"

"I can read them all," An said, feeling herself climb the ladder, feeling Jo pushing her from underneath. Finally they had climbed so high, she could see the entire city spread out beneath her. Jo was above her now, pulling her up from the waist.

"What do they say?" said Jo's voice, right next to her ear.

"Everything," said An. "That's the problem. They say *everything*. I can't absorb all that information. My brain—Kokoboro said that Humans don't have enough receptors."

Don't worry, said the voice in her head. *I'm fixing that.*

Jo pulled her through the hole in the forest floor. An made herself stand, and the two of them tottered, side by side.

"This way," gasped Jo, and they went lurching down the path.

An started to black out.

Oh no. Not now.

I'm still awake, said the voice. *I'll drive.*

Thanks a lot, said An, and slipped down into the darkness.

"Like a drunk," An said.

"What?" Jo asked her.

"Blackouts. Just like a drunk."

"An, are you all right?"

She opened her eyes. She was standing with Jo, on the command deck of a beautiful ship. She was holding Jo's hand, leaning into him with a silly grin on her face.

Both of them were wearing control suits. An wasn't wearing anything underneath hers. Jo's face was just inches away, his cheeks flushed and his mouth all soft and vulnerable, like a sleeper's mouth, like a lover's mouth.

What have you been doing!? she asked the voice.

He's so handsome! I like him.

He tried to kill me!

Nobody's perfect.

An didn't jerk her hand away. She waited until he let go of it. He looked puzzled, worried.

"I need you to be gunner, An. Can you do that or not?"

"I can," she said automatically.

"Then sit down. My eye's still not up to snuff, but I'm going to pilot, and I don't want to have to rely on auto with TTra and her boys on our tails."

He looked better than he had before she had blacked out. He looked doctored, and his bad eye was opening again. How many hours had passed?

An sat down in the gunner's chair. It was right next to the pilot's. She could see his displays just by turning her head slightly.

"This looks like Early-based technology," she said.

"It is. And I've got the best stealth features going. That's why my ship isn't in the same shape as your . . ."

"My Egg," An finished for him. She had put that pain aside, in favor of other worries. Now it came trickling back. But it wasn't as bad. This new ship was—interesting.

"You have room for a ten-man crew," she remarked, looking at the various stations around the command deck.

"Fifteen if you count engineering and medical," he said with pride.

There was even a captain's chair, positioned so it could see everyone's tacticals. And there were several view screens, which were currently displaying lush, green rain forest, as if they were windows.

"Jo," An said, awe beginning to creep into her mind, "This ship is—it must have cost—"

"A fortune. But it's just a fraction of what I inherited."

"Inherited?"

"From my father. I'll tell you about it later. First, we've got to get off."

"Let's go, then," said An, suddenly very anxious to be as far away from Cabar 4 as possible.

I was so happy about coming here, so excited about the ruins. . . . Now I could care less if I ever see them again.

An armed the weapons systems. It had been years since she had studied gunner protocol, and yet it seemed like it was just yesterday.

Yesterday.

I never studied gunner protocol.

"I—" she started to tell Jo. She felt a moment of vertigo. How did she know what she was doing? Why did her hands know? It was like trying to ride a bike after you haven't been on one for years. She would make a mistake! She would forget halfway through, and do something dangerous and stupid!

But her hands were *not* forgetting. Her mind was coming up with the procedure without a stutter or a glitch. When she relaxed and just let it happen, it was even kind of fun.

She could plug her suit into the gunner systems. Now she would be able to aim and fire with the smallest motions of her hands!

"Ready," she told Jo.

He answered by snapping on his safeties. She did the same. Their chairs swiveled to take-off position. The displays swiveled with them.

There was an amber *X* on the screen indicating the X'GBri ship. It hadn't budged from its original landing site.

"They aren't moving," said An. "Don't seem to have fired their engines in a while, either."

"That's the way we look to them, too, and we're hot. I'm willing to bet they're as well-rigged as I am."

"Wonderful," said An. "All this lovely technology and I'm still just guessing."

"You must love trouble, or you wouldn't be here."

Jo fired the engines, and they were pushed down into their chairs. They punched out through Cabar 4's thick, wet atmosphere, clearing the gravity well in painful moments. But the pushing didn't let up as much as An was used to in her Egg.

Jesus! How many gees are we going?

We're accelerating to three, answered the voice in her head.

Why do we have to go that fast, this soon?

Because we need to get to jumping distance, fast.

What!?

I'm just guessing. What do you think?

But we're not in deepsleep yet! We've gotta have sedatives! We've gotta have safety suits!

The control suits are better than safety suits.

But—

"Where are they, baby?" Jo asked over her headset. An blinked at her screen.

"Still planetside, according to your machinery."

"That'll have to do. Jump in two minutes. Get ready for a sting."

"Huh?" An said, then felt the sting in question. The suit was sedating her. "Right here?" she said. "No sleep cubicles?"

"We need to be in position as soon as we jump out again."

Ready for a fight. But An wasn't ready for anything of the kind. The sedatives were dragging her down, and she was having flashbacks about popping out of her Egg.

"Systems on automatic now," Jo said, in the same voice that had commanded her Egg to kill her.

"No, Jo," she begged, but he was counting down.

"One minute to jump. Fifty seconds. Thirty. Twenty— ten, nine, eight ... uh ... five ... four ..."

"Jo?" called An. Was he already asleep? She needed to sleep, too. She didn't want to face jump awake. It was too weird, too disorienting, too ...

Too what? It sounds interesting.

In fact, it did sound interesting. Why hadn't she ever been awake for jump? Deepsleep was to keep your body in stasis so it wouldn't weaken from the weightlessness. It conserved air supply, food, and water; it protected your mind against the boredom and the loneliness. No one had ever said that jump was dangerous when you were awake, but An was used to being asleep for it.

What would happen if you were awake? Would it hurt? Would it be too weird to stand? Or would it feel normal, like prejump?

Forget it, she told herself. *We're going under. Just forget it.*

But wait! said the voice. *You've forgotten something important!*

I wish I could forget everything, An told the voice, and then she went to sleep.

What am I forgetting? An wondered. But the question was just proper procedure, part of the mental discipline that would prevent her from taking things for granted, from letting important things become habit instead of thinking them through every time and adapting to new demands and problems.

After all, she had been an EggHead for five years now. She had learned more during that time than most people learned in their entire lives. She had mastered the art of freefall landing; and today it almost seemed like a piece of cake. But then, today she was landing on a settled world, on a field built just for that purpose, not on some wild, wet place that might send her to hell on a blast of superheated steam.

Not forgetting anything, An assured herself, then landed safely to prove it.

She popped her Egg, and let Covina's atmosphere come in. It was dry, like she liked it, and warm even though it was night on this side of the planet. Covina was very much like Storm, only a lot tamer, without the giant sandstorms that swept her homeworld. Its type-K sun was so mild, An was amazed that any life had ever had the energy to develop there.

On Covina, the plants were greener, softer, friendlier. They had big, fat leaves to let them absorb as much sunlight as possible. They had lovely, bright blooms that seemed to say, *Please come pluck me! Eat me, smell me, whatever the heck you want!* You could walk right up to one without worrying about root sensors and seed storms. The grass that was growing on the ground wouldn't poison you or try to eat you.

An climbed out of her Egg and let her boots sink into the springy stuff and the soft dirt underneath. She felt a brief pang, thinking about the naked rocks of home. Geo would have been pleased by that pang.

But An didn't have the slightest urge to go home again. Not to see Mom or Le, or even Geo. They were safely in her past, tucked away where they couldn't harm or be harmed. She preferred to keep them there.

Just now, she was off a fairly profitable run; she had

prospected a Class-M planet for Home Corp. Now she was in for some relaxation. She waited for the jeep that would take her to the transit center, enjoying the soft breeze that swept across the landing fields.

The jeep drove up about fifteen minutes later. The man who drove it was brown skinned and plain featured, like Ro had been; yet at one glance An could tell he was as different from Ro as he could be. "You in from Willow Sector?" he asked An.

"No. I was out past Morris Sector."

"You haven't heard about Lilith, then."

"What about it?"

"Vorn invasion. They've been silent for over a month now."

"No kidding." An felt the dread creep up her spine. She hadn't seen a Vorn up close since that time back on Storm.

But once since then she had seen the aftermath of a Vorn invasion, on an orbital station that had been a steady supply stopover for EggHeads for over a century. The station had circled a dead planet called Bazrain, valuable only because of its nine, mineral-rich satellites.

It had been valuable to EggHeads for other reasons. It had been a place where you could buy anything, or find out anything. Bazrain had been allowed a limited Net because of its mining operation. Of course, that legitimate Net had all sorts of not-so-legitimate extensions growing out of it. Sometimes it had seemed you could talk to just about anyone just about any*where* on that Net.

And then the Vorns killed it. And An had seen what they had done. . . .

"Are you all right, miss?" asked the man.

"Yes." An climbed into the jeep and fastened her safety harness. He drove off without preamble, jerking both of them back in their seats.

After a few moments of acceleration, he said, "It's a tough thing to hear, I guess."

"Yes," An agreed.

"All those people dead."

"All those people."

"Almost a billion colonists, from what I hear."

"My God."

"Kind of funny, though. The Vorns don't usually go after big colonies like that. Kind of makes you wonder. I heard Lilith was running their own com Net."

In fact, An had communicated with Lilith's illegal Net, which had included twenty known worlds. It hadn't been as good as Bazrain's Net had been, but it had been handy. It was just the sort of thing the Inner Worlders were always warning about. The Vorn might invade a planet using that technology, and then more super-advanced, Early-based technology would fall into enemy claws.

She looked sideways at the driver. He was placid, even a little bored. He didn't look like he was trying to solicit anti-InWorld sentiments out of her. He didn't look like he might be a snitch—not that he *would* look like one, if he was. Probably he was just the sort of fellow who loved to tell bad news.

Now why was she thinking about snitches? It wasn't illegal to have an opinion. All that time in space was making her paranoid.

The driver dropped An off at the transport station. From there, she rode the bus into town. She didn't feel lonely, didn't feel the need to connect with any of the strangers who all tried to stare at her without looking impolite. They must be wondering if she was really an Egg-Head, with all that hair.

They might also be wondering where she was from. Most of them had olive skin and auburn or brown hair. Like the plants of their world, they tried to expose as much of themselves to the sunlight as possible. They were cozy planetsiders. Once they got tired of stealing glimpses at An, they gave their sleepy attention to the news-Net vid behind the driver's station.

News Net. Back on Storm, they had called their entertainment a "Net" too. But the Net was only planet-wide on the Outer Worlds, not system wide. How Inner Worlders must laugh when they heard Outer Worlders using the term. How they must laugh at the millions of clumsy message drones people used to communicate world to world, messages taking weeks or months instead of the seconds it would take with a complex, intrasystem Net.

"Still no sign of life from Lilith, after thirty-one Standard days," said the news announcer, halting all casual conversation, making everyone on the bus sit up and take notice. "Authorities have observed heavy Vorn activity in the system—with some sources reporting sightings of as many as one hundred Mother Ships—and the question of the day seems to be: Why this resurgence in the Vorn War after so many years? Just when so many of us were hoping—*praying*—that the end was in sight? Here's a report from our correspondent, Mitaru, from Willow Sector."

Of course, since Willow Sector was one of the areas that forbade the use of intraworld Nets, the message from Mitaru was a recording. But it was fascinating, nonetheless.

"I'm speaking to you from Willow Prime," said Mitaru, who was standing on a bustling city street, the people hurrying by him hardly seemed interested in the fact that he was standing in front of a broadcast array, "which is just two hundred light years from Lilith—and the next logical target of invasion—if, indeed, the Vorns have truly started up another wave of colonization—the sort of colonization which has spread fear throughout Human settlements for the past one hundred years.

"Yet, perhaps it has been too long since those early, terrible times, when the Vorns swept out of Unknown Space like creatures from our worst nightmares. . . ."

The scene suddenly changed from Mitaru's handsome, youthful face to shocking footage of Vorn warriors storming the towers of Celestine. It was footage An had seen before, in school, at home on Storm's nets, and of course in her dreams. Beautiful Celestine, the Pearl of the Outer Worlds.

". . . Monsters from our deepest hells," Mitaru's voice continued over scenes of warfare. Human shock troops were fighting the Vorns with armored vehicles, which were quickly overrun and crippled. Human soldiers were dragged from the vehicles some of them unable to get their weapons to bear in time. . . .

An averted her eyes. Mitaru continued to talk about the downfall of Celestine, which had occurred ten years into the war. It has been an impossibly painful loss, but it may have galvanized the Human war effort. Mitaru was saying all that when An stopped listening to him.

"Bullshit," a young man was hissing, a few seats down from her. "Bull shit." He kept saying it.

"Don't you think we can win another war with the Vorns?" a woman asked him.

"It wasn't the Vorns that killed Lilith," hissed the young man.

An pricked up her ears, but he didn't say anything more. The news drifted onto another topic, something about local politics that An found indecipherable. She let her mind slip into a pleasant stupor, and mused about the evening she wanted to spend.

She was glad she had taken the time to brush Clean-Foam through her hair. It had been so tangled and greasy when she had finished the job with Home Corp. She had been covered with old sweat and grime. She always took the time to clean up with wipes and CleanFoam before reentering civilization. Most of the EggHeads in town would not have done that. They would be sitting in the bars, reeking and drinking, taking their own sweet time before checking into a hotel and indulging in a good shower.

An jumped off the transport at Fourth Street, where rumor had it the best spacer bars could be found. You could get home cooking in some of these places if you looked hard enough—and if you weren't too strict about your definitions. An walked lazily up and down, just enjoying having her feet on the ground, feeling the people around her, smelling the plant smell that only a spacer would be aware of in the middle of a big town.

Like an omen, a place called STORMY's loomed out of the neon darkness. An sauntered in, smelling the Egg-Head reek that was wafting out the front door.

She was looking for a clear table, a place where she could sit down, order a meal, and watch everyone. Her eyes drifted across a table full of men and women, all EggHeads with lean bodies and close-cropped hair. One fellow had cream-and-coffee skin, black hair, elegant cheekbones . . .

Funny that she had just been thinking about Storm and the Vorn warrior who had almost killed her. She had been thinking about the marines who had saved her life. And there he was in Stormy's, looking at her from across the room. He was older, he was an EggHead now, but it had to be him. . . .

He was staring back at her, and everyone at his table got quiet.

An had an overwhelming urge to go over and say *Hi! Remember me? You saved my life back on Storm. Buy you a drink?*

But his eyes weren't those kind of eyes. He wasn't smiling. His expression was guarded, almost suspicious. Maybe it wasn't him, after all.

Or maybe it was him, and he had gone AWOL.

"Hey!" one of the women called. "Are you an Egg-Head?"

An didn't want to yell back, so she went over and shook hands with the woman. "Yes," she said. "My name is An."

"Te," said the woman. "Sit down, if you like."

So An sat next to Te, who looked forty but might have been eighty for all An knew. Te had very pale skin. Her hair was cropped so close, An couldn't quite tell what color it was.

"That's Jo," Te said, indicating the possible ex-marine. "And that's Ra."

Ra must have been from Hel, he was so pale. His hair was that strange white that only Hel-lers seemed to grow naturally. An shivered a little at the sight of his blue eyes. But they weren't GodHead blue. A Human being was looking at her through them, not a mind laced with plant neurotransmitters.

"How do you take care of all that hair?" another woman asked her.

"I spray CleanFoam on it, brush it through, then braid it." An shrugged. "It gives me something to do on those long, in-system trips."

"Hell, I would rather read," said the woman, unconsciously brushing her hand over her own cropped hair.

"I have other things I like to do," said another woman, giggling suggestively.

Jo liked An's hair. She could tell by the way he kept looking at it, then looking away. She had considered cutting it once or twice; but it was one of the last bits of feminine identity she had left, and she hadn't been able to let go of it.

"How long have you been Egging?" Ra asked her. He was sitting companionably close to Jo, as only a very old friend would do.

"Five years," she admitted.

Ra laughed, but Jo came to her defense.

"If she's been Egging for five years, she'll probably make it for ten. Maybe even twenty."

Twenty years sounded like an awful lot, back then.

"Excuse me," she asked Jo, "have you ever been in the service?"

"No."

Something about his tone made her decide never to ask again.

An spent that night in a comfortable hotel room. She ate good food, took a long, hot shower, and enjoyed herself for a few hours before bedtime by watching Covina's excellent entertainment net.

But she didn't have pleasant dreams that night.

Funny how an EggHead could go to sleep planetside, but always woke up thinking she was in her Egg. Not that An really woke up. She only *dreamed* she woke up, and a voice was calmly talking to her from her comm.

"Bazrain Station," it announced, "we are experiencing a temporary emergency. Do not approach unless automatic guidance is available."

An shivered. She remembered the last time she had heard that. She had been traveling to Bazrain for supplies, for R&R, and to use their Net for some important messages that couldn't wait. She had heard that calm, mechanical voice, making it sound like Bazrain Station was probably only having a little technical trouble. Nothing serious. We're working on it.

So she had hooked her Egg up with the automatic systems and let them guide her in.

Don't do that now, she warned herself, remembering what she had found that last time. But it was too late. Her Egg was going in, being swallowed by a docking system that was working beautifully, looking deceptively intact.

It swallowed An's Egg and sat it gently down in a holding area until it could pressurize a receiving room for her.

I have to go in, An told herself. *I need water and air. I'll just get those things and then get the hell out of here.*

Her Egg popped open, and An found herself in a huge, dark room, not a receiving room at all. An couldn't figure out exactly where it was, except that she was somewhere on Bazrain Station, and she was about to see horrible things.

Pieces of people had been everywhere. An had seen things she still couldn't think about, even when she was dreaming.

The Vorns must still be here, somewhere, An thought. That first time, she hadn't stayed long enough to confront one of the creatures. But this time she needed things. She had to sneak in, get what she needed, and sneak out again or she would die.

An crept through a dark corridor. Her ears were alert for dry rustlings, for the vibration of Vorn wings. She heard nothing. Yet she sensed movement around her. Were other Humans creeping around, too? Survivors?

What was that?

Something had just slipped around a corner, just up ahead. It had been carrying a severed Human hand, but it hadn't looked like a Vorn. It had only been as tall as a Human. It had been dressed in a neuter suit.

Like the guards from Omsk.

"We're just cleaning up," a voice whispered to An. "We're picking up the pieces. Someone has to do it."

More people in neuter suits were passing An. They had things in their hands that An didn't want to look at.

"I just need to get air and water," she told them. "I'll get out of your way."

She slipped through a darkened doorway, hoping they wouldn't see which way she had gone. But she ran right into one of them.

From the hardness of his body, she could tell he was male. He was much taller than her, too; he towered over her. He reached up and slipped off his helmet.

He was Javici, the officer she had met on Storm.

"Don't believe them, An," he said. "Don't believe them."

Javici was an Inner Worlder, but he had left that life behind. He was ashamed of what his kin were doing. He had gone to the Outer Worlds to earn his own way.

"Just go along with them," he whispered to An.

Someone poked her hard, on the shoulder. An turned slowly, and found the Investigators behind her. She shivered at the sight of them, the enhancements that were built into their bodies and their uniforms, until you could hardly tell where the Investigators ended and their enhancements began. She had spoken with them on Regal, where she had fled after finding what was left of Bazrain Station. She had been surprised to find them there, elite Inner World forces on a backwater planet.

"Who's responsible?" snapped the chief, his artificial eyes looking right through An's skull.

"I don't know," stammered An.

"Didn't you see? Didn't you tell us you saw?"

"Pieces of people everywhere," said An.

"And who could do that to people? Who would have torn Human bodies that way?"

"Vorns, I guess—"

"You *guess*?"

"Vorns did it."

His eyes glittered with satisfaction. "And, of course," he snarled, "any Early technology that was being used here *illegally* has now been confiscated by the Vorns. We warned you about that."

"You certainly did."

"And now we shall all pay the price," he said.

"Not all of us," whispered Javici, behind An.

"Remember what happened to Celestine?" asked the Investigator, his face stern and uncompromising. "Human beings *still* are not able to live there, after what was done."

"You poisoned the place," An agreed.

"*We* poisoned it?"

"I mean—I mean the *Vorns* poisoned it," An said, hastily. "No one can live there now. That's what I heard."

The people in the neuter suits were gathering behind the Investigators. All of the were staring at An.

"Get the message?" Javici whispered. "Get the message?"

An got it all right. But she didn't want it.

And when she woke up a moment later, she did her best to forget it.

In the morning, An resolved to put all worries behind her and enjoy her holiday on Covina to the fullest. What good would it do her to agonize over what had happened to Lilith? Or on Bazrain Station? Knowing who had killed those people wouldn't make them any less dead.

But it might make An considerably less than alive.

So she forgot about politics. She treated herself to the nice hotel room with its first-rate shower facility. She indulged in towels rather than using the blower. She washed her hair every night, and got it trimmed in the hotel salon. She got a manicure and bought some pretty clothes, even though she knew perfectly well she wouldn't be able to take them with her in her Egg when she left.

You'd almost think I was dressing up for someone in particular, An thought to herself. An image of Jo would have popped into her mind then if she hadn't already been thinking of him, hadn't been incessantly doing so since the first moment she had laid eyes on him.

And was he doing the same? She saw him every night at Stormy's even though she had long since grown bored of visiting that bar. She would go every evening and have a couple of drinks with Te and the others. Jo was there every night, and he would look at her with those eyes of black glass.

Do you like me? she would wonder. *Are you as attracted to me as I am to you?*

But he never made a move in her direction. Except that he was there every night, seemingly waiting. Waiting for her?

She was driving herself crazy. During the day she would act like a woman on holiday, hopping on flyers and shopping in Covina's tourist towns, seeing the lovely little canyons that were its main attraction; swimming in Lake Wilili or picnicking in one of the meadows that sprouted on the hills that surrounded the capital city. She would indulge her skin in the warm, rosy sunlight, never ceasing to be amazed at how gentle it was.

But it would have been nice to do those things with someone else.

It would have been nice to spend the nights with him, too.

Sometimes she was sure he was her lost marine, and that he didn't want to talk to her because he had gone AWOL; that would have been a good reason to avoid her. AWOLs were always sent to gravity prisons to do Heavy Time. A prisoner could get sentenced to one hundred years and feel like he was doing a thousand—that's what everyone said. Of course, no one had ever come back from a gravity prison to talk about it.

If Jo was AWOL, then An knew she should leave him alone. But she couldn't. Every night, she admired his elegant cheekbones, the perfect shape of his jaw. She wondered how a face could be so masculine and yet so beautiful. He stared right back at her, looking at her hair, her face, her slim body. She knew he was! She had been looked at by enough men to know what it meant.

So why wouldn't he come close?

And why won't you? An asked herself. Even the others had begun to wonder. Some of the women An sat with had gotten the wrong idea.

"Are you a lesbian, An?" Gi whispered to her one night. Gi was red haired, black skinned, and a lesbian herself. But she was being curious, not pushy.

"No," An told her.

"Then why don't you go for it? What can he say? *No?* No isn't the worst thing you'll ever hear in your life."

"He doesn't want me," An whispered. "If he did, he wouldn't look so angry all the time."

"That's just testosterone looking back at you through those eyes," said Gi. "Don't let it intimidate you."

"Maybe *he's* homosexual."

"No," said Gi. "Trust me on this one."

Am I so afraid of hearing no? An wondered. Or was it something else? A tension that frightened her, made her cautious? She couldn't decide, and the days frittered away. Before she knew it, her holiday was almost over, and there was just one night left.

Of course, she spent it at Stormy's. Of course, Jo was there, too. He was sitting at a different table this time, so An couldn't even stare at him without looking obvious.

Then I won't look at him at all, she resolved, and spent the next couple of hours in torment.

She had done her hair up in a fancy twist and dressed in her sexiest clothes, and it was all being wasted on Gi and Te. And Ka, who was regaling them with her old Inner World existence and expounding paranoid theories without caring who might overhear her.

"Yeah, they killed all those people on Lilith and made it look like a Vorn invasion," she was saying. "Just you wait. They'll claim the Vorns have been driven back in a year or so, and then they'll offer Lilith up for colonization again.

Another case of OutWorlder butt saved by InWorlder wisdom. Mark my word."

An did mark Ka's word, though she wasn't certain of its real value. If you believed Ka, she was an ex-school teacher, ex-marine, ex-fancy girl—and ex-man, though you wouldn't know it if she didn't tell you. Ka claimed to have used facilities on Omsk that few people had access to. An preferred not to ask Ka too many questions; the answers might send wild birds swirling through her head, waking memories and suspicions that she preferred to keep buried.

Not that she could have paid attention to the answers, with Jo sitting so close yet so far away.

Why doesn't he come over and say good-bye? she fumed. *He knows this is my last night! I've been dropping hints all over the place! I've done everything but drop a damned handkerchief!*

"You really think you're a fancy girl with all that hair, don't you?" said an angry voice, just behind An's left shoulder.

"Huh?" said An, looking around to find an EggHead, a woman she had seen in the bar a few times but didn't know well. This woman had always sat quietly, looking blank and mildly depressed. Her hair was shaved right down to the scalp, and she smelled like she hadn't bothered to take a shower once since she had been on Covina. "Excuse me?" An asked, baffled by the woman's tone.

"Excuse me!" mocked the woman. *"Excuuuuuuse meeee!"*

"Calm down, Nu," said Gi. "Go drink yourself into a stupor, will you?"

But Nu wasn't about to engage with Gi, who was a foot taller than her. An presented a much easier target, with her petite build. Nu leaned over her, aggressively.

"What's bothering you?" An asked, though she didn't want to know.

"I think you need a haircut!" snapped Nu, and made to pull a strand out of An's fancy coif.

An slapped her hand away. "You're drunk."

"I think you need someone to cut off all that pesky hair," Nu said, without listening. "Because, girl, you've got an attitude and I'm sick of it."

"My attitude is none of your business," said An, wondering if this was a situation that warranted pulling her gun. It wasn't that she was afraid of getting beaten up— that had happened a million times when she was growing up.

But her hair was a fighting issue.

And Nu's friends looked like they were prepared to back Nu up if a forced haircut was what she had in mind.

"Fuck off, you dumb bitch," said a voice that An knew well, even though she had only heard it a few times.

It was Jo's voice.

Nu jerked her head up and stared at him, dumbfounded. He was standing, and he looked like he was prepared to throw Nu across the room. Nu's face went bright red.

Jo's face had drained of color. Even An was scared, seeing him that way.

"Leave her alone or I'm going to break your fucking neck," Jo told Nu.

"You don't—" Nu spluttered. "It's none of your—"

He just glared.

"She doesn't have any reason to flaunt that mousy hair like she thinks it makes her the queen or something!" Nu pleaded. "She's just a skinny bitch like the rest of us!"

"No she isn't," said Jo.

An twitched as Gi poked her, under the table. Gi was grinning. An couldn't do anything but hold her breath.

Nu's face was going from red to purple. She couldn't seem to open her mouth anymore; it was a thin, bloodless line.

She wanted him, too, An realized. Nu had watched

them every night, and she had got drunker and drunker. Now she had forced Jo to tell her the truth. In front of everybody.

Nu's complexion faded to a mottled gray. She jerked her body around and stumbled out of the bar.

An would have let her breath out then; but Jo looked right into her eyes. Nu wasn't the only one who had been exposed in front of everyone. Jo stared at her for an endless moment, and then he marched out of the bar, too.

"Damn it," An hissed. "Goddammit."

"Go after him," Gi said.

But An had to finish her drink before she could even get up the courage to stand.

An left Stormy's an hour later. She took the transport back to the holding field, where her Egg was waiting to be towed out the next morning. An would sleep inside her Egg, ready for takeoff an hour before dawn. She had left all of her fancy new clothes in her hotel room, with a note for the maids to keep what they wanted.

The holding field was dark and lonely. An walked among the rows, looking for her Egg, feeling like she was in some crazy hatchery. Nothing moved except for An and the warm breeze that was trying to tease her fancy coif out of shape.

From Covina she was headed to Karnak, where she was going to try for a contract from Iknaton Inc. Iknaton always paid the best rates, and An was ready to try her hand at looking for Early ruins. She was ready to go for the gold.

Too bad she hadn't gone for Jo. He wasn't anywhere in sight, and she didn't know his personal call number. She should have run out after him and . . .

And what, you big coward?

She patted the gun on her hip, making sure it was ready to use, just in case Nu was hanging around waiting for a fight. Nu was an enemy for life, that much was certain. An hoped the woman wouldn't come leaping out at her, from the shadows between the Eggs.

"It's not mousy," said a man's voice. An jumped like a cat, but she didn't draw the gun.

Jo came out from behind his own Egg.

"It's beautiful," he said. "Your hair."

"Thank you," said An.

He placed himself in front of her, not quite blocking her path.

"It looks so soft," he said. "It's the kind of hair a man wants to touch."

An held her breath, but he didn't touch her. He was waiting for a signal. She couldn't think of one.

"How are you?" she asked.

"Fine."

"Oh." She dropped her gaze, tried to think of what to say next.

"See you," he said, and walked away.

An watched him walk around his Egg, until he disappeared. She followed him.

"Jo?" she said.

He was about to climb in. He stopped, looked at her.

"What's your Egg like inside?" she asked.

"Come and see."

She did.

Jo's Egg was even more Spartan than An's, with absolutely no personal items that would reveal anything about its owner. No art prints, no bound hard copies, no pillows or comfortable artifacts. There were pictures of naked fancy girls here and there—An was intrigued to note that most of them resembled her. Jo seemed a little embarrassed that she was seeing them, now; but he made no move to take them down.

It was cramped with the two of them in there, but An

didn't mind. It was intimate that way. She could be bold and use the close conditions as an excuse to touch him.

"Do you get lonely, sometimes?" she asked him.

"All the time."

"Me, too."

"Is that why you're here?" he wondered. He still seemed to be waiting for a signal. An had no idea what more she could do to make herself more clear, without acting like a whore. He sat there cross-legged, his knee pressing into her thigh.

"I like you," she offered.

"You don't know me."

"I don't know *anyone*. Not even myself."

He considered that for a moment, then said, *"Yeah,"* almost under his breath. An marked up a small victory for herself.

"Jo, do you think I'm attractive?"

"You're beautiful," he said.

"You're very handsome."

He seemed surprised to hear that. He seemed pleased. "What do you want to do about it?" he asked.

"I want to make love," said An. "If you do."

Now he looked away. Now he was uncomfortable. That made An's heart pound. Now she wanted him more than ever.

"You're really classy," he said, struggling with the words. "I like how you—how you keep your hair long. And your face is so delicate. And you're so—you look like a dancer or something."

"I'm an EggHead," said An.

"Yeah." He laughed. His smile had an edge to it. An leaned into him and kissed his cheek. She put her hands on his chest, sliding them down, feeling the hard muscles under his flightsuit. She was going to touch his thighs, too, but he captured her hands and looked at them.

"They're so little," he said.

She let him caress her hands. It felt so good to be touched that way, to feel his warm, rough skin.

"I've had a vasectomy," he said.

Now An laughed. "I've had my tubes burned."

"Yeah, we're careful all right." He looked into her face again, still waiting for that illusive signal. An wanted him to grab her. Why wouldn't he do it?

She got an inspiration. She pulled her hands away and undid her hair. She combed it out with her fingers, spread it out over her shoulders.

He touched it. First he stroked it, then he took a handful of it and pulled her close. An tilted her head back, let her eyes go sleepy, her mouth soft. She waited for the kiss.

"I'm going to make you scream," promised Jo.

What? An wondered, but then he was kissing her. He was kissing her a little too hard, but not enough to frighten her, yet. He pulled her closer, held her almost tight enough to crack her ribs.

And he turned into a tiger.

An almost panicked at the fury of his emotions but she kept her cool. He didn't hurt her. He didn't tear her clothes when he pulled them off, he didn't bruise, or hit, or bite. He told her how beautiful she was, how he had wanted her so long. Then he held her down as if she were prey instead of a willing lover. He waited for her to climax, but then he slammed himself into her for his own.

Afterward, he held her tight.

An lay quietly, wondering how she felt about it all. Even when she had been the most scared, she had still enjoyed herself. He was exciting. His smell and his taste were still making her heart pound. But she would have liked things to be slower, less—adversarial.

"You should be more gentle," she whispered into his ear.

He didn't answer for a long moment. But An knew better than to say anything more until he had answered her.

"Maybe I don't know how to be," he said, at last.

"Do you think—it would be possible for me to teach you?"

"Teach me." He kissed her. "Right now."

An tried. By the time morning was threatening the horizon, he was treating her as if she were fine, fragile crystal. Afterward, he walked her back to her Egg.

"Maybe I'll see you on another stopover," An said.

"Maybe you will."

"Maybe we can—do this again?"

He didn't answer. "Where're you headed?" he asked, instead.

An almost didn't answer. But she didn't see the point in keeping the truth to herself. "Iknaton," she said.

"Early ruins."

"I hope."

"Don't we all," said Jo.

And then he turned and left her there without saying good-bye.

An came out of deepsleep before Jo did. At first she was surprised to see him. Hadn't he just left her alone on Covina?

But no, that was years ago, when their relationship was just beginning. Now other things were happening, important things; and she had so much to do.

She was programming a new jump into the navigational system when he woke up.

"What the hell?" he said, groggily. He looked at the new coordinates and put a restraining hand on her arm. She tried to use her control suit to complete the directive, but she wasn't plugged into navigation.

"Jezuz, An—do you know where that is?"

"The Vorn Motherworld."

"Stop it! Just tell me what you're doing!"

An sat back, impatiently. Her hands twitched with the compulsion to be at the controls again. "We have to—" she began, but the rest of the thought was not readily available.

The map, prompted the voice in her head, helpfully.

"What map?"

The one that will tell you what everyone wants to know.

"What everyone wants to know!? Everyone wants Early technology. Everyone wants to know where the ruins are."

And . . .

"And! And what? And everything!"

Jo leaned over and gripped her shoulders, making her focus on his face. "You're talking to yourself," he said. "What's wrong?"

"I'm not talking to myself, I'm talking to Kokoboro."

"Who?"

"The drip guy. You know, the donor."

You are not! said the voice.

"I am, too!"

You shouldn't call me by a separate name. It isn't healthy.

"Why does Kokoboro want you to go to the Vorn system? Is he telling you to kill yourself?"

"No, no, it's the map. He says there's a map."

I'm not a he.

"What kind of map?" demanded Jo, giving her a shake for emphasis.

"I don't know," said An.

Yes, you do.

"Why do you keep playing these guessing games with me!?"

Because if we're going to connect, you have to meet me halfway.

Jo was reaching to change the course An had plotted. She stopped him. They looked at each other wildly, distrustfully.

"Jo," begged An, "we have to go."

"You're not yourself. That drip has pushed you into some kind of schizo state."

"No! Something else has happened!" said An, but she really wasn't sure that he was wrong. After all, the voice didn't claim to be Kokoboro—

I'm not Kokoboro.

—and that only left one possibility. The nutty one. Or the bicameral one, a division in her own mind that was substituting a disembodied voice for her normal, conscious mind. But she still seemed to be thinking normally, so what was consciousness, really?

An analog of reality, based on metaphors of physical action.

Right. Uh-huh. Thanks for clarifying things.

That's an oversimplification, of course; but it's a problem I've been thinking about a lot lately, considering my own state of existence.

And exactly what is your state of existence?

A shared mind.

I see, thought An, not seeing at all.

And, of course, she was talking to herself aloud, so now Jo was really looking at her oddly. The only good thing about the situation was that, for the time being at least, he seemed to have forgotten his own crime and its tormenting guilt.

"If it isn't Kokoboro inside my head," An said, "then why was I able to work the bathtub on Cabar 4? And how did I know how to work the gunner station? The glyphs must have taught me, and I couldn't have read them without Kokoboro's RNA drip."

That's true as far as it goes, said the voice.

"You can't handle it," Jo was saying. "It's pushed you over the edge. You're acting before you can think things through."

He doesn't understand the decision process very well.

Oh, like you *do,* thought An.

People never act before thinking. It's just that they don't always know that they are *thinking.*

An tried to get up and get to the controls again. She couldn't move.

"I've locked your suit," said Jo.

"You *what*?"

"Prove you can read the glyphs," he said, relentlessly. "Tell me one thing you've learned from them. Not the bathtub thing, that's not enough. And not your gunner abilities, because I think you learned them somewhere else. Tell me something you've read, An."

"The glyphs aren't meant to be read!" cried An, then wondered what she was saying. Jo was looking at her grimly, as if she was confirming his worst suspicions.

"What are they for, then?" he asked.

"They pass on information. They pass on—they pass—oh, god—"

An fainted. But the intelligence in her mind continued to talk to her.

You're not crazy, it said. *You're just a little crowded.*

Where are you? An asked the voice.

Here, it answered.

Where is here?

With you. In here.

But where in here?

What do you mean, where? Where are you? Wouldn't you say you're in here?

Of course, I would. This is my brain.

Well, it's mine, too.

But it was mine first!

How do you know that?

Because I remember my childhood.

You remember other people's childhoods, too, like the little girl who was dying of thirst. She wasn't you, so who are you, really?

I'm An.

Once you told Jo, "I don't even know myself."

Yes, and that's my memory.

Now it's mine, too.

Are you Kokoboro?

Only if you are.

Well, I suppose that now I am Kokoboro, since his memories were implanted in my brain.

Or another way to look at it, is that now Kokoboro is you.

But then who are you? I've never heard voices before. Are you a part of my brain that deals with complex problems? You seem smarter than me.

But I can't be. I can only be as smart as you yourself are capable of being; but I don't think I was originally part of you. If I was your other half, I might appear to you as a god, or your mother; and you would feel compelled to do as I said.

Then who the hell are you?

I've been wondering that, myself.

And when did you start wondering? When did you first become aware of yourself?

On Cabar 4.

And what was the first thing you remember?

The glyphs. The wall in the little house at the end of the lane.

But I blacked out when I looked at the glyphs. I don't have any memory of seeing them.

You don't, but I do. I remember them clearly.

All right then—if you remember them so clearly, what did they say?

They said, "Come home, little one; your people are waiting."

For an endless time, An could not come back to consciousness, could not form coherent thoughts though she desperately needed to. She could feel the voice drifting with her, its thoughts as incoherent as her own, sometimes *indecipherable* from her own. Eventually they drifted together to the surface again; though An still could not wake up.

I have a theory, now, said the voice.

I do, too. Unfortunately, it involves a straitjacket.

No, no, you're not crazy. I really did come in from the outside. I think I must have come in through your eyes.

Like a virus?

You looked at the glyphs, and I was born.

How can you catch a virus just by looking at it?

How can you not catch it?

But—it's not real, it's not tangible. It's not organic!

Every time you read a book, you catch a virus. Your mind is changed by the experience. . . .

Yeah, but this is outrageous!

An idea is created, it makes copies of itself, it becomes part of you. And all that programming you drank in from the glyphs—

Programming!

Information. It was like memories, and mixed with the virus, you get me. Me, me, wonderful me!

But why?

Communication!

Who's trying to communicate with me?

Go to the Vorn system. Find the map! Then we'll know where to go, An.

Does the map tell where to find more Early ruins? That would be wonderful! An actual map! That would be the most incredible discovery of—of the millennium!

Wake up, now!

An took a deep breath and opened her eyes.

Jo was programming another jump into navigation.

"Jo," she said, "there's a map!"

"You already said that." He leaned back in his chair and sighed. "We're going to Omsk."

An felt a stab of fear. "Why?"

"To get you examined. To find out what's gone wrong with your drip."

"What if *nothing* has gone wrong?"

He closed his eyes for a moment, shutting out the possibility. "It's my fault," he said. "I drove you into this state. Now I'm going to take care of you."

"You didn't drive me into this state! I mean, I'm not *in* a state!"

Jo opened his eyes and regarded her with a sort of burned-out calmness. "I heard everything you said. When you were unconscious, you were talking to yourself."

"I was . . ." She flushed bright red. "Oh, I must have sounded—you must think I'm—"

"I have a feeling it wasn't the drip, by itself," he said, as if he hadn't heard her. "I think looking at the glyphs triggered the psychosis. Early glyphs are tricky, An; even I feel a little strange after looking at them, and I've never had a—I've never had a drip for glyphs."

Never one for glyphs. "But you're had others?"

He shrugged.

"What for, Jo?"

"I'm not the topic of discussion here, An. Quit trying to change the subject—I *heard* what you were saying to yourself. I'm not going to let you run wild under this delusion that an Early is living inside your head."

An felt a sting in her arm.

"What are you doing?" she cried.

"I'm taking you back to your doctor."

"Now? We're going to Omsk?"

"Just think of it as a short stop," said Jo.

"But, Jo, didn't anything I say make sense? When I was unconscious? Didn't *anything*?"

"Yes, baby. It made sense all right."

"I'm not crazy!"

But Jo had closed his eyes again. Everything An said just made him more sure he was right.

An was terrified. Omsk was the last place in the universe she wanted to go. Omsk was where they programmed people who didn't fit in. Omsk was run by InWorlders.

They won't try to get rid of me, will they? asked the voice in her head.

No! I don't know! No!

But what if they try to get rid of you?

An tried to call out to Jo, to get him to stop the jump. But it was too late.

An felt a nasty jolt that seemed to start in her toes and blow out through the top of her head.

"Ouch!" she snarled, and was instantly awake.

There was Omsk, artificial planetoid, ideological monstrosity, radiating a menace that far outstripped its real mass. On the tactical screen it was a black sphere whose actual features were cloaked by automatic systems that were built into every registered ship.

An was interested to note that Jo's systems were revealing more about Omsk than most did. Docking areas were illuminated by icy blue lines, and there was a ghostly red schematic overlying all with the subtitle of POSSIBLE WEAPONS ARRAY.

And then there were the incoming ships. Law-abiding citizens weren't supposed to be able to see those. What would the authorities do when they found out what Jo's ship could do?

The weapons systems on the Omsk ships were already powered up and ready. An tried to arm her own weapons, but her suit was still locked.

"Don't panic," Jo said. "I've been here before in this ship, remember? They don't know what I've got, and they don't care."

"Then why are they attacking us?" asked An, struggling in vain against her locked suit.

"It's Security. This is a rehab planet. They've always got heavy security forces."

An remembered that just fine. Omsk was the place where people got new minds if the ones they already had weren't politically correct enough. This was the place where they had scooped up her Egg and broken into it when she wasn't even out of deepsleep yet. She had hoped she would never have to come back here again for as long as she lived.

Jo was broadcasting peace codes.

"What's your business?" asked a sexless, ageless voice.

"We'd like to see Dr. Mohamonero," said Jo.

"Why?"

"Personal business."

"Are you family?"

"No."

"Only family members can make queries," said the voice.

Jo looked very surprised. He gazed at his tacticals for a long moment, reading the possibilities. While he was doing that, he said, "I don't understand—this is not the protocol I was taught for approaching Omsk."

"This is the official protocol."

"My records say otherwise—"

"We will correct your records."

Jo was starting to look as nervous as An felt.

"They're jerking us," said An. "They didn't ask me what I wanted last time I was here. They said they didn't want to know my business."

"You had an appointment last time."

"Did you, when you came looking for me? When you were here, did they question you like this?"

Jo rubbed his chin. "Dr. Mohamonero performed a procedure for me last year. I'd like to make an appointment with him for a follow-up exam."

"What sort of procedure?" demanded the voice.

"You have no right to ask me that," said Jo. "Look, what's the problem? Either I can make an appointment with my doctor or I can't. What's it got to do with you?"

There was a long silence. An watched her tactical screen, feverishly. They were bracketed by ships, but no one was making a hostile move. Yet.

"Dr. Mohamonero is on extended leave," said the voice. It was as sexless and as devoid of emotion as ever, but An's heart turned to ice.

"We've got to get out of here," she told Jo. From the look on his face, he agreed. But he was still trying to be reasonable.

"May I leave a message for him?" he asked.

"Prepare for boarding," said the voice.

Jo fired the engines.

An twitched her hand, found it unlocked. She fired her forward guns, but she aimed to blind, not to destroy.

"We'll get Heavy Time for this," said Jo through clenched teeth.

"We will if they catch us!" said An.

"Get ready for jump."

They were taking hits, but Jo's Early ship was absorbing the abuse without damage, so far. In another moment they would jump, and the others wouldn't know where they were going.

Poor Mohamonero, said the voice in her head.

Poor us! I don't want to do Heavy Time.

That's what Mo is doing.

They jumped, this time before the hypo could put them properly under. The experience didn't seem peculiar. An thought she probably could stay awake the whole time, if she weren't afraid of running out of air.

Why would they put Mohamonero in prison? An wondered.

To keep him from talking.

What do you mean?

Meet me halfway, An.

The sedatives were taking control. It was easy to slip under, to imagine herself reaching for an invisible hand, to clasp it and feel the fingers and the palm that were exactly like hers.

Yes, she told herself, and this time her inner voice was like two voices, almost perfectly blended.

Almost.

TRANSFORMATION

An dreamed she was looking for Jo. Hadn't he just been sitting next to her? But no, that was somewhere else. Now she was on Hel, a planet that wasn't anything like the frozen Norse underworld for which it was named. It was really much more like the Christian Hell: so hot, only the poles were habitable; and even there, you could only go outside at night. An was sure that the founding fathers had wanted to give Hel's name an extra *l*, but had settled for the Norse equivalent because the Ordinance To Ban Obscene Or Blasphemous Planetary Names had still been in effect.

The ordinance had been one of the funnier chapters of Human history. But lately An wasn't laughing much. She had just turned thirty, and she was considering getting her first rejuve. She was a little insecure about it, wondering if she was thinking about it too early.

Or maybe even a little late. How come she couldn't find Jo? She had found his name in the Central Directory, had left a message for him. Maybe he hadn't received it yet. He couldn't be avoiding her. Certainly not because she was looking older. He must have turned thirty himself, already. He must have had a rejuve, too, because he looked about twenty-five. Maybe she should have gotten her rejuve already. By the time she found him, she would look tired, overheated, sweaty. . . .

Old?

He wasn't at Orphee's. He wasn't at Dante's. An descended into underground tunnels, where the bulk of buildings lay protected from the worst impact of the heat. She was wandering around like a lost soul, wondering where to check next, when she saw Fallen Angels.

Jo was inside, with Ra. He hadn't seen An come in. He was busy watching a fancy girl he had obviously paid to dance naked.

An left as unobtrusively as she could.

The Egg is a lonely place. You're just one creature in the middle of a whole lot of nothingness. It was a place that taught you the truth about things, and the truth that An had learned was that her Egg wasn't the loneliest place in the Universe. So she was surprised when she heard Ra calling after her.

He caught up with her. "You were looking for Jo," he said.

An shrugged and kept walking, not trusting her emotions to stay bottled up where they belonged. Ra walked with her. They climbed back out of the tunnels, onto ground that was still so hot from the day's heat they could feel it through the soles of their boots. But they walked like they were taking a stroll through a cool meadow.

"You look great," he said. "Things must be going well for you."

"Pretty well. Found ruins on Hermes 3."

"Never heard of Hermes 3."

"That's because I'm the one who named it."

He laughed. Good EggHeads were always finding new systems. You had to risk a lot, though. You only had so many jumps before you were out of juice, maybe stranded outside Known Space.

"Te found ruins on O'Brien's planet," said Ra.

"*O'Brien's?* I thought that place was scoured over years ago."

"It was. But Te said she just had a feeling there was something more."

They were already back at An's Egg. None of the bars

were very far from parking grounds on Hel. They wanted to be instantly accessible to hot, thirsty travelers.

"What've you been up to?" asked An, and she propped herself against her Egg. He leaned over her, resting his arm on the bulkhead. He was sweating heavily from the heat, but he smelled good anyway. His eyes were dreamy, and there was alcohol on his breath.

"I prospected some new Class-Ms for Home Corp. Didn't find any Early ruins, but I kept my eyes open. Don't think you can find them on the drier planets. Earlies haven't been dead long enough for ecosystems to change much. . . ."

"Ten thousand years or so. Some places change a lot in that length of time."

"So tell me," said Ra, "what's Jo got that I haven't?"

An didn't answer him; she just smiled. He smiled back, but he seemed irritated that she hadn't said something to reassure him.

"Jo doesn't want you tonight," Ra said. "He's not about to give up a fancy girl for you."

An felt his arrow go home, but she still smiled. "You just answered your own question," she said.

"Huh?"

"What Jo has. Tact. He would never say a thing like that to me, not even if he was thinking it."

Ra looked like he was ready to slap his own face. An turned to leave, but he grabbed her wrist.

"An, I could have had a fancy girl, too. But when I saw you, I left her. For the chance to be with you. I've wanted to be with you from the first time I laid eyes on you. I think you're beautiful."

She looked at him sideways; he was always such a smartass. But he was serious now. It was as if she was seeing him for the first time. He was as light as Jo was dark. His close-cropped hair was Hel-ler white, his eyes were ice blue. His body was lean, trim, muscular in all the right places. She could smell something under the al-

cohol on his breath, a sex smell that made her wonder
what he would be like.

He must have seen the question in her eyes, because he
leaned close for a kiss. But something stopped him at the
last moment.

Ra spun around in a defensive crouch, pushing An behind him.

Jo was standing there, looking at them. The expression
on his face gave An a thrill of terror. She had to remind
herself that she had just seen Jo with another woman. She
wasn't to blame.

Ra grinned at Jo. "I thought you had other company tonight."

"I wondered why you left so suddenly," said Jo.

An backed away. She knew that these two men were as
close to being friends as two male EggHeads could get;
but they were going to fight, and there was nothing she
could do about it.

She also knew that the winner was going to want to
have sex with her, and she was going to have to decide
what to do about *that*.

She didn't see the signal that passed between them that
the fight should begin. One minute they were saying
things to each other that obviously meant something to
them, if not to An, and the next they were hitting each
other in the face and stomach.

An had never seen such a vicious fight, not even back
home, where people used to kill each other over what
channels they wanted to watch on the VidNet. Jo and Ra
had probably saved each other's lives a few times, but
that didn't mean a thing now. They were jabbing at each
other's eyes, trying to blind, trying to break noses and
ribs; and every time they succeeded in hurting each other
they cursed and tried to hurt worse, tried to get even, until
An was wondering, *Are they going to hurt me, too? Are
they going to get so mad they can't stop?*

But they did stop. It seemed like forever, but they finally started to slow down, to punch instead of jab, to stagger and take time to shake the blood and sweat out of their eyes. And Ra was losing his mad edge.

Jo wasn't. And that's why he won.

Ra put his hands up, palms open, and said, "Enough." He had to take two more punches before Jo would believe him.

"Enough," Ra said again. He looked into Jo's swollen, puffy eyes with the only one he had left that could still see. He made him believe. Jo put his hands down. He was still clenching them, but they stayed down.

Ra edged away from him and turned halfway, unwilling to present his back to Jo. But he had enough nerve left to take An's hand and kiss it with broken lips.

"The best man won," he said.

An was shaking too hard to answer.

Ra said, "See you," to Jo, and stumbled out of the picture.

Jo stood absolutely still, staring at An. "Did the best man win?" he asked, his voice still choked with anger.

An put her hand over her mouth, which did nothing with her attempt to answer him but tremble. She leaned against her Egg and closed her eyes.

After a few deep breaths she was able to say, "I was looking for you."

"I didn't know you were here."

"I left you a message."

"I didn't get it."

"Okay."

He came to stand before her with his head down. He was ashamed.

Careful, An told herself. *Careful, careful . . .*

She made herself look at his injuries. She put gentle hands on his face and tried to make him look up. But he wouldn't.

"I used to be something," he said. "I used to be someone."

An wasn't sure what he meant; but then it occurred to her he might be talking about his past, maybe about the time he (might have been) in the service.

"Come inside and let me fix you," she said.

He didn't move. She kissed his cheeks, carefully; she kissed his jaw. Seeing him so hurt broke her heart, and tears were sliding down her face before she could stop them. Jo wiped them away with swollen fingers.

He kissed her mouth; not hard, because his own mouth hurt so much.

An helped him into her Egg. From the way he was moving, she thought he probably had cracked ribs. She ran the Doc-scanner over him, found the ribs and taped them. She cleaned his face and hands with medi-wipes and gave him a hypo of painkiller.

He didn't try to interfere with her ministrations, he just worked around them. He stroked her, kissed her, looked at her. He undid her suit and worked diligently until it was off. He got rid of her underthings in the same slow, patient manner. By the time she was putting sealer on a cut under his eye, she was naked. He was halfway there himself, with an erection trying to bust out of his pants.

They had never been so tender with each other before. Looking back, there were probably things that should have been said, then and there; but An was afraid she would cry again, and TradeTown was still riding on her back with its battered women and its absent fathers.

If Jo had anything else on his mind, he didn't say it, either.

An undid his pants and straddled him. He leaned back, a willing patient. She worked herself down on him, swallowing him by small degrees. She was tight but slippery inside, the way they both liked it. When he finally went all the way home, he gasped. He wanted to start ramming, but he couldn't in that position; so he let her take charge.

She rode him slowly. She could have had a climax almost immediately; but she wanted the feeling, not the end of the feeling. She teased and played, had her gentle, inexorable fun.

When An climaxed for the first time, Jo leaned forward and took her right nipple in his mouth. He sucked it, nibbled it, then sucked and nibbled again. He altered these sensations, knowing that it would intensify her orgasm, prolong it, until her whole body would shake and convulse with it, until she would be helpless, caught in an ecstatic loop while he went back and forth, right and left, suck and nibble.

He wasn't even thinking of his own climax yet.

When An's muscles would no longer obey her commands, Jo lifted her off of him and twisted them both around until she lay under him. He slid his arms under her knees, seized her wrists and pinned her. He licked her, and she convulsed again.

He tortured her this way for a long time before he slipped his cock inside her and started to grind. He always tried to be slow at first, but it never took him long to build up speed and force. Not even now, when he was injured. She rode with him, playing the perfect receptacle.

Her second big climax marked the beginning of his first. They cried out together, going from fast, to slower, slower, hardly moving at all, then complete stop.

Full stop, thought An. *Like coming out of a jump. And now we're drifting.*

When she had calmed down, she whispered into his ear, "The best man won, Jo."

But he was already asleep. She wriggled out from under him, until the two of them were cuddled side by side. She tucked her head under his chin and closed her eyes.

She felt his warm mouth at her ear.

"Sleepcycle 0001," he whispered. "Sleepcycle 0999 . . ."

"I'm sleeping. . . ." she told him.

"Jump 1000. Abort planetfall. Abort planetfall. Sleep-cycle 1000 . . ."

"Jo, stop it. . . . I'm trying to . . . Don't say those things . . ."

"Planetfall 0999 . . ."

"No . . ."

"Emergency open 0999 . . ."

"No!"

"Emergency open 1000 . . ."

"Wait!!" screamed An, and wrenched her eyes open to darkness.

An was in the gunner's chair. It was dim, and her eyes had to adjust before she could see the navigator's chair. Jo wasn't there, of course. She felt bereft of his warmth. She could still feel his breath on her ear.

She could still hear him ordering her Egg to kill her.

I thought you were over that, she told herself. *You've got other things to worry about, now.*

Once her heart stopped hammering, she felt herself drifting back into sleep. She tried to fight it. She kept opening her eyes, thinking, *Better get up,* then closing her eyes again.

After this had happened for the third time, she knew she had been given an extra sleep drug.

An took deep breaths until she could move her arms. Her suit was no longer locked—that was a big relief. Soon she was able to sit up and keep her eyes open.

A moment later, she was able to make sense of the tac-tical screens. They had come out of jump in the Vorn system. Their stealth features were working; none of the busy craft that were swarming to and from the Mother planet had taken the slightest notice of them—yet.

There was a better way. All they had to do was broadcast the proper signals, vibrate in the right frequencies, and the Vorn would perceive them as one of their own.

She put her feet on the floor and stood up. She had taken two steps before it sunk in.

There was a gravitational field on Jo's ship. And they weren't spinning or accelerating.

It was a light field, just enough to keep your feet on the floor, probably not enough to protect your body from the long-term effects of weightlessness; but it was staggering, nonetheless. She moved across the deck toward the communications station. It was like walking on a moon; you had to adjust your energy output.

Communications was locked down; that was interesting. Did Jo think she was going to call the Vorn and tell them where she was? Well, in a way, he was right. She unlocked the station, but she didn't do anything more to it. Not without Jo's consent.

She got a sudden inspiration and searched the command chair. She found a headset and a jack.

"Jo?" she called, on ship-wide.

He didn't answer.

"Jo, where are you?"

He could hear her. He just didn't want to answer.

An went back to the gunner's chair. Her tactical screen might show her the inside of the ship, too.

It did. And there, on the shuttle deck, was a red X for Jo. It was moving around, working on something.

An memorized the layout, then ran down to the shuttle deck. She expected to see Jo right there, working in plain view. But she couldn't see him at all. "Jo?" she called.

He still wasn't answering, and she was just as sure that he could hear her.

"Stop playing games," she told him. "I'm not crazy." She went farther into the shuttle hangar and inspected the sleek craft that lay inside.

"It's beautiful, Jo," she said. "It looks about ten times more expensive than my Egg."

"It is," said Jo's voice, from nowhere.

"Even this shuttle would have been a step up for me," said An. "This ship is a whole flight of stairs."

"I could buy a fleet of these ships, now."

"Your father was that rich?"

"He was."

"He's dead now," said An, walking all the way around the craft. She knew where Jo was, but she didn't want to startle him.

"Of course, he's dead. How else could I have gotten the money?"

"Why did you have to wait?"

"He was doing Heavy Time."

"Why?" An couldn't see her reflection in the hull of the craft. Its outline seemed to shimmer a little. On a tactical screen, it would be cold, invisible.

"He was a war dissident," said Jo's voice, as cold as cloaked metal. "Heavy Time is for people who need to be punished for a long, long time."

"His enemies must have really hated him."

"You don't want to know what they did to my mother."

But An already knew. She didn't know *exactly*, of course. But she had known Jo long enough to see the legacy of what had been done. She had tried to coax him into loving her, never knowing what had happened to the other people he had loved.

"And you, Jo. For years you've been hinting that you used to be *somebody*. I never knew what you meant, until now."

"Really?" he hissed. "Could an RNA drip do that much for you?"

"And what has it done for you?" An glimpsed his face for the barest moment, darkly reflected in the depths of the shuttle's deceiving hide.

"I've had drips," he admitted. "When I had to learn things in days instead of years. And when I had to—become someone I wasn't."

"You had to become a peasant," An guessed. "What did your name used to be?"

He took so long to answer, she thought he might have forgotten what it used to be. Then, "Jokateanke," he said, making music out of the name. "Jokateanke-Re."

Re. That was more than just an honorific for achievement. It went at the end of the name of a war hero. It wasn't the sort of name an ordinary man could ever achieve. Not even by accident.

"Who was it that sabotaged my Egg?" she wondered. "Jo, or Jokateanke-Re?"

She heard nothing from him, not even a gasp of pain. Perhaps he was wondering about it himself, trying to untangle the conflicting impulses that had led him to the deed, just as An had had to untangle the conflicting voice commands in her computer codes.

"I don't know who it was," said Jo. "But I wish he was dead. I wish he would just leave me alone."

An looked up slowly, and found Jo on top of the shuttlecraft. He was standing now, looking down at her like a god on a mountain. He was frowning.

"Come down," begged An.

Jo crouched, but that was as far down as he would come.

"Don't wish him dead," said An. "He's the one who wants you to live."

"I don't want to live at your expense," Jo snapped, as if he were saying just the opposite.

"But you stayed alive all these years for *some* reason."

"—My—father."

"What did your father do that was so terrible?"

"He tried to end the Vorn war."

"How could he have done that?"

"You think he's a traitor," Jo accused wearily. "That's what anyone would think. Anyone but me."

"I *don't* think that," said An. "What I meant was, how could he have achieved it? What was his plan?"

"I don't know," said Jo. "That's probably why I'm still alive."

He slid down the side of the craft, out of An's sight.

"Come out," said An, but he didn't reappear. She shivered, and tiptoed to the corner of the craft. She almost peeked around it, but then made herself walk, instead; slowly so he wouldn't have any reason to attack.

He stood there on the other side, waiting.

"Like a nymph coming out of a lake," he said.

An took two steps closer. Three steps. Four.

"You're so beautiful," Jo said. "Every time I see you, I can't believe my eyes. Your hair is like black silk. Your eyes—are the eyes of a Chinese concubine."

"*Chinese?*" An said. "From ancient Earth."

"Not ancient. They're young, in your face."

"I didn't know you could speak this way." An took one more step toward him; but he backed away from her, as if she were the sort of nymph who lured men into the water and drowned them.

"You thought I was stupid?" he asked casually.

"Not stupid. I thought you were a plain man, like the men from back home. I thought you had escaped a place like the one I did."

"I might as well have," said Jo. "I lived in those places for a hundred years."

An's mind was humming; she was putting a new program in place, rearranging the way everything had been done before. Jo was not who she had thought he was; she would have to make a new file for *Jo*, let it saturate her cells, spread itself along short fibers and long ones, until it found its way back to her amygdala, that little almond-shaped organ in her brain that would tell her what the expression on his face meant, and what she should do about it.

She kept still, and waited for him to say what was on his mind.

"What price am I going to have to pay?" he asked her.

The question was too general. She could have answered that one for hours.

"With my life?" he said. "Do you want me to die because I tried to kill you?"

"No," said An. "You have to help me."

Those were the magic words. He didn't like them; they frightened him.

"I'm not insane, Jo. I know how I can do it."

"Do *what*?" he cried, and slammed his fist into the side of the craft. It bounced off, almost throwing him off balance. "What is so important? Why can't we just prospect like we did before? We could be rich, we could go *anywhere,* An. We're not out of juice yet, did you know that? This ship can handle fifty jumps. Can you believe it? My Egg could do four. What do you want to do that's better than that?"

"I want to get the glyphs the Vorns have been hiding."

She was as surprised by that remark as he was, but not nearly as alarmed.

"How do you know they've been hiding glyphs?" he asked suspiciously.

"It makes sense, Jo. We've been after the glyphs all these years, the X'GBris have been after them, and you know how important Early technology has been to the war effort."

"But the Vorns can't *see* the glyphs. Not like we can."

"The females can't."

He didn't understand. An was only beginning to get it herself.

"The females can't," she told him."The *males* can."

"But they get eaten. They're just slaves."

"They're not stupid. They know the glyphs are speaking to us, somehow. They're hiding them away until *they* figure out how to hear them."

"Hiding them from us," said Jo.

"Yes."

"But we could find other glyphs. We don't need the ones they have."

"We *do* need them. They've got the map."

"You don't know that! How could you know it!?"

"Because Kokoboro knew it," said An, and she was remembering what he had said in his good-bye vid: *I confess, I am the only living Human who has been allowed to study Early ruins on X'GBri and Vorn planets.* And how could he have survived an encounter with the Vorns?

"He must have known their language," said An; but she said it in a trilling, clicking series of sounds.

Jo's eyes widened. "That's Vorn," he said. "You're speaking Vorn. I'd know that sound anywhere."

"Kokoboro must have known how," she said, hoping to reassure him; but she was half lying. There was an echo to her thoughts, one that had a different tone.

Are you there? she asked the voice; instead of an answer, the question was merely reflected back at her, as if it had been asked at almost the same moment by another part of her own mind.

The infection must have progressed.

Whatever that meant.

"I know how to get in, Jo. I can do it."

His face had turned so pale his bruises were showing through. An had thought they were healed, but they were really hiding beneath the surface, waiting.

She took a chance and touched him.

"What are you afraid of?" she asked. "That I'll get us killed? That I'm going to double-cross you?"

For a moment she thought he might hit her. Then he closed his eyes. She moved closer, pressing her body into his. He didn't feel stiff at all. He felt like he wanted her to come even further inside.

"I'm afraid you'll die," he said. He let out a horrible, self-mocking laugh. "Only *I* should have the privilege of killing you."

"Stop," murmured An, as she stroked his face. "Shh."

Jo opened his eyes again. They were red, as if he had been awake for hours, worrying. "I want to keep you safe, An. I can't stand any other possibility. Not after a hundred years of—of—"

"But you brought us to Vorn," said An. "You're the one who programmed the jump here. What were your instincts telling you, Jo? That this was a risk worthy of an EggHead gamble?"

He didn't answer.

"We can salvage this whole mess," said An. "Beyond our wildest dreams. That's why you brought us here. We can do it. But we have to take those risks."

Jo's eyes watched An from the depths of a hundred-year hell. "That's what my father told me," he said.

"The difference," said An, "is that I'm right."

Jo tried to stare her down. He could have done it easily, before. But now . . .

"You've changed," he said. "You almost seem like a different person, now. You're not talking to yourself anymore."

"Are you with me?"

He nodded, and An knew she had him. "We won't need our stealth devices anymore. We need to start broadcasting some signals. I'll program them in for you."

"That Kokoboro was a smart guy," said Jo, meaning it.

An was sure he meant it. That was odd. He had turned

back into the same, stone-faced man he used to be, now that he was calm again. But he meant it. She knew it. She could see it, smell it, hear it.

Taste it.

Her senses were more alive than they had ever been before. They were telling her more than she had ever known—no. More than her mind had ever *allowed* her to know. Just now, they were telling her something she shouldn't ignore.

An turned her head, slowly, and looked around the shuttle deck.

"What's wrong?" whispered Jo.

An looked from corner to corner. She searched the spaces in between. She thought she saw a blurry spot, a distorted patch of nothingness; but when she tried to focus on it, it wasn't there.

"Who's here?" she asked.

She was answered by a clicking sound. It had two sources, one behind her and one behind Jo.

"Look out!" cried An, and tried to dive for the floor.

Something struck her spine and sent shock waves through her entire body. She lost control of her fall and went down face first.

Jo landed just inches away from her, his face twisted in a mirror of her own pain. An looked out of the corner of her eye, at the space above her body. It shifted and twisted, resolved itself into a gray giant.

GNno crouched down beside An, his face a mask of happiness.

"Now," he said, "about that map."

The Vorn war had begun two hundred years before, when Vorns had invaded Mandalay. Back then, Mandalay had been the most remote Human colony in existence. Ten thousand colonists had emigrated there, planet engineers and their families, who had dreamed of transforming the class-M planet into a paradise that would surpass Earth or even Celestine.

Mandalay would not have taken much work. It orbited one of those precious, type-G suns, from which it was exactly the right distance to prosper. From the very beginning it had seemed almost too welcoming, almost too fertile.

"Sooner or later," their historian, Kiritero, had said in his personal log, "something *must* go wrong. It's Murphy's Law! Our engineered plants and animals are thriving here, and the ecosystem of Mandalay is welcoming them as if they were long-lost kin. Every morning we wake up to nothing but joy, peace—fertility and abundance. What's wrong with this picture?"

"Nothing!" his wife had been heard to say in the background. "Quit being such a pessimist!"

And then the Vorns had swooped down on Mandalay with their Mother ship. Within the first half hour, they had killed the small group of military personnel who had been there mostly for policing purposes. The remaining colonists had not possessed any weapons. They had faced armed warriors with nothing but farming tools in their hands.

Their last hours of struggle had been partly documented by Kiritero, who had rigged recorders all over the colony and its outlying developments, hoping that in sixty years he would be able to show their grandchildren what early life had been like for Humans on Mandalay. He had been sure that this benign purpose was all that his recorders would ever serve; but safety regulations demanded that the information from those recorders must also be beamed to a message drone, which would fire straight to Celestine if emergency systems were ever activated.

Activating those systems was the last thing Kiritero had managed to do; his fate was the last event recorded.

Battle cruiser *Hizamadazo-Re* was dispatched from Mythos. It was soon joined by six other battle cruisers, whose combined firepower managed to quickly wipe out the Vorn colony that had been established on the ruins of the Human one. After Mandalay was secured, the battle cruisers tracked down the Vorn fleet, discovering it was on the way to its next target: Celestine.

The Vorn fleet was easily destroyed. They had expected no significant resistance from Humans. Almost everyone concerned had congratulated themselves on the ease of their victory. Surely the Vorn would be just as easily mopped up anywhere they could be found.

But Captain Jiroparu of the *Hizamadazo-Re* did not share that opinion. His crew had been the ones to search the Vorn cargo ships that had accompanied the Mother fleet.

They had found Human meat, hung like beef, in freezers.

"We can't predict what they might do in the future," he tried to warn the Inner World military hierarchy. "They might not be discouraged by the defeat they just suffered."

It had been a single warning, very short and concise. Jiroparu had even been believed, by some. But most military support had been withdrawn from Celestine afterward, leaving only the *Hizamadazo-Re* and one other battle cruiser to confront invaders.

And that was how Jiroparu became Jiroparu-Re. Posthumously, of course.

Celestine had been the most beautiful planet in the Outer Worlds. It was like the Olympus of ancient mythology, like Asgard. When it was destroyed, when it was *devoured*, every able-bodied man in the Outer Worlds had enlisted. Most of the able-bodied women had tried to do the same.

The rest was history.

"The Vorns are horrible monsters, fiendishly clever," newscasters were saying over Nets that were both legal and newly illegal. "They are difficult to understand and consequently difficult to kill. Anyone who doubts that should look upon their own children and imagine them hanging on a meat hook."

On most of the Outer Worlds, people didn't have to use their imaginations to see that.

So very few people wondered (out loud) if the situation would have been any different if the Vorn system were closer to the Inner Worlds. And hardly anyone seemed to notice (officially) that the Vorn war had conveniently started in time to stifle an uprising in the planetary congress that would have shifted autonomy to Celestine, away from Earth.

Jo's father had wondered, of course. He had noticed. And doing so had gotten him one hundred years of Heavy Time.

Two hundred years later, the war had lost a lot of steam; but it was like an infection that would never die out completely. Just when Outer Worlders thought they had put a cap on the situation, new skirmishes would break out, new Queen colonies would spring up where none had been suspected.

The Inner Worlders didn't have anything to worry about anymore, of course. After Celestine and five other powerful Outer Worlds were destroyed, Earth controlled everything. The Inner Worlds were utterly, impregnably secure, with nothing but the very latest and most cutting edge Early-based technology to back them up. Even the X'GBris were polite when they visited the Inner Worlds (if mockingly so).

And what had the X'GBris been doing for the past two centuries? They had been rejecting all pleas for alliance, insisting that war was not their way.

"After all, we are a Matriarchy," the Ministry of Noblewomen had insisted, their faces all pulled down in identical scowls. "We can offer you free trade, nothing more."

Two hundred years later, most of those noblewomen were dead. Two hundred years later, no one knew for sure if the X'GBris had ever engaged the Vorns in battle, even once.

Two hundred years later, TTra materialized next to Jo's stunned body, seemingly from nothingness, causing An to wonder if the X'GBris had ever even been *nervous* about the Vorns.

TTra certainly didn't look nervous at the moment. She looked happier than GNno, if possible; and he was grinning so wide his face looked read to split in half.

The X'GBris leaned possessively over the prone Humans. An got a good look at the suit TTra was wearing. She was startled to notice that it was black, not the customary X'GBri gray. Somehow, she got the feeling that the black color was not functional. It was symbolic. In this case it symbolized secrecy, underground paths, clever trickery.

Sneaky victory.

"I knew you would lead us someplace interesting, my clever little ones," TTra crowed.

"What did you say, just then?" GNno asked An. "In Vorn."

An tried to answer, but her vocal cords were paralyzed.

GNno pressed a hypo against her neck. In another moment, the painful spasms were gone. TTra did the same for Jo.

"You didn't have to stun us," An said.

"You shouldn't have startled me," said GNno cheerfully. "You may sit up now."

An and Jo obeyed him. "Nice suits," Jo said. "How long have you been here?"

"Long enough to hear all about your heroic past, Jokateanke."

"Jokateanke-*Re*," added TTra.

GNno poked An. "You haven't answered my question."

"All I said was that Kokoboro must have known the Vorn language," said An. She watched both of the X'GBris for hidden signs of fear or nervousness, but found none. They were genuinely excited, despite their proximity to the Vorn Motherworld.

"And now *you* know the Vorn language," GNno was saying.

"Yes, apparently I do."

GNno and TTra clicked their teeth at each other.

"Why are you so happy?" An asked them. "You've abandoned the ruins on Cabar 4. You've left a fortune behind."

"I sent a message drone to my sister," said TTra. "If she gets it, she'll salvage in the family name. If not, I still have *you*."

"And the aforementioned map," said GNno.

"Which you will retrieve for us, unless you want your precious Jo to be skinned alive."

TTra meant that. She wouldn't like to do it; but if An disappointed her, she would do as she threatened.

"I'm not going to let her go down there alone," said Jo.

"You are," said TTra. "You must. You are male; your risk is twice as great."

"No." Jo climbed to his feet. "You've jerked me around long enough, TTra, I'm not taking it anymore. I'm going with An."

TTra snorted with exasperation and pulled out a firearm. She aimed it at Jo and fired.

A white ball hit Jo in the chest, knocking him over. Before his body could hit the floor, the ball had exploded into white cords that wrapped tightly around him, from his shoulders to his knees.

"Goddammit, Ttra, you fucking bitch!" Jo yelled. *"Get these fucking things off me now!"*

"Stop that," TTra said calmly, "you'll make them tighter if you struggle that way."

"Get them off me, you bitch, or I'll kill you!"

"Kill me, then."

Jo stared at the X'GBri woman with murder in his eyes. "You cunt," he hissed.

"Don't try to turn my head with compliments," said TTra. She stooped and lifted Jo onto her shoulders. "This way," she called to An and GNno.

They followed her to the command bridge. CVvu and MJki were already there, sitting at the gunner and navigation stations, wearing the same symbolic black. The other two mates must have been on TTra's ship—wherever that was.

"Your stealth setup must be pretty damned impressive," An said.

TTra set Jo down at the foot of the captain's chair and seated herself. "It's no more complicated than yours. But once you and your enemies both have this kind of stealth technology, you cancel each other out. Only cleverness and aggression can give you the edge. You and Jo are so busy fighting your domestic battles, you haven't had time to use either. We have."

An glanced at GNno, whose glad mask had slipped just a bit.

"You have a plan?" she asked TTra.

"I thought you had one."

"I do, but I thought you might have everything figured out already."

"Very funny. Let's hear what you have."

An shrugged. "I'll broadcast Vorn signals and take our ship into orbit, then take the shuttle down. I'll go into the Motherhive and get the glyphs."

"There are several Motherhives."

"I'm talking about the Big Mother."

TTra scowled. "You have an invisible suit, I assume."

"No. That wouldn't help. They would smell me."

"Then how do you intend to get in?"

"I'll walk."

Even Jo was looking dubious about that. But An felt completely confident. She had no reason to feel that way; she should have been beside herself with anxiety, with rage and fear for Jo's sake.

But she *was* confident. She was calm. It was a state of mind that she was slipping into, as easily as an Early slipping into a warm bath. She didn't want to analyze it or question it, she just wanted to be there, let it happen. It was the best possible course of action, the only way to rescue the situation.

"An," Jo panted—the wrappers were beginning to interfere with his breathing—"what do you mean 'you'll 'get the glyphs?' They're carved on stone, right? Are you going to carry a whole wall? You can't do it alone."

"I'll take carriers. I'm betting they've cut them into sections."

"That's crazy—you're making wild—assumptions— just guessing—"

· TTra leaned down and inspected Jo's bindings. "Whatever you're planning to do, you'd better do it soon. He'll suffocate in an hour or two."

"You'll loosen his bindings?" An asked, trying not to beg.

"If he turns blue," said TTra, with what passed in her for compassion.

An went to communications and made her fingers fly over the keypad. GNno looked over her like a storm, but he didn't ask her what she was doing.

"Turn off the stealth system," An told CVvu.

He glanced at TTra, who nodded.

"Let's get back down to the shuttle deck," An told GNno.

He wrapped a giant hand around her upper arm and pulled her along after him. On her way past the gunner's station, she glanced at the tactical screen.

No amber *X* warned her of the X'GBri ship that must have been sitting right on top of theirs.

There must be a way to fix that, mused An.

On the way down, GNno shot sidelong glances at her. "How did you learn to speak Vorn?" he asked. "Was it the drip?"

"Yes."

He scoffed. "I would never submit to one. Never trust someone else's brain."

The shuttle deck seemed darker than it had when they had left it minutes before. But An went immediately to the shuttle and opened the door; it slid smoothly into its recess. She climbed aboard, feeling GNno's bulk right behind her.

"In fact," he whispered, "never trust your own brain, either."

He put his hand on the back of her neck. An stopped, only half attending to what he was saying and doing.

Most of her mind was miles away, planning, acting, making changes.

"I missed you," said GNno.

An was thinking about the Mother City, about the bustle and the workers who would be moving tirelessly in and out. She would go in with them, she would come out with them, and no one would question a worker about what she was doing. Only workers cared what they were doing.

"You can still change your mind about Jo," GNno said. "You may come with us, and he will still have his beautiful ship and his future." He pressed himself against her and breathed deeply of her hair.

He stiffened.

He licked her neck.

An felt him push away from her. She turned slowly and faced him. His eyes were black pools in the dark, but she could read them. They were overflowing with horror.

"You taste like a Vorn," he whispered.

"How do you know what a Vorn tastes like?" she wondered.

"Never mind that."

An didn't press him. She couldn't afford to be sidetracked from her train of thought.

From her *reprogramming*. She was shifting, going with the flow. It was surprisingly easy to do so.

"I have to be this way, GNno," she said absently.

"*How?* How can you change your chemistry?"

"I'm not changing it, not really. We all have the same chemicals in our bodies, even the Vorns. I'm just making adjustments."

"With your mind? By thinking about them?"

"Yes."

He let out a long breath. "I don't understand you."

"They'll kill me if I don't smell like them," said An.

She didn't want to explain anymore, she wanted to get going. "Tell Jo I'll be back. I'm going to succeed, GNno."

"Maybe you are," he said, and backed out of the shuttle.

An closed the door behind him and went to the pilot's station. She plugged her suit into tactical.

"Working," said CVvu's voice.

"Take us into orbit," said An.

In the background, she could hear Jo arguing with TTra. His voice seemed weak. She wished she could go to him, pull off the restraints, and hold him. *Jo, I'm so frightened,* she wanted to tell him; but the part of her that felt that way was getting smaller and smaller. That was good. The scared part would only get in the way of the smell, the language, the feelings that were coming over her—that she wasn't Human at all, but really a Vorn.

You are not Vorn, she reminded herself. *But you aren't your old self, either.*

None of us are, came an afterthought, almost as if the voice were speaking to her again.

An shivered, and strapped herself into her chair.

She was flying like a Vorn.

Their flight patterns had always seemed odd and erratic to Humans, but An saw the logic of it, now. The Vorn had had wings, once, and their flight had been a sort of speech, a ritual of communication that told who they were and what they were doing.

"I'm a worker," An's shuttle told the other Vorn ships. "I'm doing my work."

She could understand the other ships, too. They were warriors, scientists, number counters, royal mates, food gatherers, a thousand other things. They wove in and out of patterns that no longer looked chaotic to An; they had the beauty of a symphony or a ballet.

And I'm part of it. I'm not an alien.

I'm not food.

The Motherworld would have looked chaotic to the Human mind. It was a massive hive from pole to pole. It looked like someone had haphazardly thrown debris at it, and the Vorn had built their cities in the results. They were swarming over it, under it, through it, as if all the work they did was an accidental side effect of their hyperactivity.

But nothing was accidental. Everything had a purpose. An was soothed as she surveyed the Big Mother City from the air. Everything was in order, everything was running smoothly. There was plenty to eat, and no sign of the dreadful emptiness that could be seen on undeveloped worlds. The climate was carefully regulated, a lovely dry warmth would prevail.

She landed her shuttle in just the right spot. Dockworkers immediately swarmed over it, checking it for damage and covering it with the proper hive smell. An got her carrier and popped open the hatch. She had barely put her feet on the resinous pavement when she was instantly bowled over by a huge, sterile female, who gave her a vigorous washing with the soft hairs of her jaws. An licked the dock worker, doing her best to reciprocate.

The air was filled with the sounds of vibrating carapaces, thousands of bodies singing the song that Humans had heard in the deserts of the Outer Worlds, the sounds by which they had come to know their enemies:

"vvvvvvvvVVVVVVVOOOOOOOOOOOOOOO-OOOOOOORRRRRNNNNNnnnnnnnnn . . ."

When An had heard it on her homeworld, it had frightened her; but now that remembered sound seemed lonely, the sound of an isolated warrior whose queen had been destroyed.

Now it sounded different, of course. Now it sounded like home.

After she had finished her grooming, An walked into the hive.

It was a maze of entrances and tunnels, but An could smell the right way to go. This was the way to the Big Mother's nest. It was here that she caught her first whiff that all wasn't perfect on the Mother World. The tunnels carried the faint aroma of anxiety, of puzzlement.

We could finish them off with the technology we have right now. *They know they've fallen behind. No wonder they've been hiding the glyphs.*

The thought of destruction on the Mother World was making An feel insecure, so she put it firmly out of her mind. She brushed against the other workers, coming and going, some of them so big they knocked An right off her feet. She simply got up and kept walking. If any of them had relied on their eyes, they would have spotted her as an intruder instantly. But none of them did. She was one of them. The thought almost brought tears to her eyes.

But that would have made her smell wrong, so she stifled them.

A huge entrance was up ahead, and out of it wafted the most wonderful odor, one that comforted An while at the same time warning her, one that said, *Tread carefully, our Dread Mother rests here.*

An modified her gait and her odor so that they were properly humble and walked into the room with everyone else.

She didn't look at the Mother; at least, not directly. The Mother smell became a hundred times stronger, and An could feel the breathing of a giant as it vibrated the air.

The Big Mother filled most of the room. A massive leg shifted, tucking some errant eggs back into the giant mound on which the Mother was lying. The eggs were glued together with excrement; when excess material fell off, the nursery workers carried it off to use as building material in the city.

There was a noise that made An's Human mind respond with curiosity. She glanced up, and saw the Big Mother expectorating an amber-colored substance. Nursery workers were busy coating themselves under the massive jaws, carrying it off into holes where older larvae were hungrily waiting.

The Big Mother is always feeding, when she isn't eating, An reminded herself. The corner of her mind that was most Human was surprised that she wasn't frightened by the sight. The Big Mother's jaws were big enough to swallow several people at once, and she had many more legs than other Vorns. But An's new mind simply looked at the queen and said *Mother,* with something almost like affection.

An steered herself toward a passage that would take her to her goal. She had a fleeting thought about Jo, wondering if he was still bound tightly, if he could breathe.

Female, called the Big Mother, right inside An's head.

An froze. She hadn't realized that queens could talk that way with their broods.

Yes, Mother, replied her new mind, without missing a beat.

Why are you worrying about a male? The Big Mother imbued the word *male* with a disdain that wasn't cruel, but only natural for a Vorn female. *Males are for mating and eating.*

Yes, Mother.

Have I mated with the male, already? the Big Mother inquired, suspiciously. She sterilized all of her daughters when they were born; but occasionally one would retain her fertility, steal some of the Big Mother's males, and start her own city, elsewhere. This was especially true of warrior females; still, occasionally a worker would fool her. The Big Mother didn't mind her daughters having their pleasures once they were sterile (and once the Big

Mother had already mated with the male in question), but she was jealous of her power.

Very jealous.

Yes, Mother. I am infertile.

An felt a wave of approval wash over her. She grinned happily.

Some advice, said the Big Mother. *Males have two brains, one in the head and one in the abdomen. If you are hungry, once the mating has started, eat the male's head. That brain is concerned with its own survival, and spoils the mating. Once the head brain is gone, the abdomen brain will mate for hours.*

Thank you, Mother.

The Big Mother dismissed An.

She went through a little door that branched off from one of the bigger ones, like a malformed nostril. It had been made by males; An could smell them. Her heart raced at the odor; she could tell that workers weren't meant to go through it. But she was female, no male dared to stop her.

She encountered many gaily colored males along the way. Their color was not a pleasure trait—it was for other males, so they could identify each other. Many of them stopped and regarded An with puzzlement, until she stroked them, letting their inferior olfactory senses identify her. Most of the males would then go away, satisfied with her identity.

Some did not.

These followed An. They didn't try to hurt her, though they certainly could have. They were smaller than females, but they were twice An's size, with many rows of sharp teeth and four powerful jaws. These were older males. They knew how to dazzle females with hypnotic body moments and with sweet songs, entrancing them until they forgot to kill. These males were smart.

An felt admiration for them. Their tunnel wasn't flashy

or complex; it was practical, simple. It led to storage chambers, and these were loaded with blocks of stone, all covered with glyphs. Males were looking at them, sometimes touching them, discussing them with each other. An looked into every room, but her new mind led her onward, deeper into the hidey-hole.

Many males were following her now.

She felt a stab of pity for them. She would be taking glyphs away. Would they miss them? As she passed a bright green-and-yellow male, he brushed against her and paused. Something odd happened.

She recognized him.

He recognized her, too. He turned to follow her, taking his place among the others.

Now they all seemed to have the same purpose. They took An into one of the storage rooms. They lifted several of the stone blocks, many more than An could have taken on her own with just the carrier.

An searched the room for something in particular. She found it, near the back, partly obscured by other blocks.

The yellow-green male helped her move the obstructing blocks away, and An took a long look at what remained. Her mind kindled; a slow fire burned its way to the roots of her hair, the tips of her fingers and toes, then back again. In another moment, it was permanently stamped into her memory.

She turned to leave it, but the male stopped her. He picked up the map, and regarded her, patiently.

They're done with it, they don't need it any longer. And now I don't, either. But it seemed important to the male. So An took it from him.

The males escorted An back to her craft and loaded the blocks for her. Once finished, they filed away, crawling back to their holes of study and mystery.

The yellow-green male lagged behind. He looked at An through his eyes and saw her as she was.

"You have caught the virus," An said.

He replied in the clicking, chirping Vorn language, and then turned to follow the others.

An understood what he had said; especially the first word, which was *Human*. She felt a thrill of fear, but not because he had recognized her. It was the rest of the message that frightened her. It translated into something like this:

"Human, you are not my sister, but you are my sister. Pass them on."

Now An understood why they had given her the glyphs. They were viral glyphs, like the ones that had infected An. Some of the male Vorns had been infected, too. But the ones in her shuttle weren't any good to the Vorns.

They were meant for X'GBris.

What am I really doing? What's going to happen now?

An got back into the shuttle before her confusion could alter her scent. She let her new mind work on automatic, watched distantly while it moved her hands to fire the engines and to pilot through the crazy weave of traffic that tangled its way into orbit around the Motherworld.

There, among the swarm, was Jo's ship. Her real home.

Inside, TTra and her mates were waiting. They would be delighted to see the glyphs. The glyphs would be equally delighted to see them.

What did An care if the X'GBris were infected? What harm would it do? They would feel confused, disoriented. They would have an identity crisis, like An had suffered. So? It hadn't hurt her. She felt fine. She was better than she had been before.

Like a happy drug addict.

It wasn't as if she had a choice. Her new mind was driving her with an irresistible compulsion. Pass it on, pass it on.

Why? An asked herself. *What's the purpose? Is it an invasion; is it brainwashing?*

But there was no inner voice to argue with anymore. There was only a longing for the completion of a task that she could barely grasp. Pass on the virus, follow the map, and then . . .

Me, me, wonderful me, An thought, sadly. *Will I ever hear your voice inside my head again?*

The mouth of the shuttle deck gaped wide and swallowed her up. Swallowed her like the mouth of the Big Mother. An felt a twinge of regret. There was a strange beauty in the lives of the Vorns, a compelling order. But it was all an illusion. Their order had been disrupted by the war; it was about to be scattered by more potent forces. It had been infected.

An unplugged herself from tactical and went to open the door. GNno, CVvu, and MJki surged in, pushing past her. They clicked their teeth in delight when they saw her cargo.

"Break orbit," GNno snapped to MJki. "Prepare for jump."

He had spoken in an X'GBri dialect, and An had understood him. Another gift from Kokoboro? MJki obeyed with pleasure, but CVvu bristled whenever GNno got too close to him. GNno was trying to think of a way to get the other man to leave without provoking a confrontation.

They had all seemed alike, before. How could they have seemed that way?

"Could we speak out in the hall?" An asked GNno. "Privately."

"Something went wrong?" he said, his face reversing into tragedy.

"No. It's personal."

He took her by the arm and led her away from the shuttle. He did it gently, hopefully.

An had to dash his hopes. "I could tell you wanted to speak privately," she whispered. "What's wrong?"

GNno didn't answer yet. He continued to walk with

her, down the hall. She realized where they were going. They were headed for sick bay.

She started to run. In the slight gravity, she took great leaping bounds across the floor.

"Stop!" GNno commanded. He made a grab for her, but she ducked under his hand and dashed for the sick bay doors. She shoved them open and skidded to a halt in the middle of the room.

Jo was in a doctor unit. He was asleep. The life signs were stable, he was breathing normally. The cords were no longer wrapped around his body. He didn't even have on hand restraints.

"Did he faint?" asked An.

GNno took her arm again. "No."

"Then why is he here?"

GNno made her turn and look at him. He held her by both arms, not tightly, but enough to keep her from running again. His face was neither happy nor sad now. It was stuck at an unhappy place between the two.

"We're going to wipe your memories," he said.

An took the news calmly. In fact, she couldn't even feel upset about it. She couldn't feel anything at all.

"Can it be that you really believed that we were buffoons, just clowns for you to laugh at?" GNno asked. "Can it be that you really thought there was something you could tell me about brains that I didn't already know?"

"I . . ." said An thinking back to Cabar 4, and how she had wanted to laugh when he had said he talked to himself for entertainment purposes only. She had wanted to laugh for the wrong reason. She hadn't caught his joke. And now, *she* was the fool.

"We aren't like those butchers on Omsk," GNno said. "We have a finer technique. You will remember who you are. In fact, you will remember everything up to Cabar 4."

An tried to laugh, and coughed, instead. "You can be that specific?"

"If you only knew how fragile memories really are. They are nothing more than frozen cerebral codes. We will undo the bonds between them, and they will unravel."

"But how do you know which are which?" demanded An.

"Have you ever wondered why we never made war with you?"

"What does that have to do with anything?"

"We don't fight for profit, An, like Humans do. We fight for pleasure. But we understand profit. We understand it very well. We practice the fine art of the cold war."

An felt a chill creep up her spine.

"If our Early specialists hadn't disappeared, we would already control your sector. But you've helped us a great deal, An. We've been trying to recreate the Vorn smell for years, and we've always failed. We were going about it the wrong way, trying to synthesize a formula from captives and spray it on ourselves.

"But now that I've tasted you, I know how it should be done. We need something that will create the odor from *inside* our bodies. You've proven it can be done; and I have memorized the taste. This world will be dead in another year."

An stared at him in horror. How many years had she seen X'GBris as tragedy or comedy masks without seeing what lay beneath them? How many years had she been guilty of the arrogance she had thought belonged only to them?

"Don't kill the Vorns," she pleaded, knowing it was useless. "They don't deserve to be wiped out, GNno. You don't understand them any better than I understood you."

"That's an odd thing for a Human to say. Didn't the

Vorns kill Mandalay? Didn't they kill beautiful Celestine? How many millions of OutWorlders have given their lives in the war?"

"You don't understand!" An begged.

"Then enlighten me," he replied, but An could see he already knew the truth. The Vorns had not murdered, they had not acted as monsters. They had not even understood that they had been fighting intelligent beings like themselves all these years. Human beings had merely been another environmental pitfall for them, a problem that could not be overcome. The Vorns were doing what they had always done under those circumstances.

They were persisting.

"For two hundred years you have fought them," GNno said. "Now that will end. The Inner Worlds will have fewer excuses to hold you down. Perhaps we are doing you a greater favor than you realize—"

"And maybe you're not. Maybe you're just transforming the war into a civil one."

"Not any time soon," he mused. "No, it will take decades of rejoicing before OutWorlders turn on their real enemies. By then, who knows?" GNno clicked his teeth in anticipation. "We may be in a position to turn the outcome in our own favor."

"Don't you care about us at all, GNno? Don't you feel bad about what will happen to us?"

"We will do what we will do," he said. "We have our needs. Your Inner World people would understand us better, I think. They are much more like us than they are like you, despite that they share your genes."

An looked at Jo, who lay sleeping so peacefully. He looked beautiful, untouched by pain or worry. He also looked as if he had been doctored. All of his bruises were gone, his color was healthy. That was something, at least. That was some evidence of compassion.

But if GNno had been the compassionate one, now he

was the solid, unyielding rock. An sighed with defeat. "And now that you've told me all this," she said, "you'll wipe my memory. Why tell me at all, GNno? Am I your confessor?"

He frowned, then forced his mouth into a gentler line. He leaned down and kissed her, awkwardly. He couldn't resist using his tongue in the end, tickling her with it. But she didn't feel like laughing.

"When are you going to wipe us?" she said.

"Very soon. We've left orbit, now we're running to the jump point. After you translate the map for us, you'll be wiped before jump."

An let out a long sigh. A tear rolled down her cheek.

"You taste like you again," he said, sounding relieved.

"Do something for me?" she asked. "Wipe something in particular out of Jo's memory."

"The time he tried to kill you," said GNno.

"Yes."

"I was planning to. And a few other things, as well, difficult things that might make him—dangerous. Jo's wipe will be more complicated. But he has earned his respite."

"Thank you," An said, hoping that respite was what Jo was really going to get.

CVvu appeared in the doorway, rubbing his temples. "I have a terrible headache," he snarled.

How long had he been alone with the glyphs?

"I'd better get started on that map," An said, and tried not to stare at CVvu as she went out the door.

An woke up in near-darkness, with gray shadows bending over her. They spoke to each other in whispery voices, in a language she didn't understand. Someone bent close, took her face in his giant hands, and looked into her eyes.

"Do you know me?" he whispered.

Her mind eagerly chased after the information. "GNno," she whispered back.

"Yes. I have a gift for you, little An. A certain memory."

He glanced over his shoulder. The other shadows had gone, he was alone with her. But An thought she saw someone lying nearby, on another table.

"Jo?" she asked GNno.

"He is well. He has lost his burden. If you wish to lose *your* burden some day, find me. I will help."

An was surprised to hear him say that, but she couldn't remember why. She had memories of his face in other aspects: tragic, comic, angry, triumphant; but the expression he was currently wearing troubled her. He seemed to know something he hadn't known before.

"Wasn't I about to do something for you?" she asked.

"You did it."

"I don't remember what it was. Did I do it right?"

"That remains to be seen. But I suspect you did."

"Are you glad, now?"

She didn't know what had prompted her to ask that question, but it did interesting things to his face.

"Beloved enemy," he whispered, and he pressed his lips against her cheek, "good-bye."

An felt a sting in her arm, and the room darkened. It became very quiet; so quiet that An was afraid to make a noise. But her curiosity got the best of her.

"What now?" she asked.

A reddish light was pulsing off to her left. She ignored it at first; she thought she ought to lie still and wait for what was supposed to happen. But then she wondered why she thought that. Maybe she ought to get up and look after her own fate.

She rose from the table. It seemed to her that Jo was rising, too. She could see his profile in the red light.

"Stay with me, Jo," she warned him. "We can't get separated here, or we'll never see each other again."

He nodded. An turned toward the red light, and Jo followed her.

It wasn't as far away as she had thought. It was coming around the cracks of an egg-shaped door.

"They'd better seal those up," An remarked to Jo, "or the air will escape."

"That's not the void," she thought she heard him whisper back.

Something was glowing softly on the door. It changed as An bent closer to look at it. It wiggled and got larger, then shrank again. An bent very close, just inches from the surface of the door.

It was an egg that changed into a tadpolelike creature, then grew into a lizard or salamander. Then it changed back again.

"Is it alive?" An wondered. She touched it and felt nothing under her fingertips.

It sprang off the door and leapt right into her eyes. An couldn't blink in time to shut it out. She braced herself for the pain, but none came; and when she opened her eyes again, the door had sprung open. Beyond was a shifting world of sand.

"Careful," Jo breathed, behind her. "That's time."

The sand was red, like the Red Zone back on Storm; but it moved like water. It was dunes one moment, then flat the next. Masses would be piled on one side, then suddenly disappear, like foam on waves, carried away by the wind.

But one point seemed stable. There was a little hill just beyond the door that stayed the same; and on the very top lay a small, white object; an oval.

"My Egg," An cried. "That's my Egg! I've got to get it before it's buried!" And she ran through the door, onto the shifting sand.

"Don't," Jo whispered, like a ghost.

"I'm almost there. Wait for me!"

She ran up hills that tried to disintegrate beneath her; one foothold would dissolve just as she had gained the next. The Egg was just within reach. She stretched out her hand and managed to brush it with her fingertips.

The hill under the Egg disappeared. An plummeted into the new hole. New sand immediately began to fill in underneath her, slowing and breaking her fall.

"Climb!" Jo was screaming, no longer a pale ghost. "Climb out of there, An!"

An climbed, frantically. The Egg was long gone, and now she could no longer see the door. She reached the top of another hill, only to have it flatten out into a plain; then shift to one side, dragging her with it.

In another moment, it had buried her. She couldn't move, couldn't draw a breath to scream.

Something was wiggling under her right hand. It was pressed up into her palm by the pressure of the sand.

It was the Egg.

An forced her fingers to close around it, struggling against the inertia of the sand. She was blacking out from lack of air; the sand was in her mouth, her ears, her eyes, and nose. Her fingers pressed on the Egg until it cracked.

The sand fell away from her. It rolled her onto her back and dragged itself to another corner of the sky, leaving her at its edge.

In the distance, she could see the door. Jo was still there, waving and pointing at something behind her.

Someone was with him, a thin person with a wild halo of hair. She couldn't make out who it was, but now both of them were waving and pointing frantically. An turned to look, and saw a city.

It was shifting, too, but not quite like the sands were. Buildings were appearing and disappearing, but the streets stayed the same.

"Go!" she heard Jo calling, distantly. She looked for him again, in time to see the door slamming shut and the sands looming high to cover it. They rose and rushed toward her in a giant wave.

An dashed for the city with all her might. Behind her, the sands howled and roared; and they continued to do so even after she had set her foot on the pavement of the main road, but when she ventured a look over her shoulder, they had passed the city by completely.

An slowed to a walk. All around her, the buildings came and went. They had signs on them, random words in Standard and other languages. The words she knew said things like: UP, DOWN, START, ACTIVATE, FIRE, STORE, LEFT, RIGHT, sometimes accompanied by arrows that pointed in random directions or random numbers. Other words were more like pictures, and they kept changing or disappearing before An could really get a good look at them.

Finally she saw words that made sense. They said: EARLY TO BED AND EARLY TO RISE MOTEL. An ran through the door that had those words over it, before the building could go away.

Inside, things were more stable. There was a cozy if somewhat seedy lobby, with a man standing behind the front desk. He smiled at An, and she immediately liked him. He was a stout old man with a pair of almond eyes that seemed rather out of place in his pale face.

"Looking for a room?" he asked her.

"Yes, I suppose I must be," said An. She walked up to the desk and read the name tag on his blue jacket. KOKOBORO, it said.

"Room 4 is the best," Kokoboro said. "But someone is already there."

"May I have another, then?"

"Yes, but I wish you'd run up to 4 and talk to my friend, Mohamonero. He's in trouble, and he needs a hand out of it."

"What kind of trouble?"

"Heavy trouble," said Kokoboro, sadly. "You're the only one who's come. No one else knows the secret."

The letters on his name tag had shifted into something else, pictures that danced across the rectangular space as if they knew she was watching them and they wanted to put on a show.

"What secret?" asked An.

"You'll have to ask Mohamonero. He might be able to get you out of here."

"I'd better see him, then," said An. "What floor is he on?"

"The first," said Kokoboro, and he handed her a key from one of the cubby holes in the wall behind him. The numbers on the cubby hole were shifting as busily as the buildings outside.

"Careful," Kokoboro warned her. "Keep your eyes on solid things, for now."

"Thank you," said An. She turned to leave, but he called after her.

"Don't forget your suitcase," he said.

There was a big block of stone sitting in front of the desk. It had a wicker handle on its top. An picked it up and was happy to find that it was lighter than it looked.

"Good luck!" said Kokoboro, which was not an encouraging thing to hear from a hotel desk clerk.

An kept her eyes on the carpet on her way to the elevator, but that proved to be risky. The designs kept swirling and changing color. She looked at the walls next, but pictures were moving in the wallpaper. Finally she fastened her eyes on the window at the end of the hall, outside of which it was currently raining.

There was a snow storm by the time An reached the elevator; she slipped gratefully into the lift. The doors slipped shut behind her and the elevator began to move even though she hadn't pushed a button. Not that she knew which one to push; they kept changing around, and none of them ever seemed to say *1*.

The elevator stopped and opened its doors. An decided she had better jump out, or she might not have another opportunity to get off any time soon. As soon as she was off, the elevator vanished, leaving her in a drab hall with an old carpet and peeling paint on the walls.

They wanted to show her shifting pictures just like the other hall had, but they couldn't seem to muster much of anything. The door numbers were changing quite enthusiastically, however. An walked back and forth for a long time, looking for a 4.

She saw one that *might* have been part of a four; or it might have been a seven with a fancy slash on its head. She tried to get a closer look at it, to see if she could find the jagged edges of a break. But she just wasn't sure.

No harm in knocking, she thought to herself. She rapped on the door. It swung slowly inward, releasing a sound as it opened; first a moan, and then a shriek.

Inside, An found a SuperStorm. She could see it, smell it, hear it, even taste it—but she could not feel it. She didn't think about that, though. Her attention was drawn by the person who was standing in the middle of the storm.

The person was very thin and had wild hair. She couldn't see his face because the sun was behind him, shining right into her eyes.

"Are you the one who was with Jo?" she yelled over the howl of the wind. "In the doorway?"

"This isn't Room 4," the person said quietly. An could hear him perfectly. His voice was familiar.

"Are you sure?" she shouted, her voice almost lost in the wind.

"Very. Keep going. This is the most important thing you're going to do."

The door began to swing shut. An waved to the person, who waved back. "We're still praying for you," he said, just before the door closed.

"Room 4," An said, and began to look again.

When she finally found it, she was surprised she hadn't seen it before. It wasn't changing at all, just sat there above a door proclaiming *4* loudly and steadily while all else around it changed and fluxed.

An knocked on the door. From inside, a voice said, "Come in."

An opened the door.

A slim young man was sitting on the bed, watching a vid screen with almond eyes.

"Dr. Mohamonero?" An said. "Kokoboro said you needed help."

"You'd better take a look at this," he said, motioning her to join him without taking his eyes from the screen.

An closed the door behind her and went to sit next to him, setting the stone suitcase at her feet. She gazed at the screen.

A young woman was being expelled from her Egg in space. She was fighting to pull herself back in, to repressurize the Egg. An watched while the woman found her empty reserve tanks, stimmed herself in the neck with oxygen, tried to breath what was coming out of the vents. She saw the blood droplets floating, the woman blacking out, then reviving a moment later looking dazed and surprised to be alive.

She watched the woman checking her computer systems. She listened while the woman listened to the voice command codes.

She heard Jo's voice, and wept as she realized what it meant.

"My lover tried to kill me," she told Mohamonero, and sobbed like a child.

"That memory does him nothing but harm, but you need it," said Mohamonero. "You can stop it from happening again."

"There's something else I've forgotten." An stopped crying and tried to think what it was.

"We have to put your memory someplace safe," said Mohamonero. "Any ideas?"

An looked at her stone suitcase. Now she could see that there had once been some kind of writing all over it; but the characters were almost gone, as if the stone had been scoured by centuries of sandstorms. She looked under the wicker handle and found a little clasp. She tugged at it, and the case came open.

"In here?" she suggested. Mohamonero lifted his vid screen and put it into the stone suitcase. The screen was still playing scenes: A man was telling a ragged little girl, "People should never even have come to this planet, 'cause if you stumble and fall this world will soak you up like a drop of water.

"Just one tiny drop of water that shouldn't even be here," said the man's voice, just as An was closing the case.

"I'll keep this safe," said Mohamonero, "so they won't take it away from you."

"Thank you. But how do we get out of here?"

"I'm waiting for someone."

There was a knock on the door.

An was afraid to answer. But Mohamonero didn't move, so it was up to her. She went to the door and pulled it open.

"Oh!" she said. "Oh, my God!"

"Jo, answer the door."

"Hmmn?"

"Answer the door. Somebody's knocking."

An heard him rise and walk across the floor. She turned on her side and tried to snuggle into her pillow, but it wasn't very comfortable. Why was she in such an uncomfortable bed?

Jo came back and turned her over. He brushed the hair out of her face and gave her a little shake. "An," he said, "where are we?"

She opened her eyes. They were in the sick bay on Jo's ship. They had been lying on trauma couches and wearing their control suits.

"Who was at the door?" she asked.

"No one. Where the hell is this place, An? The last thing I remember, I was back on Covina, looking for you."

Covina. That was where An had been before Omsk. That was where Jo had sabotaged her Egg. She sat up.

"You were looking for me?" she asked.

"You hadn't come in yet. You were due. Jezuz, whose ship is this? It's beautiful."

"It's your ship, Jo."

He stared at her, not daring to believe it. "Don't jerk me, An."

"I'm not jerking you! We've had our memories wiped, that's why you don't recognize it."

"Prove it," said Jo.

An took him back to the command deck. "There must be an I.D. code," she said. "It should name you as the owner."

Jo looked dubious, but he found the communications station and called up the code.

"An II, 976-003-444-4" said the code, in Jo's voice. "Owner and Captain, Jokate7976842."

An blushed. She hadn't remembered that he had named the ship after her.

Jo looked thunderstruck. "That's my voice," he said. "And that was what I was going to name my ship, when I got her." He looked at An, begging for an explanation.

"Let's see if there's anything in your personal log," she stammered. She thought maybe they could access that through the captain's chair. She was right—but it took her several moments to figure out how to do it. Hadn't she been better at this before? What had GNno taken out of her memory?

Jo watched his personal log. It had only one entry in it; the one he had made after he had bought the ship.

"My father is dead," said the recorded Jo, "and that's why I'm here."

He went on to say some things about his father, then was cut off in midsentence. An looked at the command codes and discovered that most of the log had been erased.

"Sorry I can't give you better proof," she said, then shut her mouth when she saw that Jo was crying.

"You didn't remember that he was dead," An said, softly.

"No," he choked. He dropped into the chair as if his legs could no longer support him.

An knelt at his feet and put her head in his lap. "I'm

sorry," she said, over and over. "I'm sorry you had to find out that way."

"There's no good way to find out," he said, but he stroked her hair and seemed to take comfort from her. Finally he said, "Who took our memories?"

"TTra and GNno. X'GBris. Do you remember them?"

"Yes. I met them on Solis Five."

"We met them again on Cabar Four."

"We?" He lifted her chin and made her look into his eyes. "Together?"

"Yes," she said. "I told you I thought there were ruins there, and I was right. We went to Cabar Four together, but TTra must have—"

He had pulled her to her feet and was hugging her tight. "We went together?" he asked, again.

"Yes. We teamed up. I had always wanted to do that with you, but I didn't have the guts to ask. You asked me on Covina, and I was so relieved."

"So am I," said Jo. He kissed her. "I love you."

An closed her eyes and saw herself spilling out of her Egg, struggling for life. "I love you, too," she said.

Hello there, said a voice in her head. *Remember me?*

An opened her eyes. Jo hadn't spoken, he was pressing his lips against her neck, still crying a little over his father.

Is that you? she asked herself, careful not to voice the question aloud this time.

I think so.

How come you're talking to me again? I thought we were integrated now.

We had to dis-integrate, to save our memories. We had to move them.

Who made that decision!?

You did.

Oh. But where did we move our memories?

Out of the memory centers.

How could we do that?

Where there's a will, there's a way.

"Baby," murmured Jo, "you're talking to yourself."

An sighed. Why couldn't she keep quiet? "I can't help it. I had an RNA drip, Jo."

He stepped back and held her at arm's length. "A what?"

"So I could read the glyphs. I went to Omsk and got a drip, and I learned something dangerous."

She could see that this was too much information to be dumping on him at once. But what choice did she have? They might be in danger right now. . . .

"Where are we, anyway?" An went to the navigation station to have a look at the star map. A large planet was looming on tactical.

"Covina," said An. "We're right back where we started."

An sat down. Jo sat next to her, at the gunner's station. "Any suggestions?" he asked her.

She was glad that he asked, but she couldn't think of anything.

What do you think we should do? she asked the inner voice.

Beats me.

I thought you knew stuff I didn't know.

Now there's stuff we both don't know. We've shifted everything around, and we've got some holes.

Great.

"Let's find out if we're wanted by the law," said Jo.

That was an alarming thought, but an excellent suggestion. An followed him to communications and watched while he queried various governmental and business Nets. An was clean, but Jo couldn't find his name at all.

"Try adding some syllables," said An.

He finally found himself listed as Jokate. "Funny how money can give you status you haven't earned," he said.

"Jokateanke." An kissed the back of his neck. "Jokate-anke-Re. You earned that, long ago."

He didn't pull away, but his voice barely rose above a whisper when he asked, "I told you about that?"

"And your father. Heavy Time."

"Did I tell you how I earned the *Re*?"

"No."

"I'll save that for our honeymoon."

An kissed his neck again. She continued to read over his shoulder. Jo's financial resources were staggering.

"Why did I need to go to Cabar Four?" he asked. "I didn't need the money."

"The glyphs," An said.

"So? What was so great about *those* glyphs? Glyphs only mean money to me."

An straightened up, and frowned. "Hmm. Maybe you were helping me out?"

"I would have married you. That's what I want to do now."

An flushed. He turned and saw her that way. The sight seemed to reassure him. "That's my old An," he said.

"You want to get married?" she asked.

"Yes. Do you?"

Yes! cried the voice in her head.

He tried to kill me.

Nobody's perfect.

The old Jo never would have asked her. An was sure of it. Hadn't GNno told her something? He was going to do some—untangling? This Jo wasn't afraid to cry over his father, to ask An to marry him. This Jo was unburdened.

"Yes," An heard herself say.

"So why did we go to Cabar Four?"

"I thought we did it for the glyphs!"

"Was there something else there?"

An sat down on the captain's dais. She tried not to think too hard; it was like grasping for a word you can't quite remember. Jo kept quiet, respecting her concentration.

"Yes . . ." she said. "I think there was something else. But I can't remember what it was."

Do you remember? she asked herself.

Something important, said the voice, helpfully.

Jo returned to his Net-skimming. "Whatever it was, you can bet that TTra and GNno made sure we would *never* remember it. Let's get on to other things."

"What are you doing?"

"Filing a request for a marriage certificate." He tapped away on the keyboard, then looked up at her. "Come put in your code?"

He held his breath, as if he was afraid she would say no. But she didn't want to say no. The Jo who had tried to kill her had been erased.

She entered her code beside his.

For all practical purposes, they were married.

"Where do you want to honeymoon?" he asked. "Want to rent a fancy suite, planetside?"

How about right here, right now? asked the voice.

Don't be so impatient!

On the floor!

Hush!

"We haven't had time to break in the captain's quarters," said An.

"Let's fix that," said Jo. "Right now."

And they did. They locked themselves into their quarters and ordered champagne from the ship's stores. They discovered that the captain's bed had been designed to hold two—three, in a pinch.

Jo told An how he had earned the title of Re. He cried some more. Then An rolled him onto his back and licked and nibbled him until he forgot his troubles.

"I can't remember the last time I was this happy," said Jo.

"Me neither," said An.

And that's basically the problem, isn't it? asked the voice. *We can't remember.*

An was nervous as they landed Jo's ship on Covina. She was also very glad that she wouldn't be required to man the gunner's station, because those controls were looking even less familiar than navigation.

What had happened? Hadn't she been a pro at this sort of thing for years? Hadn't she landed her Egg under the worst possible conditions? And now here she was, feeling like a novice again, scared to death of making a mistake.

"You're the one who should be landing," she told Jo.

"I'm not the one who needs the practice," he said, relentlessly. "These are the best circumstances under which you'll ever land. Relax!"

"I don't think I'd better do that—"

"We're doing fine," Jo told her, but she could only feel relieved that he was monitoring everything carefully. They were locked into traffic control, anyway; so it wasn't like trying to land an Egg.

"That's a hundred times harder than this," said Jo. "I can't believe you're nervous."

"I'm just mad that I can't remember," said An.

He grunted sympathetically. But he didn't offer to take over the controls. And he was right. She would have to relearn things. They both would. And the best way to do that, they had decided, was to do things they had used to do, at least for a while.

They had talked it over the night before.

"We'll pick up where we left off," Jo had said, smoothing An's hair away from her marriage pillow. An had sighed, remembering enough about her past to realize how unhappy it had begun to make her feel.

"It won't be the same," she said, with more relief than regret. "We won't be desperate. We won't be scrambling for cash and jump juice. And in this ship, it won't be nearly as dangerous."

"It will if we do what I'm thinking of doing," Jo said.

An lifted herself on one elbow and gazed down at him. He was lying with his arms folded under his head, a far-away look in his eyes. He looked so handsome that way, she almost forgot to ask him what he meant. He met her eyes, anticipating the question.

"What would you think about going back to Cabar Four?" he asked.

Uh-oh, said the voice in An's head.

What? she asked herself.

I don't remember. But I think it would be dangerous. What do you think?

An didn't know what to think.

"We might not get out again, alive," Jo was saying. "On the other hand, if we were using our stealth features . . ."

"They caught us last time, even with our fancy technology."

"I have some ideas about that," said Jo, his eyes once again gazing into infinity. "I think I know how to step us up."

"Maybe they just planted the idea in your head," warned An.

"Maybe they did. I'm not saying it won't be dangerous. I don't want to do anything that would jeopardize your safety. You can stay here, if you want . . ."

"No! If you disappear I'll never know what happened to you!"

Jo wrapped his arms around her and pulled her down again. He kissed and nuzzled her until she relaxed.

"I don't want to take the risks I used to take," he whispered. "Not with you along. I just want to tiptoe in, see if we can find out what was such a big deal. Do you?"

An thought about it for a long moment, was surprised to realize that she did.

"We shouldn't go alone this time," she had said.

So they had put in a query with the Covina directory for friends. They had been pleased to find Ra there; and An had managed to track down Te. Both were interested in discussing business over drinks.

"This is crazy," An said, but she was excited. And then she managed to land Jo's ship without too much trouble, leading her to believe that other things could be re-learned, other skills regained.

They met with Ra and Te at Golgo's, where discreet booths could be found. Ra looked the same as he always did, but Te looked much younger than she had the last time An had seen her. She looked no more than twenty. Her hair was longer, too, and streaked with gold.

This fact was not lost on Re.

"So, you want to double date?" he asked Te, and nudged her playfully.

Te had known him long enough not to take it personally. "I'd like to put my Egg in storage," she told Jo. "And I want you to buy my accidental death and injury insurance for this trip."

"Done," said Jo.

And that was that. All that remained was to break the happy news. "We're married," An told them.

Te smiled. Ra did, too, but his smile was a little pained. "Congratulations," he said. "I knew you guys would get around to it, sooner or later." He took a long swallow of his drink and mumbled, "I was hoping it would be *later* though."

Te put her arms around him and nibbled on his ear. "I'll help you forget her," she said.

"Keep it up and I'll forget my own name."

Hmmmm . . . said the voice in An's head.

What?

All this talk about forgetting . . .

Yes?

What was the name of the guy who gave us the drip?

An groped for the name. At first she thought it might start with a *K,* but the voice said, *Mo—Moho—something—*

Jo was laughing and hugging An. "You're talking to yourself again," he said.

"Trying to remember," said An.

"You can't get past a memory wipe," said Te. "It's happened to me, twice, and I never got the information back. But that's just as well, because I'm alive and not doing Heavy Time."

Heavy Time. He's doing Heavy Time. Poor fellow.

"Isn't that what happened to my doctor?" An asked Jo.

"Huh?"

"From Omsk? Didn't we find out he was doing Heavy Time?"

"Shit, if that's true, he's lost. You can't get out of Heavy Time."

"I have a feeling this is important," said An.

Monumerano? Mohahehaha?

"I couldn't even save my own father from Heavy Time," Jo said, bitterly.

Mohamonero. That's his name. You have to see Mohamonero.

He isn't even on Omsk anymore.

Then you have to find him.

Why? I can't help him.

He has your memories.

What!?

It's very important. You have to find Mohamonero. We can't be integrated again until you do.

"Excuse me," An said. "I'm going to go look something up in the directory."

"What's up?" asked Jo, reluctant to let her go.

"I want to see if Mohamonero is still listed in the Omsk directory. Maybe I can send a message drone to him."

An got up and went to an access booth. She glanced at Jo over her shoulder, to reassure herself that he was really there, they were really married.

He looked so handsome sitting there. It was hard to leave the room. But she did.

She typed QUERY:OMSK: DR. MOHAMONERO into her terminal and waited.

I.D.? asked the Net. An typed in her number.

PLEASE HOLD.

An leaned against the booth. Five minutes went by. Six minutes. She yawned.

Someone jabbed a needle into the back of her neck.

An slipped to the floor. Her eyes were wide open; she could see who was standing over her. Four people in neuter suits stuffed her into a bag.

That was the last thing she remembered for a long time.

Years later, someone shone a light in her eyes. They asked her questions, and she heard herself answering them, but none of it made any sense. She couldn't muster the will to ask them what they wanted, where she was.

Another timeless darkness followed. And then An got another shot in her neck.

"Wake up," said the toneless, sexless voice.

"Wha—" An tried to get a look at her surroundings. All she could see was gray mesh, stretching into infinity. "Where am I?" she asked the sexless person.

"Valhalla," it droned.

"Viking Heaven?"

The person made a noise like an aborted laugh. "Valhalla 8, Heavy World Prison 45832. Welcome, dissident. You've been sentenced to indefinite time."

"Indefinite time?"

"Heavy Time," said the voice.

"Why?" gasped An. "Why!?"

"Ask Mohamonero, when you see him," said the sexless one, as it grabbed her by the back of her neck and shoved her into the mesh.

Heavy Time was Hell.

That would have seemed a simple statement, outside, back in the real universe where people cheerfully complained about work, or marriage, or taxes. They would say things like *That hurt like hell,* and never have cause to wonder how a word describing eternal torment had ever become so trivialized.

On Heavy World 54832, it was twilight all the time. The sun was a far-off blue spark that struggled across the horizon for an endless time, as if even it could not escape from prison. Sometimes it would disappear, and the world would fall into deeper darkness. It was a sunset that never heralded rest. There was no peace in the night. There was no night at all, really, just work and oblivion, torment and then an exhausted sleep that was always just a little too short.

An dreamed every night, about the life and the people she had left behind. But those memories were getting jumbled, they were fading and distorting into other shapes. She would wake to another day with nothing but death to keep her company.

Heavy Time was not meant for rehabilitation. It was not a place to put people who were being temporarily separated from the rest of humanity. Heavy Time was Hell, and people only escaped from it when they died and went to Heaven. An thought they must surely all go to Heaven, since they had already been in Hell, and why punish people twice?

That wouldn't be fair, would it?

How come people have to go to Hell in the first place? asked the voice inside An's head. It was always talking to her these days; which was good, because An was so lonely. So lonely, and tired, and worried. So desperate.

They don't, as far as I'm concerned, said An.

What about that *guy?* asked the voice.

It was talking about the person laboring in the opposite direction that An was walking. His heavy suit had CHILD MOLESTER printed in neon lights just over his visual apparatus.

Maybe he isn't really a child molester, An mused. *Maybe he's another dissident, like me.* An's headpiece said TRAITOR. She had looked for other traitors trudging back and forth between the supply stations, but she would never have time to talk to them, never have time to talk to anyone but herself. She still had air and hydro to get; she needed the air to stay alive, needed the hydro to keep the suit walking. Which one should she get first?

What if he is *a child molester?* asked the voice. *What then? Does he deserve Hell?*

If he's a child molester, why don't they give him sexuality treatments? They could reprogram him on Omsk.

Maybe they did, and it failed.

The signpost up ahead pointed in two directions. One said, AIR 2.5K, the other said, HYDRO 2.3K. An peered at her readout panel, which was just under her chin. Her air supply was nudging the red zone; her hydro was already over the line. Her suit was still moving properly.

But wait, did it stick a little, just then?

Get the air first, An.

But my suit will stop moving! I'll be trapped out here, and no one will help me! No one!

We're not out of hydro yet. They tamper with the dials to cause anxiety, to make people feel desperate all the time. We have more than it's showing there.

An had suspected that was the case for a long time. But when she was out, trying to get from base to base, she lost her confidence. It never failed. It was how they kept the prison population down, by tricking people into getting themselves killed.

Or into killing themselves on purpose.

An had stumbled across someone the other day.

When *was* the other day?

Anyway, it wasn't today, it was in the past. She had found someone prone on the blue-black ground, the hard-hard rock that was pressed down by thirty gees. An hated to look at the ground; it scared her. But she had seen the figure from a distance. She had meant to walk past it, but her conscience began to nibble at her before she was halfway there.

She leaned over the figure and activated her comm.

"Are you out of hydro?" she asked it. "I have some. I could spare a little."

She was astonished to hear those words coming out of her mouth. No one helped anyone else on Heavy Time. If she had been lying there, the others would have just trudged by.

But if they didn't show each other humanity, who would?

But the figure wasn't answering. It had MURDERER written across its helmet.

"Can you hear me?" An asked. "Move your graspers, if you can."

"I'm not out of hydro," came the whisper over her comm.

"Oh. Well—well, why . . . ?"

"I'm just tired, that's all."

"But you can't rest here. You don't have time."

"I'm not resting."

An told herself to move on, not to ask any more. Even her inner voice was silent, wiser than her.

"What do you mean?" she asked.

"You know what I mean, TRAITOR. I can't do it, anymore. It's never going to stop, it's never going to get better. There's only one way out of here."

An wanted to leave, then. But she still couldn't.

"Maybe your time will be up, soon," she said. She was rewarded with laughter that sounded more like static.

"Have you ever met anyone who came back from Heavy Time?" asked MURDERER.

An moved her suit two steps away. "Don't you want to live?" she pleaded.

"Yes," said MURDERER. "But not like this."

An turned her back. "I'm sorry," she said.

Before she could get out of comm range, MURDERER's voice whispered over the link: "Not as sorry as you're going to be ..."

Do murderers deserve to go to Hell? asked the inner voice.

They could be reprogrammed on Omsk, just like everyone else.

If they're reprogrammed, will their souls still go to Hell, after they die?

I don't believe in Hell, said An. *Not after you die.*

But this place is modeled after Hell, isn't it?

This place should not exist.

Why does it? Who thought it up?

A headless monster.

An saw the air station up ahead. There was a line of Heavy Suiters ahead of her. She got behind the last one and waited, patiently. Sometime later, someone got behind her.

No one tried to cut ahead in the line. You couldn't fight in the suits. You didn't have time or energy; and besides, they just weren't that flexible. That was probably what bureaucrats had liked about them in the first place. You could solve all prison problems with Heavy Time. No unrest, no murders, no rapes—you could even imprison men and women together.

No lawsuits for unfair treatment. No idle time in which to brew trouble.

Those fucking bureaucrats gave in, that's what happened, An told the inner voice. They made campaign promises to voters who were angry about crime. No one had the guts to tell them that there weren't any solutions. Some problems just don't have solutions; but who wants to hear that?

How did we vote? asked the voice.

The line moved, after a fashion. An didn't really mind. It was a chance to rest. They only gave you seven and three-quarters hours to rest every night. Or that's what they said, anyway. Sometimes it felt like a little more, sometimes it felt like a lot less.

Mind murder, said the voice.

That's what they should have on their helmets, agreed An.

Would you like to remember some music?

An wasn't sure she would. She could never remember an entire piece, and sometimes the very effort of trying created aggravating memory loops that played out until she wanted to pound her head. But the music was pretty, and sometimes it made things more bearable.

What do you want? she asked the voice.

It's easier for me. I'm doing it right now.

I'll listen, too, then.

So An listened to music in her head. As usual, it was incomplete, but she let it go on that way. No use fighting it. The line moved, and eventually it was her turn at the air pump. She hooked up and watched the readouts in her helmet.

These are probably wrong, she told herself. *They make you think you have more than you have or less than you have.*

We have enough, said the voice.

An unhooked and plodded off toward the next sign. It pointed two ways. One said: HYDRO 1.1K, the other said: PROTEIN 1.2K.

An was hungry, but she went for the hydro. If she had time, she would go back for the food. They didn't feed you in the bunkers.

An was skinny inside her suit. She could feel her ribs and her pelvis sticking out. There were a thousand things you needed on your trek back and forth between the bunkers every day, and you had to prioritize. You always went short on some things. An had found out early on what was most important. But what she hadn't suspected was that the things that were lowest on your list could still kill you if you didn't get enough of them. Things like vitamin C and iron. How long had it been since she had had either of those nutrients? All the protein stations gave out was bland bars.

Maybe there was protein in those bars.

Yes, An was skinny. She didn't think she was old, yet; it felt like only a few months had passed. But she would get old before her time.

We'll get rejuve, said the inner voice.

When? An asked, wearily.

When we get off.

People never get off.

Someday, we'll remember what we need to help us escape.

When will I remember?

When you find Mohamonero.

But An was beginning to doubt that Mohamonero was

there. Or if he was, he was going to the opposite bunker from her every day. One group went one way while the other group went the other, and she never had time to pay much attention to people she passed. She always tried to read their helmets, but she had never seen another one that said TRAITOR, which is surely what Mohamonero would be labeled. Assuming the labels weren't all lies, all arbitrary.

We saw another TRAITOR once.

That was true, sort of. Once An had been approached by a guard in one of the bunkers. He had been wearing a neuter suit, so at first she hadn't even known if it was a man or a woman coming on to her.

She never could tell if the guards noticed people, unless they said something specific to you in those neutered voices. You couldn't see their faces behind their visors, you couldn't smell them, and you couldn't see their bodies beneath the disguising coveralls. They just stood around with their prods, waiting for you to struggle out of your Heavy Suit; and if you went the wrong way, they zapped you.

One guard had zapped An as she headed for sleeping quarters.

"Time for shots," he said, and pointed down another hall.

An obeyed. She didn't know what was in the shots, and she had long since stopped asking. She never felt much of anything, afterward. She thought they might be immunizations, or vitamins, or placebos.

He zapped her again, directing her down another hall, the one for showers. An obeyed again. She didn't mind getting clean.

But he came into the undressing room with her. No one had ever done that before. "Strip," he commanded.

He's going to make a pass at us, the voice had said, with a tone that suggested mild titillation. An felt almost diverted herself. She stripped, but could tell nothing about his reaction.

Maybe it's a woman, suggested the voice, sounding disappointed.

But then the guard got into the shower with An. He just stood there, the water rolling off his suit and visor, while she washed her body and her hair. It felt so good under the water, An almost forgot he was there.

She stepped into one of the drying stalls. She was going to turn it on, but his hand stopped her. She was shocked by the feel of human flesh against her skin.

He had taken off his gloves.

His hands were male. They were large and square, rather nice, actually. He was holding a towel. Where would he get such a thing? Even in her EggHead days, when she had had money for luxuries, An had not seen many towels. Some of the luxury hotels boasted of them, but ordinary people used drying stalls.

He began to dry her with the towel, taking his time. An waited, wondering what would happen next.

"Were you a fancy girl?" asked the neutered voice.

"No," said An.

"You should have been."

An couldn't think of a reply.

"I've never seen one like you here, before. Usually we get ugly women."

An couldn't remember what the other women looked like. She didn't recall thinking that any of them were ugly.

"Did you get your protein today?" asked the guard.

"No," said An.

He pulled a bar out of his pocket and handed it to An. She ate it while he dried her off.

"Those have the vitamins and minerals, too," he said. "I'll try to get one to you a couple of times a week."

"Why?" asked An.

He put down the towel and put his hands on her skin again. It felt good, and that was disturbing. An was starved for human contact. He ran his hands up and down her legs, touched her pubic hair, probed her vulva with his fingertips. He turned his visor toward her face.

"You're slippery," he said.

An shrugged.

He fondled her breasts, and touched her face. An tried to imagine what was behind the visor. She thought of Jo's face, and felt an answering tingle in her groin.

But then he took his helmet off, and he wasn't anything like Jo. He was a little homely. He had small eyes and a nose with big pores all over it. His mouth was rather nice, though. He kissed An.

"We don't have time to make love properly," he said, in his own voice. "But this is something isn't it?"

"Yes," An said, though she declined to say what.

"I'll try to make life a little easier for you," he said. "That's the best I can do."

"Thank you," said An.

He put his helmet and gloves back on, then watched her while she got dressed in fresh prison issue. He put the towel in a disposal unit. Did they have so many towels that they could throw them away without caring? That seemed rather scandalous.

He took her to the shot station, where she was pierced three times, then walked her back to sleeping quarters.

He turned off at the guards' station, and An continued alone. She was too exhausted to try to see where he went. She lay down on her cot and closed her eyes.

It seemed like only a few hours later, certainly not seven and three quarters, when they were ordered out of bed again.

An trudged into the Heavy Lock with everyone else, trying not to think, trying not to worry about the impossible day ahead of her. *Put one foot in front of the other,* she told herself. *One foot in front of the other.*

Across the room, she saw someone she recognized. *Mohamonero* she thought, hopefully. But this fellow didn't look anything like Dr. Mohamonero. So why did she recognize him?

He looked back at her with small eyes, bloodshot and hopeless. He had big pores all over his nose, and a mouth that was rather nice.

They put a headpiece that said TRAITOR on his suit.

I'm so skinny, no one would want me anymore, An thought now.

She had agonized over the guard for a long time. It wasn't that she had liked him, and it wasn't just because she wouldn't be getting extra goodies. It was the look he had worn on his face. It had come back to her again and again. It had come to her in her sleep; but that time it had been Jo's face. Jo had been condemned to Heavy Time, too.

Jo isn't here, said the inner voice. *They were after us. But why?*

We won't know until we find Mohamonero.

We haven't seen any other TRAITORS *for such a long time.*

Don't trust what the headpieces say.

An didn't trust them. She didn't really believe that the guard had been punished, either. It had been a drama, orchestrated for her torment. People sat around in offices, thinking up ways to drive her crazy.

What kind of people sit around thinking up ways to drive other people crazy? asked her inner voice.

Anal retentive control freaks, said An. *Religious fanatics. Psychological sadists. Bureaucrats.*

Mind murderers.

An saw a signpost up ahead. It said: WATER 2.4K, IRON 1.6K.

An stopped dead.

I was on the hydro road. Where's the hydro?

Did we take a wrong turn? asked the voice.

No! We were on the hydro road!

I don't recognize the sign. We've never seen it before. They did something. They tricked me.

An couldn't decided what to do. Her hydro reading was well into the red now. If she backtracked to the other signpost, she would probably run out before she could get to the hydro station. But she had taken the right road, she was sure of it.

Keep going down this road, prompted the voice.

But this one goes to water.

Yes. H20. Hydro, get it? They're having a nasty joke.

An wasn't sure. She knew she couldn't backtrack, but going on didn't seem right, either. This was why she was always seeing people standing still in the roads. She always saw at least a couple every trip. They just stood there, and she never knew if they were out of hydro, or dead, or asleep, or just confused, like she was, now.

If I don't trust the signs, she asked the voice, *how will I know what to do?*

Trust our instincts.

An moved her right motivator forward. Then she moved her left. *This feels right,* she told herself, so she kept doing it.

They were such liars, here. They must lie to each other, too. They must scrabble like nasty little rats, trying to get ahead, trying to stab each other in the back.

Or were they programmed for their jobs at Omsk? Were they programmed to play certain roles, so they couldn't interfere with the wheels of justice, so they couldn't feel pity, so they couldn't feel lust and try to help an attractive inmate?

But who were the great minds behind these plots?

An staggered down the road. That last question had

made her dizzy. It must have accidentally touched on her unretrievable memories. That happened every once in a while, like when she tried to contemplate the gravity-defying devices, like her suit. She couldn't help wondering, how were they canceling out gravity? How were they doing it in the bunkers? She knew that gravity could be simulated by spinning a spacecraft or a station, or by acceleration. And Jo's ship had used Early technology to create an artificial gravity field.

(Early—that was a word that always made her dizzy.)

Those artificial fields required enormous energies to maintain. But how could you *cancel* gravity? How were they doing it?

Maybe they *weren't*. Maybe Heavy World 54832 wasn't a Heavy World. Maybe it wasn't much more than Earth Normal. Maybe guards were running around outside with nothing more than breathers and safety suits, changing signs around to confuse people.

Sometimes An thought that was true. Other times she looked at the blasted landscape, at the hard-hard ground, and was sure that it was trying to crush her, too, trying to squash her down in her Heavy Suit. It became difficult to move the suit by the end of the day.

Probably because she was tired. She had to use her muscles to make the motivators work, it really was almost like walking twenty kilometers a day.

Or was it forty kilometers? Sometimes the signs said one thing, sometimes they said another.

Maybe they were only going a few kilometers a day. It just seemed like twenty. Or forty.

There was a station up ahead. An tried to move faster, her heart pounding. *There it is! Thank goodness.*

Wait, said the voice. *Don't get in line, yet.*

But An didn't wait. She hurried over and got in line. But when she got closer, the sign said IRON.

Might as well get some, while we're here, said the voice.

An stayed in line, mostly because she felt too disappointed to move anymore. *I'm on the wrong road.*

Maybe not. And if you are, there isn't any way to fix it, so we might as well keep moving.

As long as we can.

I think we'll be able to make it back, even without the hydro.

That's because you're an optimist.

We are.

An couldn't remember ever having had iron. It came out of the same dispenser that her water came out of. Since she hadn't had water all day, the resulting sludge tasted awful.

I feel better already, said the voice in her head.

You do not. You're just saying that.

Let's keep going down this road.

An agreed. Why not? Maybe she really did have enough hydro. Maybe they could get back to the bunker without too much trouble.

Some time later, the Heavy Suit started to screech with every step of her left motivator, and she thought she was smelling burnt something-or-other inside her headpiece. Before too long, she had to work twice as hard to pull the left side forward. Her leg started cramping, and there was a dull pain in her lower back.

She saw another station. She limped toward it.

This has got to be hydro, she told herself.

The voice in her head kept silent.

The sign on the station said WATER.

An stopped.

I'm dead.

We're not dead. Let's go ahead and get water. We need it, and we won't get any more until tomorrow.

But we needed hydro more.

This is what we've got.

An stood in line. She looked at her readouts; the suit really was overheating. While she stood there, the temperature slowly went down. That was one good thing. But once, when she tried to move, the left leg froze up on her. She had to drag it forward.

What is hydro, anyway? she wondered bleakly.

Probably hydraulic fluid.

Not hydrogen, or something?

It might be hydro-something-something-something. A shortening of the name of some chemical compound.

An dragged herself forward. The leg wasn't sticking as badly now. But maybe it was getting ready to freeze permanently. Maybe she wouldn't get too much farther down this road.

By the time she had gotten to the front of the line, she was actually looking forward to tasting the water. She was very, very thirsty. No matter what might happen down the road, for now she was going to enjoy this one little pleasure.

Water was the sweetest wine in the universe. Once, after her daddy had abandoned the family, she had walked down this long desert road, and she had dreamed—

That wasn't you, that was that other little girl.

Oh—yeah.

Now it was her turn for the water. She hooked up. Her mouth tried to water at the prospect, but all she managed was a cough.

Just a few more seconds.

An waited until her readout for water said full. Then she took two shuffling steps out of line, to be polite to the person behind her. That person must be just as thirsty as she was, maybe more. She got clear of the line—that darned left leg was sticking again—and then she put her mouth against the water dispenser and pushed the button.

Nothing happened.

An tried again.

And again. And again.

Nothing was happening. She pulled back and looked at her readouts. Something was flashing on her miniature computer screen. She had never seen a message on that little screen before.

It said: TRANSFER WATER TO COOLING SYSTEM? Y/N?

An found the tiny keyboard and pushed the N button with her fingernail. She pressed her mouth against the dispenser and pushed the button.

Nothing came out.

An pulled back and looked at the screen, again. Now it was saying: SHUTDOWN IMMINENT UNLESS COOLANT PROVIDED FOR MOTIVATOR SYSTEMS.

No! I want a drink of water! I was ready for water!

We have to do it. The suit will freeze up if we don't. We'll run out of air—

I was ready for water! They set me up for water! Couldn't I just have a sip of it?

Let's ask.

So An tried to punch a query into the little keyboard. But the statement just kept flashing: SHUTDOWN IMMINENT UNLESS COOLANT PROVIDED FOR MOTIVATOR SYSTEMS. An tried to clear the screen. She succeeded, momentarily; but before she could type a new query in, the original question came back.

TRANSFER WATER TO COOLING SYSTEM? Y/N?

An sighed and punched the Y key.

Rotten Fucking Lousy Stinking Fucking BASTARDS. God damn them. God damn them to stinking hell.

Amen, said the voice.

An waited for the heat indicator to give her a green go, then tried to move her left motivator. It went stubbornly, but it went. She labored down the road toward a distant signpost. No one was coming the other way, which made her wonder how late it was. Was the day almost up? If you didn't get to the bunker in time, they made you wait outside for the entire sleep period. You could hook up to the air station just outside the bunker, but you had to sleep sanding up in your suit. You couldn't lie down in it; you might not be able to get up again.

An had spent two sleep cycles in her suit. She expected that she would probably do so again, but she hoped it wouldn't be today. Not in *this* suit, with its failing hydro systems.

That's how they kill us. We get stuck with the same suit several days in a row, and it starts to break down. This one is starting to break down.

Let's wait and see what the sign says, soothed the voice in her head.

An fixed the sign in her sights. It was a tiny little thing, so far away. She got a peculiar feeling as she watched it, a déjà vu feeling, but also a feeling of timelessness, an eternity of staring at some distant sign, some unreachable goal. She had never been able to keep her eyes on a sign-post the whole time. Her attention always drifted. Since there was nothing else to look at but blue, blasted rock, her attention always wandered inward. So she had memories of distant signposts and memories of ones close up, but never anything in between.

It was the walking that did it. The one-two rhythm made you think of nursery rhymes. Like right now, An became aware that she was singing to herself:

> *The itsy bitsy spider*
> *Went up the water spout.*
> *Down came the rain and*
> *Washed the spider out . . .*

But that left leg was dragging again, so the song was punctuated by the drag:

The IT-sy BIT-sy SPI-der
Went UP the WA-ter SPOUT

And, of course, before too long the song was beginning
to drive her crazy. And, also of course, the harder she
tried to get rid of it, the louder it screamed in her head:

> *OUT CAME THE SUN!*
> *AND DRIED UP ALL THE RAIN!*
> *AND THE ITSY BITSY SPIDER!*
> *WENT UP THE SPOUT AGAIN!*
> *WENT UP THE SPOUT AGAIN!*
> *WENT UP THE SPOUT AGAIN!*

Stop trying so hard, said the voice in her head, but she
could barely hear it over the screaming lyrics. *Don't try to
stifle it. For every thought, there's an anti-thought.*

Huh? An shouted to herself.

*In order to command yourself not to think a thought,
you must think the thought, so you'll know what you don't
want to think. But since you've thought it, you can't help
thinking it, especially if you don't want to.*

Keep talking to me. Maybe we can drown it out.

Drown what *out?*

"The itsby bitsy spider!"

See what I mean?

An supposed she did. So she relaxed and let the music
scream at her until it began to diminish, began to lose bits
of itself, and then finally petered out. An didn't bother to
feel relieved about it—she had forgotten it. She looked
ahead, and there was the signpost close up. She had no
memory of how it had looked from half the distance, or
a quarter.

They were always faraway or right there in front of
you.

This one said: HYDRO 4.6K, BUNKER 1.7K.

Ah-hah, said the voice, sadly. *This was the hydro road after all.*

But they lied about the distance.

Or we took a wrong turn.

I can't make it for four-point-six kilometers. I might as well go to the bunker.

And they would probably be mad at her for the condition of the suit. They might even make her get back into it without fixing it. Then she would have to haul it down the road to a hydro station, but that might not even help. The machinery might be too damaged to ever function properly again. The suits must be enormously expensive, and each Heavy World must have a budget it didn't dare exceed. Because the voters would get mad. An could still hear people from her hometown talking about it.

Let them die! they had said. *They're fucking criminals, they prey on honest people, so let them fucking die!*

And what had An said? How had she voted in the election? She couldn't remember. Maybe she hadn't voted at all. Maybe that was one of those issues that she just couldn't figure out, so she didn't vote on it.

And now here I am. I'm ready to cast my vote.

She walked. Up ahead, she saw the bunker. They were already flashing their warning lights. Once those lights turned red, you couldn't get in.

Lots of people farther down the road weren't going to make it tonight. An might not make it herself. The lights had turned amber. Red was next.

Walk-walk, one-two, one-two. One *drag* two, one *drag* two . . .

Someone was lying in the road. It was MURDERER. But that wasn't today, that wasn't this road.

Was it?

MURDERER had his graspers extended toward An.

"Help me!" came his voice over her comm. "I'm out of hydro!"

"I'm out, too," An said.

"No you're not! You're still moving! I'll die out here!"

The amber lights were flashing faster. An looked at her hydro reading. It said empty.

"I don't!" she pleaded. "I really don't!"

"I'll die out here! If you don't help me, who will?"

An looked at the bunker. The lights were flashing so fast now, they looked ready to explode. She began to move toward the bunker.

"Wait!" pleaded MURDERER. "Please, wait!"

"I can't," whispered An, her eyes stinging. "I'm out of hydro. I can't."

He continued to scream at her as she walked away. By the time she got through the gate, he was just a tiny cry, like some insect buzzing in her ear. Or maybe he was just her imagination, and she wasn't hearing him at all.

"There's a man stuck back on the road, out of hydro," she told the gate guards.

"I don't see anyone," said a neutered voice.

An turned to look, but the gate was closing behind her, blocking her view. The tiny voice in her ear was silenced.

An turned and went into the Heavy Lock.

"There's a man stuck out on the road," she tried to tell the guard as she climbed out of her Heavy Suit.

"So?" asked the nearest one.

"He'll die out there."

"He's a murderer. He deserves to die."

How do they know he's a murderer? asked the voice in her head.

Maybe they've got the roads under surveillance, guessed An.

Or maybe they're trying to drive us crazy again.

An didn't say anything more to the guards. She averted her eyes and headed for the sleeping quarters. But she got zapped for her trouble. The guard pointed toward another door.

"Rec Room," said the neutered voice.

An sighed. She didn't like the Rec Room. They made you sit on hard benches and watch religious programming. At first, An had been mildly amused by these; especially by the way some of the preachers worshipped the GodHeads and tried to read all sorts of elaborate interpretations into GodHead prophecies. But after a few hours of listening to these blowhards condemn to the fiery pits of hell everyone who so much as jaywalked, she started to take it personally.

But An could tune them out. She had gotten good at that. She went with the guard, trying not to look too disappointed or irritated. If she let on how much she hated it, they might make her watch longer.

The guard's helmet beeped.

"Wait." He/she turned away, and An heard a garbled conversation.

"What?" asked the neutered voice, then gave a snort of disgust and told An. "Wait here."

He/she went away. An waited.

It was rather nice, waiting. No one was poking or pushing her, and she was just close enough to the Rec Room to hear the sound of the vids without understanding the content of what people were saying. From here it almost sounded as if someone, somewhere, was having a good time.

An let herself drift into the illusion. Someone was having a good time. Things might be all right after all. Jo might . . .

Lost, Jo had said. *You can't get out of Heavy Time.*

Not even Jo could rescue her. Not even Jokateanke-Re. His own father had languished for a hundred years, and he could do nothing. Nothing. An would never see him again. How she missed him, how she wished he could hold her just one more time.

Me, too, said the voice. *I want to go home.*

But where is home? An wondered.

I don't know. They said, "Come home, little one," then something about waiting. Someone waiting.

Who do you suppose they meant?

I don't know. Maybe our mom is waiting.

Not my mom. She stopped waiting long before I left home.

Maybe it's the furry mom, in the trees. I liked her.

Maybe, An agreed, comfortingly.

The guard didn't come back. It was as if he had forgotten her. An got the feeling that no one was even watching her now, not even on a monitor. If she wanted to, she could wander off, and no one would stop her.

That sounds like fun, said the voice in her head. *Let's do that.*

An tiptoed down the hall. No one was in sight. She peeked around corners, down other halls, through doors, but found no one.

Let's see who's in the Rec Room she told herself, and almost giggled at the prospect.

The door to the Rec Room was open. There didn't seem to be anyone in there, from what An could see; but she felt compelled to look. *Just look, and if no one is there, we'll go explore some more,* said the voice in her head. This time An did giggle. It sounded a little strangled, but it felt good.

She peeked around the corner.

There was one person in the Rec Room. He sat watching one of the monitors. His back was to An. He had very black hair, with just a few strands of white creeping in at his crown. His shoulders were slumped, and he didn't move. He might have been asleep sitting up. That had happened to An a few times.

Who is it? asked the voice in her head.

I don't know. Does it matter?

Let's go look.

An wasn't sure she wanted to. If he saw her, would that be the end of her freedom? If she stepped into the room, would the monitors pick her up? They would come fetch her, and it would be back to the grind. Back to the endless walking back and forth. She couldn't stand that. No matter what, she wasn't going back to that.

We have to see his face, said the voice. *We have to.*

An almost turned away. But then her feet were moving. *That's not fair!* she told the voice in her head; but she didn't resist, since it was already too late. She was in the room now. She was approaching the man.

Now she could see his profile. His face sagged, as if he no longer had the strength or muscle tone to support it on his skull. *My face looks like that, too,* thought An.

He didn't look at her. So she moved around where he could see her.

And she could see him.

He had been handsome, once. He had tea-colored skin and almond eyes.

"Mohamonero," said An.

"Yes," he answered.

And An fell flat on her face.

Don't fall over in the suit! You can't get up if you fall over in the suit!

But An was falling, down and down the mountain of

sand. She tried to use her motivators to stop, but they always moved just a moment too late. *I'm out of hydro! Why didn't I get the hydro!?*

An rolled down the hill of shifting sand; then it lifted her up again, to a pinnacle where she could see the bunker. But it wasn't the bunker! It was the city, that shifty place where she had lost her memory.

An tried to move her motivators toward the city, but the sand was sinking again, and this time it was burying her.

At least this time I've got a Heavy Suit. I won't suffocate.

Not for a while, anyway.

The sand buried her completely. She couldn't move her motivators; but her graspers could wiggle a little. She looked through her sensors and tried to see the sand. It wasn't red sand, it was blue, the color of Heavy World 54832. But she saw something white glistening just beyond her right grasper.

My Egg! That's my Egg!

She wiggled the graspers until they were around the perfect Egg. Then, without really understanding why, she cracked it open.

The sand fell way from her, leaving her on the edge of the city.

"Hurray!" cried An.

And then her suit cracked open, just like an Egg. It popped open just like that other Egg that had tried to spit her into the void. "No!" An screamed, and this time she wasn't able to grasp anything on the way out, to stop herself from being squirted into methane gas and thirty gees. Foolishly, she held her breath, hoping for one last second of life.

If I'm in thirty gees, how come it feels like Earth normal?

An opened her eyes. She was on the Heavy World all right; but she had been right all along. It was a lie. There

were no thirty gees. But what about the methane? She let
out the breath she was holding—not that she really had a
choice at that point. In another moment, she couldn't help
sucking one in.

It was good air.

Ah-hah! Another lie!

An felt like dancing. No more stumbling around in a
Heavy Suit, no more weariness, no more desperation!

The city, said the voice in her head.

"Oh, yeah . . ." An turned and looked at the shifting
city. It was just as she remembered it—or thought she remembered it. She walked down the main road and right
into its heart. That's when she caught a whiff of a difference.

Some of the words and symbols that were phasing in
and out seemed more definite. Others were blurrier, and
seemed hardly willing to manifest themselves at all.

We'd better hurry, warned the voice in An's head; so
she started to run. She ran down the main road and all the
way to the Early To Bed and Early To Rise Motel, which
now sported a large, neon arrow that pointed straight
down to the lobby as if to say, *Yeah, yeah, this is the
place, so HURRY-HURRY-HURRY!*

An took a flying leap at the lobby doors as they were
starting to shift out again. She just managed to pass
through before they disappeared.

She landed flat on her face. It gave her a feeling of déjà
vu, but she ignored it and got to her feet. The lobby was
empty, and there was no one behind the desk.

"Well, I'm here," called An. "Now what?"

Someone rushed out of the back office at the sound of
her voice and stood behind the desk. He wasn't the other
guy, but he sort of looked like him. He wasn't as old, and
his face was more tan than red. His eyes were blue instead of almond, and his name badge said *Geo.*

"Where's Kokoboro?" asked An.

"He had to move on," said Geo. "We all do, eventually, and he was glad to go. But that other fellow is still here, the guy in room 4. He's waiting for you."

He handed her the key. An smiled at him; he was so friendly, almost fatherly, and seemed very familiar. If she could just wait and think a moment, she would know him.

She glanced at the wall behind him. Some of the numbers had stopped shifting in and out, and were frozen in some indecipherable halfway state. Others were frantically pulsing, as if they were about to go on the fritz, too.

"Better hurry," said Geo.

"Thank you," said An, and ran down the hall.

The elevator should have been standing open, waiting for her; but the only hole An could find was a glowing cave which breathed damp odors at her. Nothing else looked even remotely appropriate; even the wallpaper seemed to be losing its ability to convey information. It tried to shift as An walked along, but only managed to disappear entirely.

The cave was the only option then. She went in.

The cave became a tunnel, and even seemed rather friendly, though a bit too stinky for her tastes. Up ahead, something big was breathing loudly.

I'd better not disturb her, An thought to herself. *I don't smell right anymore.*

There was a branching of the tunnel, which went past a large opening through which the breathing was coming. An turned up a branch that seemed to climb, avoiding the hole with its dread and beloved occupant, hoping that this other way would lead her up to the room where Mohamonero was waiting.

Worker, demanded an imperious voice in her head.

Yes, Mother? replied An.

You're thinking about a male?

Yes, Mother.

Have I mated with this male, yet?

I don't know, Mother.

A wave of rage emanated out of the hole and up the tunnel, chasing An up and up toward a distant opening that was bordered by retractable doors.

The elevator! said a friendly voice in An's head.

But Mother was already sticking her maw out the hole, probing with a very long tongue.

Come back here, worker! How dare you mate with a male before I've done so!

I'm not going to mate with him, Mother!

What else? What else could you possibly do with a male, except eat him, which you are certainly not allowed to do until I've mated with him first!

I'm not—I haven't—I just was—er—I mean, he isn't—!

Come here, worker! Mother commanded, and An could hear the tongue bouncing along right behind her. It was a very sticky tongue, and if she didn't get into that elevator and close the doors, Mother would drag her down and consume her until there was nothing left of her memory at all except dead wallpaper and frozen numbers.

Bounce, bounce, bounce, came the tongue, and An pounded her feet and lifted her knees like a sprinter about to jump over the most important hurdle in her life. Up ahead, the doors seemed to open wider, as if to make her passage easier. She took a leap, felt the hot sticky thing behind her make a stab at her back. It burned her with saliva, but she landed in the elevator.

The doors slammed shut.

"Safe!" shouted the control panel, forming a face that looked almost like the desk clerk, Geo.

"Room 4, please!" cried An.

"My pleasure," said the control panel. The face disappeared, and the elevator lurched up.

It tried to stop several times, then seemed to change its mind just as the doors were about to open. Finally it stopped halfway between floors. One of the doors screeched open, and An had to climb up to get out.

"You did your best," she told the elevator. "Thank you."

This floor was a little livelier than the other had been, with wallpaper that still moved, if slowly, and numbers that shifted back and forth, if sleepily. At the end of the hall was room 4.

An would have run to it, but a creeping fear made her go slowly and carefully. What if it disappeared just as she got to it? She had to walk slowly and keep her eyes on it. She had to concentrate, to watch it getting closer and closer. One-two, one-two, one-two ...

> *The itsy bitsy spider*
> *Went up the water spout. . . .*

There it is, An told herself. *Room 4. Right there.* One-two, one-two, one-two.

> *Down came the rain.*
> *And washed the spider out.*

"Room 4. Right there."

> *Out came the sun.*
> *And dried up all the rain.*

An let the song play in her head. That was okay; just as long as she kept her eyes on the door. She was one quarter there, then halfway. How strange that was! To see a place when she was halfway there. Usually things were only faraway or up close.

> *Then the itsy bitsy spider.*
> *Went up the spout again.*

Now she was three-quarters of the way. And now she was there. And now—An put her hand out and made a fist. She knocked on the door.

The door swung open. She was standing on the other side of it. But this version of her was healthy, well fed and well rested. It gaped at her in shock, recognizing itself in her.

"Oh, my God!" her self said, and then it vanished.

"Waking up," An said. "Poor me, with the Heavy World still ahead."

Mohamonero was still sitting on the bed, only now he looked very thin and tired. He was watching the vid screen, which had only one thing on it: the animated glyph of an amphibian, flowing from egg to adult and back again.

There was a stone suitcase between his feet.

"At last you've come," he said, without looking at her. "At last. I've waited so long."

"I'm so sorry," said An. "I couldn't help it."

"I know. Come get your suitcase now."

An went into the room. She leaned down—trying not to get between him and the screen, since he was so absorbed in it—and picked up the case.

It had looked so heavy, but it was light. She lifted it to chest level and examined it, looking for the clasp. While she was looking, she heard a crisp *snap,* and the top popped open. The lid swung slowly back.

"Look inside," said Mohamonero.

An peeked over the edge. It was dark in there, but something was softly glowing, amber, with little traces of gold as it flicked its tail. It turned its tiny face up toward her and smiled.

"You're just a salamander," said An.

"What do you mean *just* a salamander?" asked the tiny amphibian. "Don't I have the most complex genes of any species, on any planet? Look at me, me, wonderful me!"

An leaned closer. The salamander grinned wider, and his glowing eyes burned into hers. "You see?" he asked. "You see?"

"I think so . . ." said An.

"Well, kiddo, you ain't seen nothin' yet!"

The salamander leaped from the box, right into An's eyes. She tried to drop the box, tried to blink, but it was too late. She felt it come in through her visual cortex and ignite the surrounding neurons, until a million identical salamanders were rushing through her networks, causing resonances that recreated wiped cerebral codes, evoking so many emotions, sounds, tastes, sights, smells; memories that had echoes all the way down into her snake brain, all the way down into the most primitive part of her. Her limbic system fired in alarm. Her brain was trying to filter out the overwhelming stimuli, to no avail.

Oh, well, said the voice in her mind. *If you can't beat 'em, join 'em.*

"Okay," said An.

And they did.

When An woke, she was lying on her face, in something sticky. She struggled to her knees, dragging her head up last. It felt like a lead ball on the end of her neck. Something wet poured down her face to the tune of her throbbing heart.

"What a mess," said a voice.

An opened her eyes. She saw the fuzzy image of a man sitting on a hard bench. He was looking at her, not at the vid screen behind her.

"Mohamonero," she said.

"My name is Mo now. They told me so."

"I like Mo better, anyway," said An. She wiped at her face with her sleeve, trying to soak up the wet stuff.

"You're making it worse," remarked Mohamonero.

"It feels broken," said An, feeling her nose, tenderly.

"It's not. It's the shape it was before you fell on it. You broke a vessel open; the bleeding should stop soon."

An started to nod, then regretted the gesture. "How long have I been lying here?"

"An hour at least."

"No one came to get me?"

"No one came at all."

An stared at Mohamonero until the fuzz focused into clarity. He looked yeas older than when she had last seen him. He looked tired and ill. An knew perfectly well what had wrought the change in him. It was branded into her own flesh.

"I've been looking for you," she told him.

"Why?" he asked, hardly seeming to care.

"The two of us are getting out of here."

"How do you propose to do that?" He looked back at the vid screen without waiting for her answer. He had already dismissed the idea.

"We're going to walk out, Mo. We're going to get up and leave this hall, and we're going to find a way out."

He didn't answer, but a tear rolled down his cheek.

"I'm not getting into another one of those Heavy Suits, ever again," said An. "I will die first."

"Will you?" whispered Mohamonero. "I said that, once."

"Take my hand, Mo. Let's walk out of this room." An stood, carefully, and extended her hand.

Mohamonero didn't move. "They're watching us, you know. On the remotes."

"No, they're not."

Now he did look. "What do you mean?"

"Something has happened. It happened even before I came into the room. My guard was called away, and he didn't come back. You and I were supposed to be kept apart, yet here we are. And no one has come."

"They just want to see what we'll do. They didn't get

the information they wanted out of either of us, so maybe they think we'll tell each other something important. Now that they've had time to break us."

"No. I think it was an accident."

He closed his eyes, then dragged them open again with great effort. "How could you think that? After so many months here?"

"Seeing you has returned all of my memories, and now I know how to get out of here."

"How?" he asked, his tone hinting at hope.

"Walk," said An. "Take my hand."

"Is Kokoboro still in there with you?"

"Yes."

"And someone else, I see. An Early?"

An's hand trembled. "How did you know?"

"I went digging through Kokoboro's files. That's how I ended up here."

He took her hand and stood. "Why not?" he said. "It will be novel to do something different."

They turned together, and saw the guard. He was standing just inside the door, his helmet turned toward them. He was holding a cup in his gloved hands.

An knew who he was.

He walked over to them, slowly, and extended the cup to An. It was full of water. "Drink," he said, in a neutered voice.

An drank the water, gratefully. She tasted her own blood in it, but hardly noticed. The taste was sweet, and her body was starved for it.

"Come with me," said the guard.

An had to help Mohamonero walk. All of the energy seemed to have drained out of his body at the sight of the guard. But he went, passively. The guard took his other arm and the three of them made their way down the hall.

"In here," said the guard. He touched the wall, triggering a mechanism that An could not see until after he had touched it. A door slid open, and they went through. The door slid shut behind them again.

They walked down a short hall and into a locker room. Another guard was lying on the floor. An thought he was the one who had taken her to the Rec Room. He wasn't moving.

The guard opened a storage cabinet, where uniforms were neatly folded and piled.

"Put them on," he ordered.

Mohamonero gaped at him, but An immediately pulled out uniforms for the two of them. She stripped off her prison issue and scrambled into the clothes.

Mohamonero moved more slowly, but he picked up speed as he went, and his face assumed an expression of grim determination.

The guard came over with two helmets. He handed one to Mohamonero, who struggled into it. He looked at An for a moment, as if wondering if he should find a way to clean the blood off her face.

"We'll get it later," An told him. He nodded, and slipped the helmet over her head.

As soon as An sealed it, it lit up inside with readouts and system reports. Through the visor she could see much more clearly than with her naked eyes. Controls appeared on walls that had been blank before.

"Will they be able to pick us up on remote?" she asked the guard, and heard her own voice neutered by the helmet.

"Not anymore," he remarked, and motioned for them to follow him.

They went down another hall, through a couple of automated security checkpoints. At these, the guard lifted his visor and let a light beam strike the center of his eye. An wished his back were not to her, so she could look at his naked face. But she could wait a little longer.

Once past the second checkpoint, they entered a control

room with view screens. The screens revealed several scenes of prison facilities and prisoners. The guards watching the screens were dead. Someone had shot them all in the head. He must have had a silencer, because no one had apparently noticed that the others were being shot.

He didn't stop to let An and Mohamonero stare at the dead. He walked right through the room and out another door. This led through a series of halls, and eventually admitted them into a Heavy Lock.

Four Heavy Suits stood waiting. But these weren't the miserable, poorly built things that An and Mohamonero were used to. These were beautiful, gleaming machines, bristling with features.

"Climb in," said the guard.

These suits were so big, you could get in with your guard helmet on. "See the jack inside?" came a voice over the suit's intercom. There was a jack inside the headpiece. "It goes into the socket on the right side of your neckpiece," said the guard.

An plugged in. Her helmet lit up with a set of new readouts. She understood all of them, perfectly. She hoped Mohamonero had a clue as to what his meant, too.

"Ready?" asked the guard.

"Yes," said An and Mohamonero together.

The guard opened the Heavy Lock and trudged out into the blasted landscape. They followed him.

They didn't walk on any road An had ever seen before. These were guard roads. Sometimes she saw piles of signs lying at the side, and one of her suspicions was grimly confirmed.

They left the road before too long, and trudged over wild terrain. The guard stopped from time to time, turning his suit this way and that, as if casting for a direction. Then he would start off again, as if certain of where he was going.

An knew he wasn't certain at all. But he was making a good guess, and she was willing to take her chances with him.

The minutes dragged into slow hours, until the indicators in An's suit were starting to nudge empty on several accounts. She started to lag slightly behind the other two. They had to stop and wait for her, and she was beginning to wonder if they were going to have to drag her the rest of the way.

"Did you know you can drag yourself with your graspers if your motivators freeze up?" Mohamonero asked suddenly. "I had to do that, once. I almost died. They didn't help me at all. Not at all."

"That's over now," said the guard, and he pointed at an empty spot on the horizon.

"Your ship?" guessed An.

He couldn't nod. He simply trudged toward the empty spot. They followed him, hopefully.

When they were just a few yards from the ship, An could see a few ripples in what otherwise looked like empty air. Then a hole opened in the blasted blue. The guard trudged into it. Mohamonero followed him, and An came last.

Whatever the bunkers were using to cancel out thirty gees, this ship had it, too. When the Heavy Lock had closed behind them, and the atmosphere had normalized, they were able to climb out of their Suits. The guard took off his helmet, and there was Jo.

His eyes were now cobalt blue.

"I had to get new ones," he told An. "You can't get a job as a prison guard unless you submit to a retinal scan. My old retinas belonged to Jokateanke-Re."

An pressed her cheek against his and held it there for a long time.

It should have been a long, hard climb out of a gravity well of thirty gees. An never would have made it out in her Egg.

But Jo's ship was different. It blasted out almost as quickly as it had done on Cabar 4. An thought surely they must look hot to anyone watching from the surface, or from orbit. But no one had detected the *An II* when Ra and Te had brought it in; and maybe the same was true now that they were taking it out again.

Maybe.

"Accelerating at five gees," grunted Ra, with wonder still managing to squeeze itself out of his strained throat.

"Get ready for jump," said Jo.

"Where to? Where can we hide, now that we've done this?"

"I know where," said An, straining over Ra's station to fix coordinates.

"Jo?" asked Ra, doubtfully.

"Just as long as it's out of here," Jo croaked.

But Te was not satisfied with that. "An, where are we going?"

"To a wormhole," said An, locking the coordinates. She couldn't allow any arguments now. Then the acceleration forced her back into her chair, which was ridiculous. Jo's ship had canceled out the gravity of a Heavy World; it could cancel this feeling of acceleration, too. It wasn't doing everything it was capable of, probably because its Human designers just hadn't thought it mattered.

"Anyone coming?" Jo asked over her headset.

"Not on my screen. But who knows?"

Everyone was sunk into his or her chair now, taking short breaths and waiting for the sting that would come before jump. An tried to look at Mohamonero, who was at the science station. He had been silent since the Heavy Lock had closed behind them. He had merely gazed at An, waiting. He thought he knew what he was waiting for, but he was wrong. He didn't know everything; not quite.

"An?" asked Te, from Ops.

An felt the sting. "What is it, Te?"

"No one has ever found a wormhole before. How come you know where one is?"

"It's on the map," said An.

"What map?" everyone asked together. Everyone but Mohamonero.

"The Early map," said An. "The one we found on Vorn."

Five, four, three, two, one . . . said the countdown on An's screen. Then came the jump, and the silence.

It was a silence full of questions, from Ra and Te, and especially from Jo. But An would answer them when they came out again. She would answer all of them.

Even the one they hadn't asked, yet.

An stood in the shower, letting recycled water wash over the months' worth of blood, grime, and misery that had coated her on Heavy World 54832. She let the heat soak into her skin. In prison, she had never been warm enough. There had been no blankets on the sleeping cots, and the clothing was always just a little too thin.

She stood there until the water shut off and the readout said: TANK DEPLETED. PLEASE WAIT FIFTEEN MINUTES FOR RECYCLING TO COMPLETE.

An didn't wait. She was clean enough. She went into the drying stall and let the mechanism labor over her mass of hair.

"They wanted to cut your hair," said a voice. "But our supervisor liked it, so he wouldn't let them."

An knew the voice, but she still shivered, thinking of the guard on Heavy World 54832. She looked over her shoulder at Jo, who was sitting on a padded bench, watching her.

"How long were you there?" she asked him.

"Four months. Arrived two months after you. I had to call about a dozen old favors in from friends of my father's. I had to rub their faces in their own shame."

"I was there only six months?"

"Yes."

"I wasn't sure. Sometimes I thought it was years."

"My father didn't last a year."

An separated strands of her hair with her fingers, gazing at him through the resulting curtain. He wanted to talk about his father, but he also *didn't* want to talk about him. She ventured a question, anyway.

"Jo, you said he was there a hundred years."

"That's what I had thought. But that's just how long they waited before they let go of his money. They earned interest on it all that time."

So they hadn't even bothered to tell him that his father was dead. An remembered all the days she had spent trudging back and forth, hopeless, thinking that no one in the universe was suffering as much as she. How wrong she had been.

Jo said, "I had always wondered what kind of guy would become a prison guard on a Heavy World. Now I know. They should have a sign in their recruiting office saying: ONLY SADISTIC ASSHOLES NEED APPLY. Every one of them. Sadistic, dumb bastards."

"They changed the signs around," said An, still mad about it.

"That's the least they did, baby. While we were there, ten people died because of tricks they played."

He was looking at her body now. An was ashamed of what he must be seeing.

"Don't cover yourself," he said. "You're beautiful, even when you're skinny."

He frowned as he remembered something else.

"I was afraid to take my eyes off you, An. My supervisor noticed, and he thought up a joke to play on you. I was supposed to come on to you in the shower. But at the last minute, he took my place."

He brightened for a moment. "Did you see him in the control room?"

"No," said An.

"You probably didn't recognize him with half his head blown away."

An turned off the stall. She fussed with her hair for a moment, but the intensity of his scrutiny made every movement seem false and awkward. He wanted her to come to him, to put her arms around him. So she did.

"It wasn't all for nothing," she whispered. "I got my memory back."

"Did you get mine, too?" wondered Jo.

He was pulling her down into his lap. He was undoing his fly. She straddled him and moaned as his penis slid into her. They didn't move, didn't try to push and grind; just held each other in that close embrace.

"I don't remember what's so important about a map,"

said Jo. "I don't remember going to Vorn, or why the hell I would even do such a thing."

An kissed his ear. "Mohamonero is the one who gave me the drip, remember?"

"I figured that much out by myself."

"On Cabar-Four, I was infected with an Early virus. A mental virus, Jo. An intelligence."

He didn't answer. His silence seemed more bemused than suspicious.

"The virus included a directive. It forced me to go to Vorn, to find a map. The map reveals other Early worlds, on the other side of the galaxy. It also reveals the whereabouts of a wormhole that will take us there."

"No one has ever traveled through a wormhole before," said Jo. "That's just theoretical."

"Someone has."

"Who? How do you know?"

"I think the X'GBri have done it. Maybe the Vorn, too."

Jo snorted. "Then what's the point of going, if they've already been there? They've probably plundered all the ruins by now! Why don't you just let me take us all into hiding?"

"How long can we hide, Jo? We escaped from a heavy prison. We're as good as dead, if we stay on this side."

"We can buy new identities, new faces . . ."

"You know the best reason we should go, Jo? They don't want us to. They don't want us to find those Early worlds."

He didn't answer that. He just held her tighter. He was afraid of the wormhole, maybe of what was on the other side. *How much does he really remember?* she wondered.

"You should see it on the screen," said Jo. "Or rather, you should see what it's doing. It's pulling everything in this system inside itself. How could we travel through it and live? We'll be crushed. And with the time distortion, the crushing will take forever."

"We won't be crushed."

"How can you be so confident?"

How could she, really? The intelligence in her brain was confident. It had grown so far into her neural net, she was incapable of doubting it.

"Do you trust me?" she asked him.

He pulled her tight enough to make breathing a serious effort.

"I dreamed I killed you," he whispered.

An tensed. GNno had promised.

"Every night in Heavy Prison, I dreamed I had made some mistake, and you died. I woke up in a cold sweat every morning, and it was all I could do to keep from blowing everything and trying to get you out right then and there."

An wanted to say, *You did the right thing* and *It worked out the way it should have,* but those words seemed so lame. Heavy Time was the worst thing that had ever happened to either of them. In fact, it was even worse than Jo's murder attempt. He didn't remember it, and An's brain had been through so many sortings and re-sortings now, she could barely muster any pain over that betrayal anymore. All she wanted was that Jo shouldn't remember it, ever.

"I waited a hundred years, believing my father was still alive. I kept myself alive, kept myself young, kept myself *up to date* with drips. I thought that was Hell. But it was nothing compared to just a few months of watching you suffer."

He began to rock her, gently. She rode with him. They both needed it. They deserved it.

"I was the one who made you use your water for your cooling systems," he said. "They wanted you to freeze up. They wanted to watch you drag yourself with your graspers, like poor Mo."

"I'm glad you were watching out for me. I would have drunk the water."

He shifted slightly, pushed deeper inside her. "This may be our last time," he said.

"It won't. I promise."

He might have believed her promise, but he wasn't taking anything for granted. He rocked her with that same, slow rhythm far longer than most men would have bothered. It struck An that this was the first time he had ever gone slow for her, without her asking. He wanted to make it last forever.

Of course, it didn't. She climaxed first, and then he did. His penis softened, slipped out of her, and he had to make do with just holding her with his arms.

"Have you wondered," he asked, "just why the Earlies would want us to know where they used to live? What was in it for them?"

He was still trying to talk her out of it. He knew he couldn't, but he couldn't help himself.

"They loved to pass on information," said An. "Everything in their culture was based on it. They were communicators, first and foremost."

"Most people stop talking when they die."

An laughed. "Not Earlies. Maybe they *couldn't* stop talking. Maybe they had a species-wide obsessive-compulsive disorder, and they just decided to make the best of it."

Now he laughed. He even sounded a little amused. But he didn't want to let go of her. He didn't want her to walk out of that room and take them all on a wild ride through the Early Express.

An looked into his eyes. It was odd seeing the cobalt where there used to be fathomless black. But it was still Jo inside them, still the man she wanted, despite everything.

"Did you remember that I love you?" she asked him.

A tear slid out of one of those eyes. Something seemed to go with it, something that he was better off without.

"Yes," he said.

He helped An off of his lap, and gave her body one last appraisal. "My skinny nymph," he said. He watched her while she cleaned herself and dressed.

An buttoned the last of her buttons, and gave him a crisp salute.

"Ready?" she asked.

"Ready," he agreed.

He took her hand, and held it tight all the way up to the bridge.

Ra was sitting at navigation, Te at Ops, and Mohamonero at the science station. They were all staring at Ra's tactical screen when An and Jo came in.

"You're going to take us into that?" asked Ra.

"Not exactly into," said An. "Sort of around it. Sort of through it."

"Sort of," he said. "Is there a physicist in the house?"

"I need to sit where you're sitting," said An.

Ra looked at Jo before he would get up. Jo gave him a short nod, and Ra switched over to the gunner's station.

"How long will the trip take?" asked Te, who was sitting with her hands folded passively in her lap. She was afraid, but that wasn't a new emotion for an EggHead. That was an old friend.

"You'll sleep during the trip," said An.

"Is it like jump?" asked Te.

"Sort of."

Mohamonero laughed. "You haven't mentioned the time distortion. All of you are aware of this, yes? You have no family who will miss you for the next several years?"

He frowned as he remembered he was speaking to Egg-

Heads. None of them had families who were waiting for them. "They murdered my wife and made me watch," he said. "My children and grandchildren think I'm dead. That's for the best, don't you think?"

"It's for the best," said Jo.

"And we'll sleep," said Mohamonero, "while An guides us through time."

An glanced at Jo. He was looking at the tactical display of the wormhole. A muscle in his jaw jumped, but he said, "Yes," without hesitation. He was the kind of man who could roll all of his chances into one ball and risk them with his best throw. He had always been that kind of man, even when he had been coming apart. "An will pilot the ship," he said. "The rest of us will sleep."

He plugged in his control suit and fastened his restraints. Te and Mohamonero did the same. Ra was slower to follow. He looked at the screen and then down at his suit. He looked at the screen again.

"Just so you know," he said to no one in particular, "I'm really fifty years old."

He plugged his suit in, but hesitated before fastening his restraints.

"I never thought I was going to live forever," he said.

"We're going to make it through," said An.

"I believe you," he said, but didn't speak the rest of the thought behind his eyes: *That's what I'm afraid of.* He fastened his restraints and gave her the thumb's up sign.

An plugged in her own suit, but canceled the sedative. She would be wide awake all the way through. She might be the first human who had ever gone through a wormhole alive. She had no idea what the sensation would be like—or perhaps she *did* know, on some level. Because she wasn't afraid.

She heard Ra gasp as he was stung by the sedative. Only then did she fire the thrusters. She didn't want them to be afraid as they fell into the whirlpool. She kept her eyes on tactical and searched for their current.

The star had been pulling them closer all along. It enhanced the speed of their acceleration now that An had fired the engines. Once inside, the wormhole would take them along, spitting them out on the other side from its twin.

An fastened her restraints and breathed a sigh of satisfaction. They had been accelerating toward the star; now they were sucked into the current, pulled into that part of the system that An's mind had marked with a mental arrow that said: BEGIN HERE.

Things got very strange.

The shifting patterns flowed right off the screens and into the ship. An almost felt as if they weren't in a self-contained environment at all; yet she was breathing oxygen. They were not instantly crushed by gravity, but they would be if she didn't keep up with the changes. It all reminded her of something.

"Careful," Jo had breathed, behind her. *"That's time."* She had been looking out of an egg-shaped door, at red sand that flowed and changed. She had run out onto the sand, and climbed, scrambled, rolled to keep from falling into a gulf and/or being buried. That's what she was doing now. The difference was this time she was succeeding.

On the other side of all this is the shifty city, where the glyphs all chatter and sing to you, trying to tell you everything at once. The Early To Bed And Early To Rise Motel will check us all into room 4, and there ...

"Communication will occur," said An. Was anyone awake to hear her? Probably not, because even though time had ceased to mean what it usually meant—for them, at least—time had still passed them by. Or rather, they were passing time by. They were flying through it, and it was not marking them.

Integration has occurred, she told herself. She and the Wonderful Me were one now. It was funny, when she thought about the usual outcome of a viral infection. Viruses always tried to change everything into themselves; you either fought them off, or they killed you.

The virus had succeeded in changing An into itself. Maybe because it had changed into her, as well; and now they were something new, something better.

Or at least something more complicated, thought An, and laughed at her own joke. She laughed, and piloted the spacecraft with such ease, drawing on Kokoboro's expertise and on all of the information from all of the glyphs she had seen. *Pass it on, pass it on!* they had all seemed to say at the end, and now she would.

Her hands were clever on the controls. Her memory flashed back to a time when that had not been the case, when she had landed her first Egg.

She had gone through the classes with good grades, had qualified on every test. She had ventured forth on her first expedition, feeling so proud of herself, so confident.

But when she had been confronted with her first landing on an unsettled world, had made her first mistakes and found that she was panicked, confused, without a clue of what to do, she had asked herself, *My God, what have I done? What have I gotten myself into?* And she had missed her old, simpler jobs. She had missed the vacuum nozzle and the parasite probe. She had longed desperately to go back to them, to change her mind.

But it had been too late. She had descended into the atmosphere and then made every mistake it had been possible to make. And somehow, miraculously, she had survived anyway, without even damaging her Egg.

Talk about luck. Maybe that had been all she had really had going for her in the first place. After all, luck was what led her to Omsk and Kokoboro's RNA drip. Luck was what had led her to Cabar 4, where the virus lay waiting for Kokoboro, who had searched for it for so long. Yes, he had known there was a virus for Humans, but he probably hadn't recorded that information on his hello/farewell tape. That would have frightened her off.

Luck. She had had both good and bad. But it wasn't luck that was guiding her now. It was skill and intelligence.

"You're doing beautifully," said a familiar voice, behind her. An didn't turn. She couldn't afford to take her eyes off her work.

But she smiled as she said, "Thank you, Ro."

She could feel him standing behind her. She could imagine what he must look like, his hair wild and filthy, his eyes so sane.

"This is the last time I'll be able to speak with you," he said.

An didn't ask why. She knew. Ro was dead now. He had died years ago. He was speaking to her from the past.

"Godweed charges a high price," she said.

"So does an Early virus." Ro laughed. "But you wouldn't give it up now if you could. And neither would I."

"I'll give the Earlies your message. I'm sure they can help you find a way to live as GodHeads without wasting away."

"They have already succeeded in doing something we failed to do," Ro admitted. "They have connected with the Vorns. When we tried to do that, their nest-mates killed them, because of the Godweed smell."

"No wonder they were afraid of you."

"And you were, too. Are you still?"

"No," An said, and felt regret creeping into her triumph. "Will we ever meet again, Ro? As ourselves?"

"Even Godweed can't reveal that secret."

"Stay with me as long as you can. Please."

"I'll always be with you, An. Just look for me at the Early To Bed Early To Rise Motel." He laughed, and An laughed with him, hearing him fade and fade, until he was just a memory again. A precious memory.

Almost done, she told herself. *Almost there.* How she wished Kokoboro could see it with his own eyes.

Listen carefully now, Kokoboro had said. *This is important. I suspect that the Earlies are—*

"I suspect that the Earlies are, too," said An, and the wormhole spit them out of its other side, into new space.

An triggered stims for everyone else, and waited for them to wake as she accelerated away from the wormhole. It had captured a binary pair, a red giant and a white dwarf that was slowly devouring a red river from its giant companion. This binary pair were orbited by three large, outer planets. An's sensors analyzed the second one and found it to be one and three-quarters gees, with no appreciable atmosphere; yet it was covered with lights and other obvious signs of development.

"Welcome to Shifty City," said An. She took them into orbit around the planet, and waited.

Jo woke up first. His eyes focused on An's tactical screen,

"What's that?" he demanded. He wasn't referring to the planet; he was referring to the ships orbiting it with them.

"That nearest ship is Vorn," said An. "The next nearest is X'GBri. I don't recognize some of the others on screen."

She paused, hoping that he would be as excited about the prospect of meeting new races as she was. But he still didn't know enough.

"And—?" he snapped.

"We won't have much longer to wait," said An.

"Wait," mumbled Ra as he woke. "We have to wait? What time is it? Did we sleep long?"

"Twenty minutes or twenty years, depending on how you look at it," said An.

"What are we doing here, An?" mumbled Te, who was

struggling with her restraints even as she was waking up. "That's a Vorn ship! What are we doing here? What is this, an ambush?"

Te shrugged off the last of her restraints and dove for the gunner's station. Ra gaped at her, too startled to stop her.

Dr. Mohamonero dove at Te's feet and knocked her off balance. As soon as she was down, he clambered over her and tried to hold her down with the weight of his body. "It's not an ambush," he said urgently. "It's not what you think, Te!"

"Get off me! That's a Vorn ship!"

"Those are males on that ship," said Mohamonero, and he risked a look at An. "Isn't that so? Kokoboro said the males use their eyes more than the females. . . ."

"Those are probably males and renegade females," said An. "And those X'GBri ships must be populated by the missing linguists. Remember the missing linguists, Jo?"

"No."

"These people got here the same way I did. They used a map."

"I thought you were the one with the map," said Jo. He got up and stood behind An, but he made no attempt to alter their orbit, or move toward the gunner's controls. "I thought you were the one who caught the virus."

"Viruses are designed to be passed on," said An.

"Why? Why did the Earlies want us all to come to this side of the galaxy?"

"You can ask them when they get here."

For the first time since his memory had been wiped, Jo looked at An as if she were crazy. "They've been dead for over ten thousand years, An. No one has ever found a sign of life in *any* of those ruins."

"We *have* found life, Jo. The glyphs are alive. They infected me. They infected the people on those other ships out there."

"That's a damned metaphor! Glyphs are not people—"

"Jo, the Earlies are alive—"

"In your *head* they're alive; it's not the same thing!"

"*No,* they're alive, they really are alive. They didn't die—don't you understand? They just moved to a new neighborhood!"

"Incoming!" snapped Ra.

An and Jo turned back to her tactical screen. An switched on the outside monitors, giving them a seventy-five-degree view of space off their bow. No ships were visible to the naked eye.

"They must be using stealth tech," said Ra.

"No, hold your fire," said An. "Look there."

No one could see anything, not even An. But her gut told her something was coming. In fact, in a way it was already there. An's brain was singing a welcome and giving her a sense of homecoming she had never felt before. The emotion almost brought tears to her eyes, but she didn't let it. She wanted to see them arrive.

The Early ship was at first visible only as a burning line, vertical in relation to them. Then the line was intersected through its middle. A two-dimensional image of a ship unfolded from these two lines, then became three-dimensional.

"Doesn't look like anything I've ever seen before," said Ra. "Our computer doesn't have a reference for it."

Everyone jumped as a loud beeping sounded, and they checked their stations to see where it was coming from.

"Communications!" cried An, and she ran to the unoccupied station. She put her hand on the console and prepared to open a link with the Early ship.

She paused, and looked back at Jo. He sat down at navigation, waiting for her signal.

All of them were waiting, expecting An to make everything clear. *This is it,* she told herself. *Now I get to find*

*out if I really know what's going to be on the screen when
I make the call.*

An touched open a link and activated the forward screen. A glowing image immediately sprang to life. An looked into its burning eyes and smiled.

Not exactly a salamander, but close enough.

The Early raised a six-fingered hand and spoke to her in Standard.

"Hello, little one. We have been waiting."

"Hello, Mom," said An, with a relief and joy that almost overwhelmed her. This was better than the way she had felt with the Furry Mother. This was what she should have had with her Human mother.

"I'm sorry it took me so long," An told Mom.

"And I grieve for your hardships, even while I celebrate your arrival," said Mom. "Welcome home."

An had to wipe away a tear. But she wasn't too choked up to ask another question. Her curiosity was too hungry to be silenced.

"Are GNno and TTra are already here?"

"They are. And another you have met, a Vorn male who passed you important information."

An tore her eyes away from the sight of Mom just long enough to see if the others were listening, if they were taking in what was really being said. "Why did you infect me?" she asked, for their benefit, because she already knew.

"We had little in common," Mom replied. "But there is an important thing."

"Curiosity," said An. "Burning, driving curiosity."

"Burning and driving, yes. The Vorns and the X'GBris share this trait; and so do some other neighbors you have yet to meet."

"Jo, do you understand now?" An pleaded. "*This* is why the Inner Worlders didn't want us to find out too much about the Earlies."

"Because they could bring us all together?" said Jo. "But how are they doing it?"

"Common ground," said Mom.

Jo shook his head. "This planet?"

"The virus." Mom appeared to smile; but the gesture was really one of acceptance, of relaxation, rather than humor. "You are one of us now."

The others gaped at An. "What does she mean by that?" whispered Te.

"All of us who share the virus understand each other," said An. "That's what she means."

And the truth dawned on Jo. "That's why they put you in prison. And Mohamonero. You know how to end the war."

"They would have just killed us if that was all they were worried about," said Mohamonero. "They tucked us away for another reason. Because we might know how to talk to *them*. And they might need us to do that some day. So they thought they would break us, first, and then . . ."

Mohamonero went to stand beside An, where the Early could see him clearly. "I have a message for you. Kokoboro says hello."

"Hello to Kokoboro," said Mom as she gazed back at Mohamonero. "Kokoboro is dead, yes?"

"Partly," said Mohamonero. "Part of his mind lives inside An. He had wanted to meet you all his life; and this is the only way he could accomplish it."

Mom smiled wide again. "We have done the same. We have left parts of ourselves all over the galaxy."

"Why?" said Jo. "What's in it for you?"

"To *talk*," said Mom. "That's what's in it for us."

Jo frowned. An thought he must be thinking about the ruins, about the way the glyphs chattered and danced under the eyes. Jo nodded, and his shoulders lost some of their tension.

"Then let's *talk*," he said.

"Where shall we meet?" said An. "What rituals shall we observe?"

"Your ship, your rituals," replied Mom, and then added, "this time," and made a gesture that was much closer to the Human concept of a smile, though it was really far more complex and meaningful.

An grinned at her, knowing she wouldn't be misunderstood.

"We're waiting," she said.

Mom made another gesture, this one more a laugh than a smile. "Waiting?" she said, and conveyed, with yet another gesture, the passage of millennia since the virus glyphs were first conceived. "Kiddo, you don't know the meaning of the word!"

"No, but I will," An promised. "Soon."

The Early terminated the link, and the screen went dark.

An turned to her friends. Ra was too shocked to know what to think yet; Te was looking at her with deep suspicion.

Mohamonero was crying. He sat back down at the science station and turned his back to them.

An went to Jo. His face was the one that mattered the most to her. She gazed at him for a moment, then took his hands.

"Are you sorry?" she asked.

"No," he said. Then, "Yes. I'm sorry my father went to prison for nothing. I'm sorry he couldn't see what I saw today."

"We've never known what we needed to know when we needed to know it," said An. *Until now,* she added to herself. It would be best to keep that thought private for a while longer.

He was gazing at her hands now. *Such pretty little hands,* he was thinking. He was glad to be holding them, and he didn't have a clue that he had almost killed them.

He didn't know now, and he wouldn't ever. That information belonged in the past, with dead fathers and broken eggshells.

"We won't need a wormhole to get back home again," An said. "We'll have Early technology. We'll be able to make thousands of jumps per trip, instead of just one. And when we go back to Inner World Congress, and we have the Earlies with us, do you know what the Inner Worlders will do?"

"They'll shit," said Jo.

An smiled. "Kind of makes it all worthwhile, doesn't it?"

He didn't answer. He just gazed at her with wonder, with hope.

"Come on," said An. "The Age of Information is calling."

He rose, trusting her; and he and the others followed An from the room, down to the shuttle deck where visitors were arriving: Vorns, X'GBris, Earlies, and people from parts of the galaxy yet to be visited.

To *talk*.

Almost, An could see another walking with them, a ghost with wild hair. "You think you're going to talk now?" he said, laughing. "Just wait until *we* get involved in the conversation."

Just wait, An agreed. *But not for much longer.*

Not for much longer at all.

Don't miss Emily Devenport's
fascinating new novel about an
extraordinary young woman
and her superhuman mentors
in their search for
the ultimate paradise.

The Kronos Condition

to be published in 1997

It was time to be murdered.

Sally sat in her customary place on the bus. They had been driving for many hours; though it didn't feel like it had been that long. In fact, it only felt like minutes, when Sally really thought about it.

But it must have been hours, because they had started in that parking lot and driven down a road that looked brand new, through the heart of those impossible mountains. Now they had almost reached the first summit; the clouds were floating by underneath them.

They had seen no one in all that time. The bus and the Volvo appeared to be alone.

Who built the road, then? Sally wondered vaguely, then worried that Marc might be listening to her thoughts. But he wasn't listening.

His mind was in Olympus.

Sally tried hard not to laugh. It would have been a nervous laugh. They were coming close to the place where they would be pushed over the edge, and Sally was waiting to activate the secret Mastermind. She was ready, but she couldn't help being nervous.

Soon she could go on automatic, and she wouldn't be so damned conscious of everything that had happened.

Not to mention everything that was *supposed* to have happened.

She remembered all the details. The sounds of their

footfalls in the empty Indian School. The feeling of doom, as if some hungry beast were waiting for them in the girl's rest room. She remembered putting her hand on the door.

She remembered the stall where the Gate was waiting. How the light had crept around the edges.

And then?

The Gate had been there. She was sure of that. But now its details were fading in her memory, and that was odd. It had been anti-climactic, somehow. No one had been waiting for them on the other side. No challenge had been issued, no struggle had ensued. And now they were driving the bus and that silly Volvo again, through mountains that certainly seemed wondrous, certainly deserved to be explored. But were they the mountains of Olympus?

The Three thought so. Sally's Secret Mind was working hard to make sure of that. It had painted a picture of different events for The Three as they had passed through the Gate; it had tinted the whole event with wonder and triumph. They were still glowing with it. It had enthralled The Three with that wonderful memory that was so close to what they had hoped for, they were going deeper into it with every moment that they contemplated it, basked in it. But they had one little detail to take care of, first.

They had to dispose of the children.

They had thought they would do it from the heights of Olympus, with god-like remote control. But there were too many peaks to choose from, and they weren't quite gods yet. Apparently that was going to take some work. They would settle for driving these old vehicles one last time. This might even be better; they could savor one more act of murder while they were still Human. Surely when they became gods they would be above all that.

As they were going around one of the curves, Sally caught a glimpse of the Volvo, behind them. She saw Ted and Susanna in the front seat. Their faces were bland, quite normal in appearance, but she knew they were as enthralled as Marc.

Where are we, really? she allowed herself to wonder. She had thought they would encounter something. Some-*one*. Why had she thought so? And why did she *still* think so?

The road, maybe. But the road seemed a little too convenient, like it had appeared simply because they needed it.

The bus lurched to a stop.

Sally grabbed the armrest, her heart pounding. *So soon? It's going to happen* now?

Be ready, warned her Secret Mind.

Sally forced herself back in her seat. Marc was putting the engine in idle and setting the brake. He got up. She waited for him to turn and look at her. But he didn't even pause. He didn't look at *any* of the Kids as he climbed off the bus. He left the door open.

He didn't even say goodbye.

Sally took the deep breaths she would be needing for the next step. Or they were supposed to be deep breaths. They sounded more like sobs. Tears streamed down her face and mingled with the sweat of her terror.

She wouldn't be able to start until after they had gone over the cliff. There would be a moment of free-fall.

Sally took a brief inventory of the Kids. They were dazed, but no longer under the Thrall. The Three didn't know that, and Sally didn't want to blow it at the last moment. She would have to work fast, once the fall started. She would have to be steady and sure.

Ted and Susanna climbed out of their Volvo. Marc went to stand beside them, at the edge of the cliff. They all wanted to get a good view. The ground was far below, and obscured by clouds; but Marc could enhance their sight with his powers. Seeing every moment of the show wouldn't be a problem at all.

Sally looked into their minds. She saw what they expected to happen. She carefully recorded every image, every nuance of feeling.

Ready? asked her Secret Mind. *Here he goes . . .*

The brake came undone with a *clunk*.

THE CLOUDSHIPS OF ORION
by P. K. McAllister

SIDURI'S NET

When an unstable comet severely damages *Siduri's Net's* mothership, the once unified gypsies become a people divided. Only the siren call of even rarer molecular treasures can save both ships—if the crew survives. Can Pov Janusz, cloudship Sailmaster, guide *Siduri's Net* through the dangers of comet dust and newborn stars to harvest the rich minerals of deep space? (453190—$4.99)

MAIA'S VEIL

What should have been a triumphant return for Sailmaster Pov and the crew of the cloudship *Siduri's Net* quickly escalated into a dangerous confrontation. For Net's mother ship, *Siduri's Dance*, had done the unthinkable in exchange for its own survival. Now Rom, Slav, and Greek must each choose between virtual enslavement and a perilous flight to the unknowns of the Pleiades. (453204—$4.99)

from 〔Roc〕

*Prices slightly higher in Canada.